DEATH FOR ART'S SAKE

A Mallard Melodrama

Book 4

R J Williams

Published: 2026 by The Book Reality Experience,
Leschenault, Western Australia
ISBN: 9781923454378 - Paperback
ISBN: 9781923454385 - eBook
*

Cover Design by Brittany Wilson | Brittwilsonart.com

For Marjan, Ian, Steve and PK
my good friends at the Book Bazaar

Other books by R J Williams

A Fitting End

Death in Earnest

Sovereign Risk

Chapter 1

'Friends, before we disperse, I have an announcement to make.' Oswald Lamont looked down from the lectern. All the benches ranged on either side of the aisle were occupied. A dozen community members unable to find seats stood at the back of the barn, while a scattering of infants and young children amused themselves quietly under the watchful eyes of two young women.

'Today, a member of our community has set out on her journey to that place we call The Blessed Plot.' Oswald waited for the buzz of excitable comments that always greeted such announcements, to die down.

'Catherine Swain, known to us as a dedicated and selfless upholder of our ideals, has been deemed worthy to take the path that we all aspire to follow and will soon take her place in our sister community. She has asked me to convey her good wishes to all here and her hope that more of you will shortly follow in her footsteps.'

The hall echoed with an upswell of chatter as his audience shared their reactions to the news. Oswald stepped down and passed along the aisle, nodding and smiling to community members.

'Blessed Plot? Still peddling that mystical claptrap. Tell the truth, Oswald. She's cleared out, had enough of *the simple life*, as you call it.' The man blocking Oswald's path made no effort to conceal his contempt. Dressed in a well-worn dark suit with a white collarless shirt and grey muffler, he stood with feet planted apart, thumbs hooked into his waistcoat pockets. Arnold Wright took pride in plain clothes and plain speaking.

Nose to nose, the two figures stood in sharp contrast to one another. Arnold, the spare, sinewy working man with close cropped dark hair and sharp aquiline features, facing the aesthete, dressed in a facsimile of Russian peasant dress: white smock colourfully embroidered at the neck and cuffs, and baggy sage-green trousers tucked into calf-high soft leather boots. Although his loose clothing served to disguise the flabbiness beneath, Oswald's pink-cheeked moon face, framed by shoulder-length brown hair parted down the middle, gave him the appearance of a chubby page-boy.

'Time and a place, dear chap. Time and a place. If you want to air a grievance, there's no need to trouble everyone else.' Oswald's condescending smile and tone of voice were calculated to irritate. 'What is the matter this time?'

Arnold growled. 'You know what the matter is.'

Oswald glanced around, noting that most of the gathering was dispersing. One or two cast a look in their direction, then went on their way. All, that is, save a group of men dressed in similar plain fashion to Arnold. Stern-faced, they shuffled closer to form a loose phalanx behind him.

'I see. Well, contrary to what you think brother Arnold, the wages you and your fellow craftsmen receive are a fair apportionment of the revenues we earn. I need hardly remind you that we are a commonwealth, giving freely of our skill and knowledge and sharing the bounty of our labours. These are the principles to which we have all agreed. To be our own masters, beholden to no outsiders. A community of equals striving for the common good and dedicated to the creation of objects of beauty and utility.'

'Spare me the sermon. I, and the others here, we're real socialists, we don't just play at it, and we're true craftsmen. Proper artisans who know the value of what we create.'

'Indeed. No one here would deny your worth. And as socialists, you must surely adhere to the dictum, *from each according to his abilities, to each according to his need.* You all came here to get away from the exploitation of masters, capitalists who feed like vultures on the toil of honest workers. And let's not forget another reason why this community appeals to those who value freedom. Here we have no hypocritical moralising about the natural interplay of the sexes. Here, we are all at liberty to form such attachments as suit our natures as human beings, without the straitjacket of the church or state. I know that many of you have taken full advantage of those freedoms.'

Oswald paused to gauge the effect of his words. Some of the men at Arnold's shoulder nodded, others shook their heads, still others remained expressionless, while one or two winked and nudged their neighbours.

Arnold glared at those behind him then turned back to Oswald. 'Don't think you'll get away with spouting that *each according to his ability* stuff to me. What do you contribute? A bit of pottery, the odd etching. How much does that fetch? And not just you – the rest of your dreamers and simple-lifers too. It's us that carry this community.'

Oswald's smile didn't falter. 'What do I contribute? Now let me consider. Everything you see around you. The land. The buildings. Your rent-free habitation. In short, everything that makes this community of ours possible. Will that do?'

The murmur of conversation that greeted his words told Oswald everything he needed to know. For every expression in the negative, five voices were raised in agreement.

'Well, I think that concludes our little tête-à-tête, don't you, Arnold?' Oswald stepped around his accuser and passed through the little crowd, wishing everyone a cheery 'good night'.

Chapter 2

'Wasn't she good? Barely a whimper during the whole ceremony.' Verity looked fondly at the sleeping bundle in Olivia's arms.

'She's such a darling, I must say. Cora, her nurse, says she's not seen a more contented young soul.'

'She must take after you then, Olivia. When Mortie and I were christened, it seems he bawled the church down from start to finish.'

'I heard that.' Mortimer appeared at Olivia's side. 'I was told that it was you who wailed throughout the service.'

'Your memory plays tricks on you, brother. There, look, you've woken Sylvia with that gruff voice of yours.'

'Gruff, indeed, why I barely spoke above a whisper. Was I gruff, Olivia?'

'Perhaps it's time we all went through for tea. Cora, would you take Sylvia to the nursery?'

'Yes, ma'am.'

Verity followed Mortimer and Olivia into the drawing room. While her brother and her sister-in-law joined Olivia's parents near the fireplace, she gravitated to the group occupying two sofas near the French-windows overlooking Thorneycroft's rose garden.

'Thick as thieves, I see.'

Mary Phillips and George Benson turned their heads in her direction. Opposite them sat 'disreputable Uncle Ambrose', as she and Mortimer fondly referred to him - her late father's cousin, valued for his kindness and unbridled eccentricity.

'Aha, Verity, come and sit with me.' Ambrose patted the sofa next to him. 'Shall I be mother?' he offered, picking up the teapot on the table in front of him and pouring a cup of Darjeeling. 'These eclairs are simply wonderful. Do take one. I've had two already and fancy I'll have another.'

Verity eyed the tiered cake stand and opted for a slice of the Battenberg sponge.

Ambrose succumbed to temptation. Never lost for words, he was temporarily silenced, savouring the rich mixture of choux pastry, cream and chocolate.

George and Mary sat side by side. He studiously picked at a loose thread on his sleeve, while she leaned forward as though to speak, but hesitated.

Verity put down her cup and saucer. 'Curious, isn't it? There we are, all three in London, yet it takes a christening in Oxfordshire to bring us together.'

Mary shuffled uneasily.

George gave up on the thread. 'But you've only just returned from France.'

'Yes,' Mary chimed in. 'You went away at the beginning of December.'

'And I returned a month ago. Did neither of you think to call on me? Or must it always fall to me to initiate things?'

'But…' Mary began, reddening.

Ambrose put his plate down with a clatter. 'Good Lord, is this how you three greet one another after all that you've been through together? Three of the people whom I hold most dear, behaving like strangers. The reason that we four are able to be here today is because we are all devoted to one-another. Do the perils that we've encountered together mean so little? Larkford Grange, murderous Fenians, German assassins?'

'Yes, but I was only saying -'

'Never mind that, Verity. If you three find it so difficult to hold a polite conversation, I shall appoint myself moderator. Mary, why don't you tell us about your latest triumph on the stage?'

'Oh, very well. I'm still with Phillip's company. Our forthcoming production starts next week at the Doric. I feel a bit of a fraud, really, but Phillip says I'm more than equal to the role.'

'Of course. Who could doubt it?' Ambrose said in mock indignation.

Mary smiled. 'I haven't told you what the role is yet, Ambrose.'

'No matter. You have the measure of any role in the theatre, my dear. What can it be? Lady Macbeth? Cleopatra, perhaps?'

'No.' Mary couldn't suppress a laugh. 'It's Paula in *The Second Mrs Tanqueray.*'

Ambrose looked vague.

'By Pinero. Mrs Patrick Campell played her a few years back. That's why I felt a bit of a fraud. Following in such footsteps.'

'A woman with a past. Something of a departure from your previous roles. And a tragic ending. Your career is flourishing, Mary. I never doubted that it would.' All traces of Verity's caustic manner had vanished.

'Oh, thank you, Verity.'

'Is Edward in it?' George asked.

'He plays a doctor this time, Gordon Jayne.'

'There now, this is more like it,' Ambrose slapped the arm of the sofa. 'Your turn, George. What adventures can you regale us with?'

'I'd like to think my adventurous days are over, Ambrose.' George gave Verity a pointed look, earning an amused smile. 'It's bread and butter investigations from now on. I'm pursuing an embezzlement case. It seems someone has been salting away a tidy sum of my client's money for years.'

'And you're about to unmask him?'

'The suspect is a woman, as a matter of fact, Verity.'

'Then she must have had a good reason. Was she being exploited?'

George grinned. 'Oh, she had a reason alright. It's called greed.'

Ambrose forestalled Verity's riposte. 'I've discovered a new interest – you needn't all look at me like that. It's nothing outlandish. I have purchased a bicycle. A Raleigh. What a boon it is. Master of the highways and byways of the county, that's me.'

'Oh.' Mary giggled at the mental image of Ambrose hurtling through the countryside, scattering people and animals unfortunate enough to find themselves in his path. 'I beg your pardon, Ambrose. Do you travel far?' she asked, striving to maintain a straight face.

'Far and near. You see, I have a purpose. I make brass rubbings.'

An awkward silence greeted Ambrose's statement.

Verity broke the spell. 'Forgive me, Ambrose, I've always considered brass rubbing to be a pursuit of schoolboys. A hobby, like philately.'

'Then let me enlighten you. Monumental brasses represent a most wonderful and intriguing historical record. We have more in this country than anywhere on the continent, you know. And it is certainly not the sole preserve of schoolboys. I have some very fine rubbings at the Lodge. Please come and see them.'

Mary snorted. 'Oh dear, there I go again. It sounded like *come up and see my etchings.*'

Ambrose affected a look of utter mortification. 'The very thought. Am I not a pillar of rectitude?' Unable to maintain the pose any longer, he shook with laughter; 'e – etchings, eh?' he stammered, dabbing at his eyes.

'That leaves you, Verity,' George reached across to pour himself another cup of tea.

'Yes, well, I'm sure it will come as no surprise when I say that I'm writing a series of articles for *The Englishwoman's Review*. The editor is most encouraging of the subject.'

'Which is?' George stirred his tea.

'The subject of the series is *History's Forgotten Women*. You see, in a world run by – and for – men, women who have achieved great things are all too often consigned to the margins, or forgotten altogether. My next article concerns Aphra Behn.'

George put his teaspoon down. 'Who?'

Mary and Ambrose looked blankly at Verity.

'There we are. Not one of you has a clue who she was, do you? Aphra Behn was one of the most remarkable writers of the Restoration period. Playwright, poet and novelist, she was easily the equal of her male peers. And a spy for Charles the Second to boot. But who would know that today?'

'Bravo, Verity, she sounds fascinating. Didn't fall prey to the Merry Monarch, did she?' Ambrose asked.

'For heaven's sake, why would you assume that she was his mistress, or anyone else's for that matter? The point is that she was her own woman, succeeding in a man's world through her talents and strength of character.'

'Now, I wonder who else might fit that description.' Ambrose looked archly at Verity and winked.

'Oh, very droll, Ambrose. Well, if none of you is inclined to treat the matter seriously, let's change the subject.' Verity reached for her handbag. 'I expect that I'm not the only one who has received one of these,' she said, withdrawing a printed card and placing it on the table.

Mary leaned over to read it. 'Oh yes, I have one too. Isn't it enterprising of them? I'm certainly going to attend.'

George nodded. 'Yes, I wouldn't miss it.'

'Be a good excuse to come up to town.' Ambrose produced an identical card from his jacket pocket.

'Yes, well, there's one more thing I should tell you all. I'm leaving Montagu Square. It's what I'd always intended. Mortimer kindly allowed me to stay after Father's death, but now that he and Olivia have little Sylvia, they'll want to make use of their townhouse from time to time.'

'Oh, I'd quite forgotten that the house had passed to Mortie,' said Mary. 'It's difficult to imagine you living anywhere else. Where will you go?'

'I've found just the place. A rather charming little house in Eaton Terrace.'

'Belgravia, isn't it?'

'Yes. And I've persuaded Elsie to come with me as my housekeeper. Mortie grumbled a bit about that, but I'm sure Olivia will want to make her own decisions about servants. I'm in the throes of furnishing the place. As soon as it's shipshape, you must all pay me a visit. No excuses. Especially you, George.'

Chapter 3

It had been a rewarding afternoon. Verity loved to spend time at Liberty's, the department store. Often, she was content simply to wander from floor to floor, admiring the variety of goods on display and treating herself to a length of Indian silk or exquisitely crafted *objets d'art*. Now, however, she had a very particular purpose in mind – to furnish her new house.

The Mallard townhouse in Montagu Square was richly appointed, but in her late parents' style. Verity would bring her own taste to the fore in her new home. A modern look as befitted the approach of a new century. Furniture, wallpaper, curtains, rugs – her shopping list was extensive.

'Will that be all for now, madam?'

'Yes, for the time being. When can you deliver?'

'Let me see… would tomorrow afternoon be suitable?'

'Perfectly.'

On her way to the door, Verity stopped before a mirror to admire the silver and enamel brooch she simply hadn't been able to resist adding to her purchases.

'Aren't those Celtic designs simply divine?'

Verity turned. The dark-haired young woman standing behind her smiled. 'I hope I didn't startle you. I have such a passion for exquisite design. My name's Stella Miles, by the way.'

'Verity Mallard.'

The woman's smile widened. She wore her jet-black hair down in defiance of convention, cascading over her shoulders. Verity glanced at her dress, a loose and flowing affair in rose pink with long puffed sleeves. It had a medieval look.

'Please don't think me forward, but I perceive that you have an appreciation for beautiful objects in the aesthetic style.'

Verity nodded. 'If you mean objects in the Arts and Crafts tradition, then yes.'

'I adore the honesty of the movement. Beauty and utility in harmony. The products of true craftsmanship rather than mass-produced commodities.' Stella reached into a capacious velvet bag hanging from her shoulder. 'Please accept one of these,' she said, handing Verity a leaflet. 'It's an exhibition of decorative arts presented by the Chase Manor Community. Have you heard of it?'

'No, I can't say I have.'

'They have dedicated themselves to living in harmony with nature. Theirs is a community of talented artists and artisans with no distinctions of class, and with equality between the sexes.'

'Sounds rather utopian. Does it work?'

'It's wonderful. I'm proud to say I'm part of it. It's changed my life in so many ways.' Stella's eyes gleamed.

'Where is this community situated?'

'In Herefordshire. The manor stands in fifty acres near the village of Monk's Fallow. It's idyllic, truly.'

'I dare say your exhibition will be most interesting, but I have no plans to visit Herefordshire.'

Stella looked puzzled, then laughed. 'Ah, no, the exhibition is here in London.'

Verity scrutinised the leaflet in her hand, noting the venue: Arrowfield Hall, Highgate. 'Oh, I see. Well, I'll give it consideration.'

'Oh, I do hope you'll come. I work in stained glass. I'll have several pieces on display.'

***

Seated in her drawing room at Eaton Terrace, Verity opened her diary. It had been a busy week. She'd spent two half-days volunteering her services at Bart's hospital. Her article on Aphra Behn for *The Englishwoman's Review* had required several hours of her time, and then there was a lecture on women's suffrage she'd attended in Bloomsbury. Turning to the next day's entry, she made a note about the furniture delivery from Liberty's. There was only one other mention for that day –

6.30 pm Invitation to attend A & R Cotton, Pawnbrokers

At the christening, Mary had said she would be attending. George too. And Ambrose. But last week he'd gone and fallen off his bicycle. A cracked rib, contusions and a severe blow to his dignity, said his letter to Verity. Sadly, he would have to decline.

Alfie and Dick Cotton's invitation called it a *soiree*, no less, on the occasion of the grand opening of their new enterprise.

Pawnbrokers, indeed? Verity wondered why on earth the brothers had decided to set themselves up in trade. Legitimate trade at that. Tomorrow, she'd make sure she got to the bottom of it. In any event, it would be a pleasure to see them again.

The drawing room was empty apart from her chair and the small table in front of her. Tomorrow it would be transformed. Verity let her mind wander, imagining the new furniture, rugs and curtains, in situ.

What was it that young woman, Stella Miles, had said? *Beauty and utility in harmony. That's precisely what I wish to achieve*, thought Verity, fishing in her handbag for Stella's leaflet.

She'd dismissed the idea of attending the exhibition as soon as she'd left Liberty's. Much as she admired the Arts and Crafts style, she could indulge her tastes sufficiently through Liberty's and similar emporia in London. She could be assured of the quality of *their* wares, whereas who knew what she would find at an exhibition mounted by some communal group in Herefordshire? Verity imagined a collection of homespun objects of a decidedly amateur variety.

She'd heard of such communities, driven by idealism, setting themselves apart from conventional everyday society. Some sought simple self-sufficiency, living off the land. Others sought spiritual fulfilment. While this Chase Manor Community, it seemed, had dedicated itself to the decorative arts.

Such ideas could succeed, as William Morris had shown. Several of the items she had bought were from Morris & Co. But for every such success, she didn't doubt that there were many failures, driven by enthusiasm rather than talent.

Verity put the leaflet aside.

She was on her way to the kitchen to speak to Elsie about dinner when the thought struck her. What if she *were* to attend, not on her own account, but with her journalist's hat on? Not that she would present herself in that capacity. This Chase Manor Community might provide material for an article. Ever on the lookout for stories, Verity decided she might after all take up Stella's invitation to attend their exhibition.

Chapter 4

The bell vibrated on its spring as Verity opened the door and stepped across the threshold.

She was the last to arrive. Familiar faces turned in her direction. Mary and George stood side by side, overshadowed by a huge stuffed brown bear of distinctly moth-eaten appearance.

Before she could apologise for her lateness, Alfie Cotton came scurrying out from behind the counter.

'Miss Mallard. So good of you to come. Not the sort of place you're used to.' Alfie rubbed his hands together nervously.

'Goodness Alfie, did you imagine I'd miss seeing this… Alladin's cave of yours? And we know each other too well for formality. No *Miss Mallard*, please.'

Verity looked around at the jumble of objects spread around the shop. Assorted armchairs, hat stands, occasional tables, various items of taxidermy besides the bear. Longcase clocks, carriage clocks, timepieces of all types. Several violins arranged on a shelf. A bugle, trumpets, a trombone, and was that a tuba? Pottery, crockery, glassware. Umbrellas and walking sticks. Rugs on the floor, and rugs rolled up in a pile in the corner. A ship in a bottle. In a glass display cabinet behind the counter, she glimpsed trays of jewellery.

'My word, so much. So many items. But how long have you been open, Alfie? Surely it would have taken months to acquire all this. Ah, but where are my manners? Dick!' Verity advanced to the counter. 'It's so good to see you again. Are you keeping well?'

Dick Cotton flushed and grinned. 'Very well, Miss… sorry, Verity.'

A movement behind Dick's shoulder drew her attention. A woman, short and slight, wearing a plain maroon cotton dress, her brown hair drawn back in a bun, came and stood at Dick's side. Alfie cleared his throat. 'Ladies and gentlemen. It gives Dick and me great pleasure to invite you to our 'umble premises. Now, before I say more, let me introduce our sister, Mrs Nelly Fowler.'

The woman bobbed her head in acknowledgement.

'I know it will come as a bit of a surprise to learn that we have a sister. It's not a secret or anything, but our dear old Nel has just come back to us from Australia. Yes, all the way from Melbourne. Sad to say, Nel's husband, Stanley, passed away, and now she's here working with Dick and me in the shop.' Alfie nodded to his sister, who disappeared through the door at the rear of the shop, returning in a few moments with a tray laden with glasses of champagne.

'Come on round, Nel, and serve our guests,' Alfie beckoned.

Alfie took the last glass and held it aloft. 'A quick toast to absent friends.'

'Absent friends.'

After a moment of solemnity, in remembrance of Alfie and Dick's cousin Benny, Mary was the first to speak.

'You *are* a dark horse, Alfie. You too, Dick. Who would have thought of you two keeping a shop, never mind a pawnbroker's?'

'Well, it's…'

'Yes, Mary, that's just what I was thinking. It doesn't sound like their cup of tea at all,' Verity chimed in.

'Well, I can…'

'Remarkable, isn't it? What do you think?' Mary turned to George.

'I think that you and Verity should allow Alfie to talk. Go on, Alfie, before they can get another word in.'

'Righto. You see, this place is a gift, in a manner of speaking. It's thanks to a certain person as put some money our way. Enough to buy this shop and all the stock. It was…'

'Quilter?' said George. 'I'd like to think that his conscience got the better of him, but I left him in no doubt that I'd see his career in ruins if he didn't do right by Benny's family.'

'Benny's old mum got a tidy sum, and quite right too. Dick and me weren't expecting nothing but then he turns up with a cheque.'

'To buy your silence about the Jubilee business.'

'Yes. "A token of appreciation from a grateful nation" is how he put it. But we knew what it meant all right.'

'But a pawnbroker's, Alfie?' Verity took him by the arm. 'A newsagent perhaps or a pub, but why a pawnshop?'

Alfie winked at George.

George gave a wry smile. 'Let's say that it presents certain opportunities to dispose of goods that may have been acquired by unconventional means.'

'Ah, I see. Perhaps it's best not to dwell on that. But doesn't a pawnbroker require a licence?'

George nodded. 'I understand a magistrate must first issue a certificate on the basis of the applicant's good character. Did Quilter help with that too, Alfie?'

'He put in a good word. Mind you, Dick and me's never been charged with anything. Coppers could never prove nothing. Now then, that's enough of all that. Nel, come and top up everyone's glasses, would you, love?'

***

Three empty champagne bottles stood on the counter. Nel had just appeared with another. George looked at his wristwatch. 'I'd better not, thanks, Alfie. There's an early morning surveillance I need to do. Speaking of which, I suppose you and Dick will be too busy with the shop to help me in future.'

'Oh, I think we could still do a spot of work for you, guv. Nel's the one who'll be running this place most of the time.'

'Very good. Anyway, thank you for a pleasant evening. Are you two ladies staying or can I interest you in sharing a cab?'

Verity put her empty glass on the counter. 'Very gallant of you, George. Mary, will you join us?'

'Oh.' Mary drained her glass. 'Yes, thank you, Geo… look – outside!' Mary's scream drowned the sound of her glass splintering as it hit the floor, but not the crash of a brick shattering a window pane and thudding to a halt at George's feet.

Alfie dashed to the door with George and Dick at his heels.

Under a streetlight on the other side of the road, stood a middle-aged couple, arm in arm, gaping at the shop.

'Did you see them?' Alfie shouted. 'Did you see who chucked that brick?'

The man began stuttering until the woman shushed him. 'Let me tell him, Norman, or we'll be here all night. We saw it all right. Three of them. Rough looking types, I must say. One of them threw it, then they all ran along the street and round the corner. Shocking. Come on, Norman, let's get home.'

Alfie thanked their departing backs.

'Not a random act of violence, was it, Alfie?' George looked back at the shop.

'No, guv.'

'Upset someone, have you? An unhappy customer?'

Alfie shook his head and turned away.

Dick whispered. 'It's the King brothers again.'

'The toughs who said you owed them money? But that was months ago.'

'Now they want paying to make sure the shop don't come to no harm. They called last week demanding ten quid a week. Insurance, they called it, didn't they, Alfie?'

George snorted. 'The law would call it demanding money with menaces. Did you report it to the police?'

Alfie scoffed. 'Do me a favour.'

'So, what now?'

'Dunno. They would never have pulled a stunt like this if Benny was still alive.'

'It will only get worse unless they're stopped.'

'Course it will. As if I don't know that,' Alfie snapped. 'Sorry, George, I'm not having a go at you. I'll have to come up with something.'

George slapped him on the back. 'Come on, let's get back inside.'

'How good of you to join us now that we women have swept up the broken glass.' Verity stood with broom in hand while Nel carried the glass away in a bucket.

'Who was it?' Mary asked, still shaken. 'Why would someone throw a brick through the window?'

'Never mind that now.' George smiled reassuringly. 'Let's get you home. And Verity, if you're ready? I'll hail a cab.'

Verity turned to Alfie. 'Whatever is behind this, don't feel you must deal with it on your own. I owe you a great deal, so do George and Mary.'

Alfie nodded and forced a smile. 'Not the evening Dick and me planned. Sorry you had to get caught up in this.'

Verity took his hand and squeezed it. 'I meant what I just said.'

***

George waited on the doorstep until Mary closed the door of her lodgings behind her, then rejoined Verity in the hansom cab.

'It's all very well fobbing Mary off with your tale of it being the work of some drunken louts just throwing a brick for the hell of it on their way home from the pub. Now tell me the real story, George.'

Fifteen minutes later, the cab halted in Eaton Terrace.

'There's no need to escort me to the door, George. Your plan sounds ambitious, but I believe it could work. Let me know if you need my help to convince Alfie and Dick. And before I forget, you and Mary must come and see my new home. Looks quite handsome from the outside, doesn't it? But wait until you see my new furnishings. I'll send you both invitations. Good night.'

George watched until Verity disappeared inside before signalling to the cabbie to move off.

Chapter 5

Oswald unloaded the stoneware vases from the kiln and carried them through to the studio for glazing. Taking his cloak from a hook on the back of the door, he wrapped it around himself before stepping out into the yard. Over to his left, the lights in the furniture workshop provided some illumination as he crossed the yard to enter the kitchen garden and take the path to the house, guided by the lantern hanging outside the kitchen door.

'Ah, you're back.'

The woman standing at the kitchen range turned. 'I only arrived twenty minutes ago. Seth met me with the trap at Hereford station.'

At forty-eight, Ursula Lamont was five years older than her husband. Her dark brown hair, streaked with grey, was drawn tightly back and knotted in a plait extending to the small of her back. A large, embroidered sunflower embellished the front of her loose indigo smock.

'How was the journey?'

'Perfectly miserable when I started out. Mist and persistent rain all the way down to the town. But the train ride was comfortable enough. I had a compartment to myself most of the way. It's such a desolate place at this time of year. I couldn't wait to get away. Next time, you can be the escort. Blessed Plot, indeed!' Ursula gave a humourless laugh.

'And what of your charge?'

'We had some difficulty with her just after we arrived, because the sedative must have been insufficient. It's as well the place is remote. She became quite hysterical. However, Maynard took her in hand.'

'How is she now?'

'Comatose when I left. I've entrusted her to Maynard. You know how he works. It took six weeks last time, but he assures me he will get her to sign. Then Pryce-Thomas will handle the legal niceties.'

'Very good.' Oswald rubbed his hands together. 'Now, to other matters. I received a letter from Dornford this morning. The hall is ready. All that remains is to arrange transport for the exhibits. That gives us five days.'

'Can we expect many visitors?'

'Judging by the number of leaflets handed out, I'd say we can.'

'Excellent. Some new blood for our community and, perhaps, another candidate for The Blessed Plot?' Ursula's lips parted in a vulpine grin.

***

'George, come in. I'm not expecting Mary for another ten minutes. Come through to the drawing room.'

'If the hall's anything to go by, you've not spared any expense.' George removed his hat and coat.

'I've been quite indulgent, it's true. That rug was simply irresistible. I'll wait until Mary arrives to give you a proper viewing. Will you join me in a sherry?'

George took a seat while Verity turned to the sideboard and poured two glasses of manzanilla from a decanter.

'You've spoken to Alfie and Dick?' Verity handed a glass to George.

'Yes, last night… Mmm, this sherry's very good.'

'I've discovered an excellent wine merchant nearby. Now, what did they say?'

'I'd like to tell you that they jumped at the suggestion. The truth is, they were not fully convinced. They worried that it might backfire on them, and they're concerned about my safety.'

'That's understandable. And it's good of them to be concerned on your behalf. Did they agree in the end, though?'

George nodded. 'They were persuaded, but not by me.'

Verity narrowed her eyes.

'It was their sister, Nel. Mrs Fowler. I know she didn't say much when we attended the shop the other night – just stayed in the background. Well, I certainly saw another side of her last night. She told her brothers in no uncertain terms that the Kings needed to be put in their place. "If my Stanley was here, he wouldn't have a bar of it", she said. "We had some nasty types giving us grief back in St Kilda. Stanley and a couple of his good mates saw them off and no mistake". She's a redoubtable woman when she's roused.'

'Bravo. A woman after my own heart. When do you propose to put the plan into action?'

'It will take me a few days to complete one of my investigations. The rest of my work can wait for a while. I'll become Bob Watson next Monday.'

'You'll be sure to warn me. I'll need to give Elsie and the other servants the evening off.'

'Of course. And I'll have to speak to Inspector Tweed.'

'Oh yes, I almost forgot about that. Do you think he'll co-operate?'

'Let's hope so. If not, I could always mention Quilter's name,' George grinned.

'Oh dear, you nearly made me spill my sherry. Ah, there's Mary at the door.' Verity glanced at the clock on the mantelpiece. 'Wonders will never cease. She's actually early.'

Chapter 6

The banner over the entrance to Arrowfield Hall proclaimed *An Exhibition of Arts and Crafts by the Chase Manor Community* in swirling Celtic lettering. Verity passed underneath it, ascended some steps and crossed the vestibule.

Her first impressions were underwhelming. Arrowfield Hall's modest interior of plain cream walls and floorboards stained a dull brown made an uninspiring backdrop for the exhibition. Even the Parish Hall in Flaxminton, the village close to Thorneycroft, had more to recommend it.

Parallel lines of trestle tables extended along each side displaying a variety of decorative objects. She saw ceramics, jewellery, clocks, silverware, fabrics and embroidery. A display of furniture occupied the centre space. Each display was attended by one or more of what she assumed to be members of the Chase Manor Community. Distinguished by their unconventional clothing and air of determined amiability, they all appeared to be female.

As she progressed along one side of the hall, she had to admit that although the surroundings left much to be desired, the exhibits themselves were a revelation. *Quite as fine as anything at Liberty's,* she conceded.

Stopping to examine a casket of finely wrought silver on copper, inset with cabochons of semi-precious stones, she attracted the attention of the young woman in attendance, whose dress could be considered an exhibit in itself. Its bodice and skirt were covered in embroidery, depicting scenes from Aesop's fables, leaving only her puffed sleeves unadorned.

'Exquisite.' Verity put the casket down. 'Is this your work?'

'Heaven's, no, it's not mine. This is where my talents lie,' she smiled, extending her arms and pirouetting to display the back of her dress, featuring motifs illustrating the tale of 'The Tortoise and the Hare'.

'Remarkable,' Verity said encouragingly.

'Isn't it? Elspeth's needlework is simply exceptional.'

Verity recognised the voice in her ear. 'Miss Miles, hello again.'

'Stella, please. You came. I'm so glad. Do allow me to show you around. My own work is over on the other side.'

'Very well.'

As they passed along the row of trestle tables, Stella introduced other community members. Not only were they all young women, but they were also uniformly welcoming, almost to the point of being gushing. And so well spoken. Verity was reminded of her finishing school companions, trained to subordinate their individual natures beneath a veneer of genteel behaviour.

'Now, my stained glass awaits.' Stella pointed to a colourful display on the opposite side of the hall.

Verity turned to follow her. 'Stella, one moment.'

'Yes, what is it? Oh, of course, how remiss of me.' Stella joined Verity facing a plain wooden screen covered in green baize displaying a montage of photographs. 'This is our community. Let me show you.'

Verity listened as Stella pointed to each photograph. The entire community posing as a group. Men and women at work indoors and outside in gardens and meadows. A large stone barn, workshops and cottages. And at the centre of the display – a photograph of a limestone manor house. Standing at the entrance were three figures – a middle-aged couple and a younger man.

'Our inspiration and the leaders of our community,' Stella explained. 'Oswald and Ursula have dedicated themselves to beauty and to lives lived in harmony with nature. We owe them everything. I count myself blessed to be a part of it.'

'And the younger person?'

'Our hope for the future, Verity. Their son, Dornford.'

Stella's voice and expression conveyed such adulation that Verity had to suppress her usual disdain for displays of public emotion. For an instant, she wondered whether her idea of pursuing a story about the community was advisable. How could she pose as an adherent when the entire ethos of such an arrangement struck her as absurd and self-indulgent? What compelled people to become involved in such things?

The journalist in her overcame her doubts. Utopia versus human nature. Surely, there was a story to be had in that unlikely pairing?

'They sound like remarkable people.'

'Oh, they are. And one of them is here today,' Stella whispered.

'Yes?'

Stella nodded excitedly. 'Wait here.'

She scurried off, leaving Verity to observe the comings and goings around her. A crowd filled the room, milling around the displays. Several minutes elapsed before she caught sight of Stella emerging from the throng. At her side walked a figure from the photograph – Dornford. A head taller than Stella, his lanky frame was clothed in a suit of dark green velvet over a white shirt, the soft collar open at the neck. His smooth cheeks, full lips, dimpled chin and mop of loose black curls seemed faintly Byronic to Verity. As Stella pointed her out, Dornford's dark eyes met hers and his lips parted, revealing a flash of even white teeth.

'Miss Mallard, Stella tells me you have an eye for the aesthetic.' He adopted a theatrical stance, hips to the fore, leaning back and gazing at Verity as though examining a painting.

'I take pleasure in beautiful objects, if that's what you mean, Mr …?'

'Ah, I'm simply Dornford. Surnames are so bourgeois, don't you think?'

Verity stayed silent just long enough to unsettle him. Holding his gaze until he blinked and looked away, his smile fading.

'Stella has been telling me about your community at Chase Manor. It sounds most interesting.'

Dornford arched his eyebrows. 'In what way do you find us interesting?'

'The notion of a community existing at arm's length from everyday society and dedicating itself to a set of ideals. That such a community might thrive and remain true to its purpose is intriguing. It seems a most worthwhile endeavour.'

Dornford's smile returned. 'Perhaps it strikes you as a rather romantic way of life. But we're practical people, first and foremost. As you can see from this exhibition, we are genuine artisans, not dilettantes. We rely on the sale of our work. Although we spurn convention, we are also dependent on the everyday world for our sustainment.'

'Yes, the quality of the pieces here is quite outstanding. What is your craft, if I may ask?'

'Uh…' His pale cheeks flushed.

'Dornford's talents extend far beyond mere manual work.' Stella gazed adoringly at her companion. 'He is our artistic conscience. His sensibilities guide our efforts. The beauty you see around you stems from him.'

Dornford brightened. 'We all contribute in our own way. You see, the community is greater than any individual.' His posture and tone dripped condescension. 'May I ask, do you have creative talents? Verity, isn't it?'

'Oh, I'm more of a lover of art than a creator. I play the piano quite proficiently and I can turn my hand to flower arranging. Does that count?'

'Hmm, well, I suppose…'

Stella interrupted. 'It's the desire to allow one's creative side to flourish that's important. There are several members of our community who doubted themselves at first. But given the right environment and a willingness to learn, everyone can develop the most remarkable abilities. You should see for yourself, Verity. Come to Chase Manor. We offer retreats for those who wish to discover more about us. Learn a craft or simply find peace. That's how I started.'

'What's this? Are you two haranguing this lady about the virtues of the communal life? I'm sure she didn't come here with the expectation of being preached to.' Elspeth threaded her arm through Dornford's. 'They'll detain you all day, extolling the virtues of the place. Do feel free to walk away and continue to enjoy the exhibition,' she continued, smiling at Verity, then pouting up at Dornford.

'Oh no. I expressed an interest. They are simply satisfying my curiosity. I'm keen to know more.'

'Yes.' Stella leaned forward from Dornford's other side to catch Elspeth's eye. 'Verity should come on retreat. I'm sure she'd find it rewarding.'

Elspeth gave Verity a searching look. 'If you're genuinely curious about us, Verity, by all means come to our next retreat. Stella will tell you all about it. Now, if you'll excuse us, I must drag my fiancé away. Perhaps we'll meet again at Chase Manor.'

Verity watched them pass through the crowd. In the centre of the hall, they stopped briefly and turned to look back.

'Now, come over to the stained-glass display and let me tell you all about the next retreat.' Verity allowed Stella to take her elbow and steer her away.

Chapter 7

'Drat the man. He insists I postpone any plans to ride my bicycle for at least a month.' Ambrose limped from the front door of his home at Thorneycroft Lodge to the drawing room, leaning on a stick. 'Nice of you to call, Mortimer. Excuse my tetchiness.'

'Dr Stevens only has your best interests at heart. Not getting any younger, are you?'

'Hardly on my last legs.' Ambrose sank into an armchair. 'This inactivity is driving me to distraction. Poor Mrs Elkins is feeling the strain, too. I'm not a willing invalid and it shows, I'm afraid.'

Mortimer nodded sympathetically. 'Perhaps I have the solution. A change of scene for you, and some peace and quiet for Mrs Elkins.'

'Not planning to pack me off to a sanatorium, are you?'

'Hmm, hadn't thought of that, but now you've brought the subject up…'

'Over my dead body.'

Mortimer grinned. 'Actually, I have something else entirely, in mind. Would a spell in London do the trick? Olivia and I are taking up residence at Montagu Square for a few weeks. Sylvia is old enough to travel, and Olivia will relish a break from country life, much as she enjoys it here. Join us.'

'I do believe I'm feeling better already.' Ambrose flexed his leg, masking the sharp stab of pain. 'London. Just the tonic. And Verity. I'm all curiosity to see this new house of hers.'

'We leave on Wednesday by the ten-thirty train from Bicester. Have your portmanteau packed and ready. I'll write to Verity this afternoon. Now, I must be on my way. Estate business awaits.'

Ambrose watched Mortimer take up the reins of the dogcart and set off toward the estate office. *London, eh?* Returning to the drawing room, he picked up the day's edition of *The Times*.

Mrs Elkins arrived with the tea tray as the clock in the hall sounded. Ambrose noticed neither his housekeeper nor the persistent striking of the eleventh hour. A photograph on page eight of a reception at the Guildhall commanded his attention.

'Your tea, Mr Mallard.' She waited for Ambrose to emerge from behind the newspaper. To no avail. The tray grew heavier. She set it down firmly with a clink of china.

'What? Tea?' Ambrose lowered the newspaper. Mrs Elkins' footsteps faded as she returned to the kitchen.

The Lord Mayor, Sir John Moore, greets Sir Neville and Lady Ternan, the caption read. Ambrose took another look. Was it? Older of course, and the hair was styled differently, but that face? The eyes, with their look of cool detachment, were hers to a tee, and that upturned nose… It had to be. Lady Ternan, eh? She was plain Violet Mason when he'd known her in Bombay – and certainly no lady.

Chapter 8

George Benson climbed the stairs to the third floor, keeping clear of the rickety banister. The wailing of a baby gave way to a drunken shouting match between a man and a woman, as he passed the scratched and flaking doors of his neighbours' tenements. The pervasive smell of boiled cabbage that filled his nostrils as soon as he entered the building followed him upwards, almost, but not quite, masking the reek of urine.

There were worse places than this. At least his shilling a day bought a room of his own. For many of the poor souls inhabiting the teeming warrens of the East End, the best they could hope for was a flea-ridden dormitory bed in a squalid, common lodging house.

Nolan, the caretaker on the ground floor, had eyed him suspiciously, demanding a week's rent in advance before handing over the key.

The number 12 was crudely painted in white. Room 12 at 64 Brick Lane would be his home for the next few days. George slid the pack off his shoulders and dropped it on the pitifully thin, stained mattress. The bedsprings creaked in protest. Stepping to the widow, he lifted the sash, allowing a fitful breeze to freshen the musty air within.

After unrolling the bedroll strapped to the top of his pack, he set about making the place at least barely habitable.

Fifteen minutes later, he sat on the bed, contemplating his surroundings. A small deal table and two rickety bentwood chairs stood in the middle of the chamber. George had wiped the table as best he could with a cloth from his pack. In an alcove by the door, stood a small brown cupboard, one of its two doors missing.

The fire grate opposite his bed was thick with ash, which had spilled out onto the bare dark floorboards. Plaster walls, once painted white, had faded to grey with the laths showing through in places. The one splash of colour relieving the drabness came from a pair of curtains hanging dejectedly from a rail above the window. Even though stained and ragged, one could still see a pattern of violets on a lemon background.

To George, it would be no more than a bivouac, a place to sleep. He'd not avail himself of the communal kitchen on the ground floor, nor the noisome pair of privies in the backyard. There was a public bathhouse around the corner and a barbershop for his daily shave. He'd eat out. All his pack contained was a pair of plain grey blankets, a small cushion to serve as a pillow, a fresh shirt, a change of underwear, and a candleholder with three wax candles. Also, most importantly, a bottle of Glen Grant and a battered tin mug.

He'd wondered whether it was really necessary to subject himself to such privation, but if his pretence of being a servant recently dismissed from his position was to hold water, he'd need to play the part to the full.

At least George could congratulate himself on recruiting Inspector Tweed to the cause. He recalled the policeman's expression of suspicion and disdain, which greeted his appearance at the front desk at Bow Street Police Station.

'I'm a busy man, Mr Benson. Why do you wish to see me?'

'Perhaps we could speak in private, Inspector. I have information of a confidential nature.'

Tweed looked up at the clock on the wall. 'It's hardly convenient.'

'Well, if you're too busy to prevent a serious crime, perhaps the Superintendent might spare some time?' George spoke loudly enough for the desk sergeant to look in their direction.

'I'll give you five minutes. Follow me.' Tweed led the way down a corridor of plain cream walls and a dark tiled floor. Opening the third door on the left, he waved George inside a room containing a table and two chairs.

'You see, Inspector —'

'I know you, don't I? No, don't tell me.' Tweed searched his mind. 'Never forget a face… yes – the Diamond Jubilee. You and a couple of East End ne'er-do-wells were involved in a commotion on London Bridge. I had to arrest you.'

'But you later released us because we were simply defending ourselves from a group of drunken louts. Surely you remember that.'

'Hmm, ye-es. Very well.' Tweed's eyes suddenly narrowed. 'But you invoked Colonel Quilter's name as well, as I recall. Does your visit here have anything to do with him? I have strict instructions from the Commissioner to report any approaches from that quarter.'

George sighed. 'It has nothing to do with him.' *Thank God*, he added under his breath. 'Inspector, can we just take a seat and I'll explain why I'm here? It won't take up much of your time.'

Tweed nodded.

'You've heard of the King brothers.' George began.

'Yes, scions of a family of Whitechapel criminals. They have certainly come to our attention. Thus far, we have only had cause to arrest one of them on a minor public nuisance charge. Bound over to keep the peace.'

'Well, they're certainly not keeping the peace. I can assure you of that.'

'Granted. From what I hear, they have ambitions to carve out a prominent place for themselves among the criminal underworld. Theft, extortion, that kind of thing. But the city is teeming with their sort, and we've not been presented with evidence of wrongdoing on their part. Is that all you have to tell me?' Tweed sat back and folded his arms.

'What if a situation were to arise in which the police had the opportunity to catch them red-handed in the commission of a crime? A feather in your cap, Inspector?'

Tweed unfolded his arms. 'Who are you, Benson?'

'I'm a private investigator, Inspector, and this is my proposition.'

George smiled at the memory of that conversation. Rising from the bed, he shut the window and left Room 12, locking the door behind him.

***

'The Black Lion in Hanbury Street or The Bell in Brick Lane, them's their usual boozers,' Alfie had told him back at the pawnshop. 'They're usually propping up the bar in one or the other, most evenings. You can't miss them, guv, just look for three large geezers with great big mops of curly straw-coloured hair. Honest, they remind me of circus clowns. All they'd need is some greasepaint and those funny shoes clowns wear. Not that anyone would say so out loud. Sammy, the eldest, is a bit taller than the other two, and he's got a squint. Very sensitive about it, too.'

The Bell was just a stone's throw from George's lodgings. He tried there first. The public bar was packed, but no one there looked remotely like the King brothers. In respectable parts of the city, he'd not expect to find women in a pub, but here both sexes mingled. George poked his head round the door of the snug, empty save for a young couple whispering together in the corner.

A few minutes' walk brought him to The Black Lion. Half a dozen men and a couple of women stood outside, lounging against the wall with drinks in hand. George threaded his way through the smoke-filled bar. In a scuffed dark tweed jacket, trousers with frayed bottoms, and a flat cap and muffler, he blended in. Finding a spot at the bar between two labouring types crouched over pints of bitter, and a wizened old fellow with a small mongrel and a persistent cough, he caught the barman's eye.

'Pint of Trueman's best.' George reverted to the broad Gloucestershire accent of his youth.

While the barman pulled the tap handle, George took in his surroundings. There was no sign of the Kings. Since his plan relied on staging a chance encounter with them, he could hardly ask the barman whether they'd already been and gone. He'd stay for as long as it took to drink his pint. If they didn't show up, he'd head back to the Bell and try his luck there.

'Thanks.' George pushed two coppers across the bar counter and took his glass to an empty table. He watched the steady comings and goings. Working men mostly, calling in for a well-earned pint after a day's graft, as well as a smattering of shady characters. George recognised the type. But there was no sign of the curly, fair-haired trio that Alfie had described.

Then there were the women. Some in the company of men, some sharing a gossip and a glass of gin or cheap port with friends. And others, like the young thing, hardly more than a girl, pulling at his sleeve and whispering suggestively in his ear.

George shook his head and pulled his sleeve away. 'Here's a tanner. Get yourself some dinner,' he said, earning a scowl as she scooped up the coin and flounced away to proposition a portly man reading a newspaper in the corner.

Returning to his beer, George took a deep draft of ale and felt in his jacket pocket, closing his fingers around the ring, feeling the smoothness of the emerald sitting in its gold mounting.

A flurry of movement near the front door made him put his pint down. A knot of men who had been standing together drinking and talking, split in two to permit the passage of a tall man, like a school of fish parting at the approach of a predator. Dressed in a three-piece suit topped off with a bowler hat, he walked straight up to the bar. The drinkers who had been leaning on it moments earlier, moved hurriedly away. The barman waited nervously, polishing a glass with a towel.

An eerie silence pervaded the pub. 'Pint of the usual, Terence.' The newcomer's voice struck George as strangely calm and reasonable, quite at odds with the fear his presence seemed to inspire.

The fair curls sprouting under the bowler left George in no doubt that the fellow's surname was King. As the man stood alone, raising his glass to his lips, the murmur of conversation returned, but at a subdued level. Just as George was wondering where the other two could be, the door swung open. Dressed identically to their brother, they joined him at the bar. Standing side by side, while the barman poured two more ales, George concluded that the first arrival must be Sammy, a head taller than his siblings and with a distracting squint.

He watched as the trio settled into their drinks, clearly at ease, and indulging in some light-hearted banter by the look of it, though George couldn't hear what they were saying. Ten minutes passed. He gathered his courage and swallowed the last of his pint.

Crossing the floor, George felt as though every eye in the place was on him. The barman's expression didn't help. Clearly, the fellow was astonished that anyone would be so foolhardy as to approach while the brothers were in possession of the bar.

'Another pint, please.'

As though drawn by an invisible force, the three brothers turned in unison. Three pairs of eyes looked him up and down.

The barman stood back, a picture of indecision until Sammy turned to him and nodded.

Not a word was said, as George's pint was poured.

The barman set it on the counter.

'That will be three more pints, Terence. I can see that this gentleman must have come to pay his respects. Nice of him to buy us all a drink, I'm sure.' Sammy fixed his stony gaze on George.

'Oh, yes – um, three more pints.' George echoed, looking away and focussing on his glass.

The barman finished pouring. 'That's eightpence then.'

'Right you are,' George rummaged in his pocket. He counted four pennies on the bar and rummaged again. 'Oh, blast.' The contents of his pocket clattered onto the floor at his feet. Swiftly, he bent to pick them up. One by one, four coppers – and the emerald ring. Hurriedly, he pocketed it and put the coins on the bar.

With a shy smile and a nod to the brothers, George reached for his pint and turned away.

'Nice ring you've got there.' Sammy's voice stopped George in his tracks.

'I said that's a nice ring. What do you reckon, Reg?'

'Yeah. Let's have a butcher's, - whatever your name is?' Reg agreed in a voice half an octave higher than his brother's.

George looked over his shoulder.

'Come here,' Sammy beckoned with his index finger.

George put his pint on the counter.

'Don't sound like you come from round here,' Sammy leaned casually on the bar.

'Country boy, ain't 'e.' Freddy moved to hem George in between his brothers.

'I'm from Tewksbury. And who would you gents be?' George took a sip of his beer.

Sammy grinned. 'You really ain't from round here, are you? If you was, you'd know who we are. Just ask anyone who the King brothers are. They'll soon put you right. So – let's see that ring of yours then.'

George reached into his pocket. Ignoring Sammy's outstretched palm, he worked the ring on to his little finger before withdrawing his hand and holding it up for inspection.

Sammy's grin vanished. His hand closed around George's wrist. 'Hand it over.'

George shook his head.

Sammy tightened his grip. 'We can do this the easy way or the hard way. You take it off your finger and hand it over, or Freddy here will be happy to chop off your pinkie. Show him.'

Freddy leaned in close and unbuttoned his jacket. George saw a wooden handle protruding from a leather sheath strapped to his shoulder. Freddy only needed to lift it a couple of inches. The butcher's cleaver was small but more than adequate to amputate a finger, or a whole hand, for that matter.

'Look, gents, shaking me down for one ring is all very well. I'm hardly going to take on the three of you. Anyway, violence is not my style. What if I was to offer you an opportunity worth more than fifty rings like this one?'

George staggered as Reg grabbed his collar from behind. 'Don't try worming your way out of it.'

'All right, have it your way. You can have the ring. If you're happy to pass up a small fortune, that's up to you.'

'Terence.'

'Yes, Sammy.'

'We're going to need your back parlour.'

'What? Now?'

'No, in six months' time – course I mean now.' Sammy glared at the barman. 'Half an hour, that's all.'

Terence lifted a flap on the bar counter.

Prodded unceremoniously through the parlour door, George found himself seated at a table, facing Sammy, with Freddie and Reg on either side.

'What's your name?' Sammy sat back, arms folded.

'Bob – Bob Watson.'

'Come on then, Bob. Start talking.'

George recited his story. He'd lost his place as a footman – well, more of a butler, really. His sister in Stroud had fallen ill. Widow she was, with two young ones. He didn't think his mistress would miss a few coins from her purse. Nor had she. It wasn't enough though, not enough for doctor's fees and medicine.

He thought he had the house more or less to himself. The cook had a half-day off, and Florence the lady's maid was accompanying the mistress to the shops. Young Agnes, the parlourmaid and general dogsbody, had popped out on an errand. It was the perfect opportunity to steal into the mistress's boudoir and search through her jewellery. She must have a lot of it, judging by the way she adorned herself with rings and brooches, necklaces and earrings, and God knows what?

'Thought if I was careful and only took a smaller item or two, she mightn't miss them.'

He'd only managed to pocket the ring and a cameo brooch. How was he to know that his mistress had met an old friend in Bond Street and sent Florence back home while she and her friend went off to have high tea? God, his heart had almost stopped when the bedroom door opened and there she stood. He'd stammered something about hearing a noise and coming to investigate, but Flo was no fool and hard as nails.

He didn't wait for the inevitable, ran up to the attic and changed out of his livery, packed his things and left.

'I got a few bob from pawning the brooch. Enough to pay for lodgings for a while. But I know where she keeps her jewels. There's diamonds, gold, really expensive stuff, and here's the thing, her brother's getting married this Saturday. She'll be away in the country, and she's bound to have Flo with her. The coast will be clear on Friday night.'

'But the other servants will still be there.' Sammy drummed his fingers on the table. 'What about them?'

'Old Mrs Harris, the cook, is half deaf. She'll be sound asleep by midnight, and Agnes, too. That's when we go in, nice and quiet.' George produced a key from his jacket. 'Servants' entrance. It's not bolted. This will get us in without making a noise. Then we tiptoe up to the mistress's bedroom. We can be out of there with the jewels in a jiffy and no one the wiser till the mistress gets back.'

'Gotcher!' Freddy laughed and banged his fist on the table. 'Thanks very much, Bob. We'll just take that key off you and do the job on our own then. How's that, Sammy?'

'Yes, Freddie, except Bob here hasn't told us where the bleedin' 'ouse is?'

'He will if I get me cleaver out.'

'Look, there's no need for any nasty business.' George spoke directly to Sammy. 'I could give you an address right now, but how would you know it was the right one? There's enough in this for all of us, no need for anyone to get greedy. And you'll need me to find your way around the house, otherwise you'll all be blundering about. Look, we meet at my lodgings on Friday at eleven. I take you there. We do the job and go back to my place to divvy up the loot. I only want a few bits and pieces. You can have the rest. Then I'm buggering off to the country.'

Chapter 9

'That brings us to our next retreat.' Oswald addressed the other members of the Council of Guidance. The title had been his idea. Although the community espoused the notion that all were equal, in practice a show of hands could hardly be organised every time a decision had to be made. And, in truth, most community members would rather devote themselves to their creative endeavours than to what might be termed mundane administrative matters.

The Council of Guidance was created for the very purpose of shouldering such a burden. Not a governing body, of course, simply an enabler. Gently steering a course for the good of all.

As the founder, it naturally fell to Oswald to chair the Council. He also chose its members. His wife Ursula sat at his right hand, his son Dornford to his left. By virtue of their engagement, Elspeth Forsyth, Dornford's fiancée, had been admitted to the Council. She sat between Dornford and the remaining member, Aquinas Thorpe. Distinguished by his saturnine features and black hair flowing down to his shoulders, Aquinas led the Arthurian faction.

Steeped in the romance and mysticism of Arthurian legend, as depicted in Thomas Malory's *Le Morte d'Arthur*, Aquinas and his followers formed a distinct grouping within the Chase Manor Community and dressed accordingly. His costume of a high-necked crimson brocaded jacket, alternating purple and crimson stockings, and pointed soft leather shoes, was an especially flamboyant example.

'Elspeth, you have the list of applicants,' Oswald turned to his prospective daughter-in-law. 'Pray enlighten us,' he added, leaning back with a self-satisfied smile and clasping his hands over his paunch.

'We have four persons desirous of attending.' Elspeth referred to her notes. 'Gregory Manning describes himself as a seeker after perfection, no less. It seems he came down from Cambridge last year and has spent some time travelling on the Continent. Reluctant to commit himself to *quotidian mundanity,* as he puts it, he sees our community as a gateway to a nobler way of life.'

'A young man searching for meaning, nothing unusual there,' Ursula commented. 'Naïve and impressionable, one assumes. Do we know anything else about him?'

'He writes from an address in Mayfair,' Elspeth responded.

'Encouraging.' Ursula smiled at Oswald.

'Oh, and he sent a photograph of himself,' Elspeth placed a sepia print on the table.

The image showed a painfully thin young man wearing a light serge lounge suit, a wing-collared shirt and a polka-dot bow tie, sitting stiffly at a desk. He was turned towards the camera, his eyes goggling behind thick lenses. His prominent cheekbones and short, fair hair, oiled down and parted in the middle, accentuated his slight build.

Ursula snorted. 'Looks as though he'd blow away in a moderate gust. Not a candidate for your round table, I fancy, Aquinas?'

'I think we could safely assume that Excalibur would have remained undrawn should Mr Manning have attempted to retrieve it,' Aquinas drawled, with his customary note of world-weariness.

'Malleable and unlikely to present difficulties, is my view,' Oswald slid the photograph back to Elspeth. 'Let's admit him. Does anyone disagree?' Ursula shook her head, followed by Dornford and Elspeth. Aquinas merely shrugged.

'Very well. He's admitted.' Oswald pronounced. 'Who's next, Elspeth?'

'Next, we have a Miss Caroline Hislop. She writes from Droitwich Spa and states that she is a recent alumna of the Glasgow School of Art.'

'Really? Then the young lady – I assume she must be young – has some talent to offer us?'

'She mentions having designed and produced book illustrations, gesso panels, and also repoussé metalwork. She's even included a couple of small illustrations. I must say they look rather good.' Elspeth produced two pieces of card, each measuring nine inches square.

The first, an exquisitely detailed botanical illustration of foxgloves, drew appreciative comments from everyone.

The second, a beautifully rendered watercolour of King Arthur's body being conveyed to Avalon, was pored over eagerly by Aquinas, in a most uncharacteristic display of enthusiasm. 'Sublime,' he breathed.

'Someone to take under your wing, perhaps, Aquinas?' Oswald smirked.

'That would depend on her other attributes,' Ursula gave Aquinas a thin-lipped smile. 'She's not provided a photograph, so we can't tell whether she might aspire to become another of your Guineveres.'

'You do me an injustice, Ursula. I live according to the code of chivalry. No matter how comely she may or may not be, Miss Hislop has undeniable talent. She must be admitted.' Aquinas fixed his belligerent gaze on Ursula and Oswald.

'She has my vote,' Dornford interjected. 'What do you say, Elspeth, my love?'

'Yes, certainly.'

'There's nothing to indicate how she's placed fortune-wise, I suppose?' asked Ursula.

Elspeth shook her head. 'No, but surely…'

'Our first consideration must be her contribution to our aesthetic aims.' Oswald turned to his wife. 'I think we can all agree, on the evidence before us, that she should make a worthy addition to our community. If she turns out to be endowed financially as well as artistically, so much the better.'

'Very well, admit her. Who do we have next?'

Elspeth returned to her notes. 'Next, we have… Mr Joseph Braithwaite, who says he's a master woodworker. He writes that he was a guildsman under Charles Ashbee at the Guild and School of Handicrafts at Essex House in London until its closure, and is now a member of a small handicrafts co-operative in Cheshire. His ambition, he says, is to devote himself to the furtherance of socialism. He talks at length about social ownership of the means of production, then there's something about a post-capitalist system. I must say, I found it rather heavy going. Anyway, he mentions that he was encouraged to write to us by none other than our very own Arnold Wright.'

Oswald groaned. 'No. I'll not countenance another troublemaker. Arnold will not be permitted to turn this community into a nest of revolutionaries. Give the man an inch and he'll be demanding that we make over the house, the estate, everything, to some form of collective ownership.'

Ursula nodded vigorously. 'The last thing we need is another Arnold Wright. He must not be admitted.'

'Not an ounce of romantic sensibility in Wright and his ilk. Socialism – ugh.' Aquinas shuddered.

'And the last candidate?' Oswald glanced at his wristwatch. 'I'm conscious of the time. Can we deal with this quickly, please?'

'Well, the final applicant is a person that Dornford and I have met. Her name is Miss Verity Mallard.'

'Yes, and she is most certainly comely, though not in the Guinevere sense, Aquinas,' Dornford added with a broad grin. 'Not one of your impressionable, ethereal types, but her looks…'

Elspeth's glare dissuaded him from elucidating further.

'We met her at our exhibition in London. I as good as invited her to come on retreat. I must say I doubted that she would take me up on it, but she has.'

'Why? Does she possess any artistic talent, Elspeth?' said Ursula, polishing her spectacles.

'Her interest stems from her aesthetic sensibility. She does not profess any practical skills, but…'

'Then why encourage her?' Ursula replaced her spectacles and glared at Elspeth.

'She attended the exhibition after meeting Stella at Liberty's.' Elspeth steadily returned Ursula's gaze. 'Stella overheard her placing an order for furnishings. In excess of a hundred pounds' worth, according to Stella. Having met Miss Mallard, she strikes me as an affluent woman of taste. Why not see if we can harness her wealth?'

Ursula shrugged and turned to her husband. 'I'll leave it to you.'

'Hmm. I'm inclined to admit her. Otherwise, we'll only have two for the retreat. She clearly has money. Yes, I say admit her. Elspeth, would you be so good as to write letters of invitation to the three successful applicants? And inform Mr Braithwaite that, regrettably, we cannot accommodate him. Now then, supper calls.'

Chapter 10

'Best if we cross two at a time. Don't want to attract the attention of any nosey neighbours who may still be awake. Sammy and I'll go first. Wait two minutes, then you two follow. Don't rush, just walk natural.'

'Think we're stupid?' Freddy grumbled. 'We've done over 'ouses before, lots of times.'

'Course you have. Anyway, two minutes. Come on then, Sammy, this way,' George pulled up the collar of his overcoat and stepped off the kerb, closing his hand around the key in his pocket. The tradesman's entrance was in the basement. At the top of the steps, he paused, then led the way cautiously to the small courtyard below.

George waited for Sammy to light the lantern he'd brought with him, then fitted the key in the lock. A half turn and George pushed the door open. Hovering in the doorway, he and Sammy awaited the others. Freddie negotiated the steps without incident, followed by Reg, gripping a Gladstone bag to carry the loot away.

With all four safely inside, George closed the door and took the lantern from Sammy, leading the brothers in Indian file along a corridor and past the servants' parlour to a flight of stairs. 'One at a time and tread lightly,' he whispered.

Emerging into the hall, George shone his lantern back down the stairwell to guide the others. Freddy's protestation that they'd done this before was evident from the brothers' stealthy progress, showing a degree of discipline which George hadn't expected. The only sound was the ticking of Verity's long-case clock.

Moments later, the four of them gathered outside Verity's bedroom. George turned the door handle and waved the others through, then pointed his lantern to illuminate the dressing table. In accordance with the briefing he'd given them, the King brothers removed two caskets from the top right-hand drawer. Sammy weighed one of them in his hands and gestured to George to bring his lantern closer, giving a quiet chuckle as the contents were revealed. Having also satisfied himself as to the contents of the second casket, he motioned Reg to open the Gladstone bag.

'I'll take that,' Freddy whispered in George's ear, gripping his wrist and wrenching the lantern from his grasp.

'Oi, what's going on?' George hissed.

An open clasp-knife in Sammy's hand gleamed in the lantern's glow an inch from his face.

'Thanks for the guided tour, Bobby. Won't be needing you no more. You just cool your heels here for a while. Try and follow us and I'll 'ave yer guts for garters. Got it?'

George kept his eyes on the knife and nodded. He watched Freddy leading his brothers out of the room and onto the landing. The lantern light faded as they descended the stairs. 'One – two – three – four,' he counted under his breath.

A shrill whistle blast shattered the silence. Boots pounded from several directions. Lantern beams danced about.

'Stand still!' Inspector Tweed's stentorian command echoed around the house. 'Take them, men.'

Looking over the banister, George observed the King brothers huddled together, dazzled by the bullseye lanterns shining in their faces, hemmed in by a crowd of constables, truncheons at the ready. Sammy obeyed Tweed's order to drop the knife. A sergeant secured the Gladstone bag and opened it for Tweed's inspection. 'You're all under arrest. Sergeant, get the cuffs on them and take them out to the black maria.'

George stepped back from the banister. 'Keep your mouths shut,' he heard Sammy mutter to his brothers as they were led away.

'Is it safe to come down?' George looked up at the attic landing. Verity's face flickered in the light from the lamp she held aloft.

'Yes, they've gone.'

Verity joined him.

'Bravo, George, or should I say, Bob? Alfie and Dick will be delighted.'

'And relieved. It's just as well it all went to plan. I'd hate to admit to Nel Fowler that the King brothers were still at large.'

'Come down to the drawing room. I believe a nightcap is called for.'

'Scotch?'

George nodded, sinking into one of Verity's new armchairs.

'I gave the servants tickets to the music hall and booked them into a little hotel in Earl's Court for the night.' Verity handed George his glass. 'A toast?'

'To Inspector Tweed and the fine men of the Metropolitan Police,' George proposed, clinking glasses.

Verity downed her scotch and sat down.

'What did you tell the servants? I can't imagine Elsie just toddling off for the night without asking questions.'

'I told them the truth, or part of it, anyway. I said that the police had discovered that burglars were planning to break in and that a trap was being set. They might have thought I was having an assignation, otherwise.'

'Hmm, I take your point. Well, they'll be behind bars by now. Tweed will have them up before the magistrate in the morning, and then it will be off to Pentonville until the trial.'

'And my jewellery?'

'Tweed swore on his honour that they will be returned as soon as the formalities are completed. I'll go round and collect them tomorrow, if you like?'

'No, George, we will both go. Another scotch?'

***

'All three of them?' Alfie danced a little jig, almost upsetting an elephant's foot full of walking sticks in his delight. 'Dick, Nel! Come out here. The rozzers have got the King brothers. They're banged up.'

Nel emerged, wiping her hands on her apron. 'Mr Benson, you're a marvel and no mistake. And you too, miss, begging your pardon. Letting those crooks into your house. I hope they didn't do no damage.'

'Thank you, Nel. No, there was no damage.'

Dick was heard thundering down the stairs, emerging in the shop a moment later.

'It's true then,' he beamed. 'They're all in the clink?'

George nodded. 'They won't be troubling anyone for a good while.'

'Now then,' Alfie produced a chair for Verity, dusting the seat with his handkerchief. 'Let's hear all about it.'

George held the floor, describing how the brothers had taken the bait. 'It got a bit sticky once or twice, but greed overcame any suspicions they had. After The Black Lion, they walked me back to my lodgings. One look at that place convinced them that Bob Watson was what he said he was.'

'I never thought I'd have a good word to say about coppers, but that Inspector Tweed's done us a right favour.'

'Yes, Alfie, it was a good collar, won't do him any harm. Verity and I paid him a call earlier. It seems that Sammy tried to bargain with him, offered Bob Watson's name as an accomplice. Gave him the address of Bob's lodgings. Tried to say that he was the mastermind.'

'Did he now?'

George laughed. 'Tweed played along, said he'd bring Bob in. Then he comes back to Sammy and says, "You'll have to do better than that, my lad. There's no Bob Watson at Brick Lane or anywhere else. You're behind all this".'

Chapter 11

Mortimer and Olivia planned to stay in town for a month at least. 'You're welcome to stay for as long as you wish, Ambrose,' Mortimer had offered. 'You needn't accompany us back home if you want to spend more time in the city.'

'Oh, I dare say I'll yearn to be back in the country once I've exhausted the fleshpots of London.' Ambrose had replied with a wink.

Fleshpots indeed. Ambrose sat on the bed. The journey from Thorneycroft left him fatigued. His bicycling accident took more out of him than he cared to admit. Stirring himself to unpack his suitcase, he mused over what he might do to pass the time. Firstly, he looked forward to visiting Verity in her new house. Then there was George. And Mary, he must see her too. And the Cottons, of course.

What else? He'd fleetingly thought about pursuing his interest in brass rubbing. There'd be a wealth of opportunities in London, but the prospect soon paled. Perhaps Verity was right, maybe it was best left to schoolboys.

With everything unpacked and stowed in the wardrobe and the chest of drawers, Ambrose closed his suitcase and clicked the locks shut. There was something else he might do, he thought, recalling the newspaper article that had caught his attention back at Thorneycroft Lodge. What would Lady Ternan say when confronted with her shady past in the shape of Ambrose Mallard?

A knock on the door interrupted his reverie. 'Yes, what is it?'

'Begging your pardon, sir, Mr Mortimer asks, would you come down to the drawing room? Miss Verity has just arrived.'

'Ah, thank you, uh…'

'It's Susan,' the young housemaid said shyly, bobbing a curtsey and hastening away downstairs.

'Verity, how delightful,' Ambrose made his entrance, arms outstretched.

'Are you quite recovered?' Verity felt the breath being squeezed out of her in Ambrose's enthusiastic embrace.

'On the mend. Most definitely on the mend.'

'Yes, so it seems.' Verity detached herself and took a step back.

'Ambrose is dying to see your place in Eaton Terrace,' Mortimer appeared at Verity's elbow with Olivia on his arm. 'And so are we.'

'How thrilling to furnish your own home. A blank canvas, so to speak. Is it very modern?' Olivia asked.

'Quite modern. You must all come and see it. Come for lunch. Bring Sylvia too. How is she, by the way?'

'Thriving,' Olivia announced with obvious maternal pleasure. 'Will you be staying for tea?'

'No, I must fly, I'm afraid. Journalistic deadlines wait for no woman.' Verity read Olivia's disappointment in her expression. 'I'm sorry, my dear. I don't mean to seem rude. The weekend is entirely free. Shall we say lunch on Saturday?'

'Why, yes. I think we're free, aren't we, Mortimer?'

'On Saturday? Yes, we have nothing arranged.'

'Shall we say noon then? And don't forget to bring Sylvia. I'm dying to play the doting aunt.'

'I'll see you out.' Ambrose offered Verity his arm.

'Gallant as always,' Verity allowed herself to be led out into the hall.

Ambrose flashed a smile. 'I have a question for you. In your comings and goings in town, have you come across a Lady Ternan?'

'No. Why do you ask?'

'Mmm, it's not something I can go into here and now.' Ambrose shuffled uneasily.

'My word, now I am intrigued.'

'Oh, look, it's nothing. Forget I asked.'

'Forgive me for teasing. I won't pry into your private affairs. No doubt you have good reason for asking.'

'Well, I was rather hoping that you might have some knowledge of her whereabouts here in London.'

'I'm afraid not, Ambrose. But I have an idea. Why don't you drop George a note? He'd be only too glad to help an old friend. Now then, I must away.'

Ambrose returned to the drawing room, finding Mortimer and Olivia deep in conversation. Not wishing to intrude, he excused himself. 'Just need to rest the old leg,' he said. 'I'll be down for tea.'

It wasn't purely an excuse. His leg was troubling him. Up in his room, Ambrose lay on the bed, gazing vacantly at the ceiling.

It was at one of the lowest points in his time in India that he'd crossed paths with Violet Mason. Cheated by his partner in crime, Thakur Singh, Ambrose found himself in

Bombay with depleted funds and no immediate prospect of gainful employment.

The Saffron Salon was a favourite of expatriate men of middle rank: traders, clerks, railway officials, shipping brokers and the like. Even some civil servants. Outwardly, it offered a clubbish venue for dining and drinking, card playing, and billiards. Behind the scenes, however, it catered for less seemly activities.

While he was no innocent, Ambrose was genuinely unaware that beyond an anonymous curtained door, a flight of stairs led up to a suite of rooms where ladies of ill repute, as they might be termed in polite society, entertained their guests.

Increasingly desperate for money, he'd been drawn to the card tables to try his luck at pontoon. Despite fluctuating fortunes, his winnings kept his head above water. He became something of a fixture.

Within this male domain, Mrs Violet Mason stood out. *The proprietress*, as she referred to herself, ruled her establishment with a blend of female charm and no-nonsense resolve when the occasion demanded it. Though short in stature, her outsized personality commanded the respect and admiration of her clientele.

Rumour had it that Mr Mason had a shady past, something about a banking scandal back in London, though no one seemed to be clear as to the exact nature of his transgression. In any case, the man was dead. Whatever his history, he'd apparently left his wife well provided for.

Ambrose recalled the evening when the swish of her skirt and her alluring fragrance had made him look up from his cards to admire the sight of her passing through the room. At the door, she turned and caught his gaze. The hint of a smile she bestowed upon him led ultimately to their becoming lovers.

Raven haired, with coal-black eyes and skin almost translucently pale, she successfully presented herself as in her early twenties; only a close look at the faint creases in the corners of her eyes provided any hint that she'd not see thirty again.

The dalliance lasted for two intoxicating months, then cooled. Not on his part; she firmly but kindly let him know the affair was over. Along the way, he'd discovered to his surprise, that there was more to The Saffron Salon than met the eye. Although it shocked him at first, the confident insouciance with which she'd disclosed the fact that the upper floor of her establishment was a brothel somehow made it seem unremarkable. 'It's a service, Ambrose. There's nothing tawdry about it. My girls are well cared for, and my gentlemen are both appreciative and discreet.'

They remained friends. Well aware of his precarious financial position, Violet offered him employment. Had it come from anyone but her, he'd have scoffed at the prospect of becoming bookkeeper to a bordello. And not just the establishment above the salon. There was another, also in Bombay, and a third in Poona.

Violet was a generous employer. Within six months, Ambrose had accumulated sufficient wealth to move from his cramped quarters in a rundown part of the city, to a comfortable villa with servants at his beck and call.

If he was honest with himself, he knew it couldn't last. The end came swiftly. A junior clerk in the British administration, having indulged in too many glasses of punch at an official reception, let slip that The Saffron Salon was more than the gentlemen's club it purported to be. The man's immediate superior would have taken the young man aside and carpeted him in private. No sense in creating a lot of unpleasantness. However, his wife, who had also witnessed the young man's indiscretion, had other ideas.

By sheer good fortune, Ambrose had just turned the corner on his way to work when the sight of three police officers escorting Violet to a waiting carriage stopped him in his tracks.

He turned on his heel and went to ground in his bungalow, dreading the prospect of a knock on the door by the authorities. Within a week, he'd packed up his belongings and decamped to Bangalore. He'd heard nothing of Violet since.

Chapter 12

'Do look at this hallstand, Mortimer, and that mirror. What an adorable copper frame. I love that ornamentation. Coiled leaves, do you see?' Olivia's admiration of Verity's furnishings was obvious from the moment she crossed the threshold.

Eagerly following Verity's tour through the ground and first floors, she imagined how the townhouse at Montagu Square might be transformed. Not a complete metamorphosis such as Verity had accomplished, but the introduction of some modern, less traditional touches.

Mary Phillips tripped lightly after them, adding her own expressions of approval. Following a few paces behind, Mortimer, Ambrose and George did their best to show an interest for form's sake. Not that the three women paid them any attention.

Luncheon followed.

'By the way,' Verity turned to Ambrose. 'I've already mentioned to George that you were seeking the whereabouts of Lady Ternan.'

'Eh?' Ambrose's cheeks glowed a slightly darker shade of red than his whiskers.

'Lady Ternan, Ambrose?' Mortimer seized on his relative's obvious embarrassment.

'Oh, she's just someone that I knew in another life. Just an acquaintance. It's nothing really.'

Mortimer grinned.

'Really, Mortimer, it's not important.' Ambrose's normal poise and easy manner deserted him.

'I'm sure we needn't intrude on Ambrose's private business,' Olivia intervened diplomatically. 'A change of subject, I think?'

'Just before we do.' George pushed a slip of paper across the table. 'The lady's address. It only took a glance through the social columns of the newspapers.'

Ambrose slipped the note into his pocket with a muttered 'Thank you'.

Olivia gave him an encouraging smile, then turned to Verity. 'Why don't you tell us what you're writing at the moment?'

'Oh, still *History's Forgotten Women*. I've submitted my piece on Aphra Behn.'

'And who's to be the next fallen woman?' Mortimer quipped.

'I shan't rise to the bait. That's exactly the sort of vacuous statement I would expect from you, dear brother. My next subject is Artemisia Gentileschi. There now, any the wiser?'

Verity smiled condescendingly at her brother's blank expression.

'She was an Italian Baroque painter, dear.' Olivia came to her husband's aid. 'Highly regarded in her time, but sadly neglected these days.'

'Bravo, Olivia.' Verity clapped her hands. 'There you are, Mortimer. Your wife knows of her.'

'I came upon her by chance. Some of her works featured in a book on seventeenth-century painters that I discovered in the library at home. I must say some of her subject matter is rather confronting.'

'Yes, women severing men's heads and the like. I find them quite engaging. A cautionary tale for any males who underestimate the boldness of the so-called weaker sex.' Verity turned her head to include George and Ambrose in her remark.

'Better run up the white flag, you chaps.' Ambrose seemed to have recovered his poise. 'Verity has us trapped on a lee shore with all her guns brought to bear.'

'We'll promise to read it when it's published,' George offered. 'No doubt we'll find it improving.'

'No doubt. However, you will have to wait. I will be engaged in quite another enterprise for the next three weeks or so.'

Verity paused for effect.

'I'm having a spell in the country. Herefordshire. A place called Chase Manor.'

'We're all ears,' Mary said encouragingly.

It's an arts and crafts community. Quite talented, too. I attended an exhibition of theirs in Highgate.'

'Goodness,' Mary exclaimed. 'I attended an exhibition of watercolours just last week, but it never occurred to me to go and reside with the artist. Has someone in this community taken your fancy, Verity? Is that it?'

'I'm sorry to disappoint you, dear. It's nothing of the sort. I'm pursuing a story. They're one of these utopian groups. You know – otherworldly, dedicated to their art. At least that's the public face they present. It made me wonder whether the reality matches their ideals.'

'Are they amenable to a journalist poking about?' George asked. 'From what I've read, these communities guard their privacy. I dare say some of them wouldn't want the public to know what they get up to – free love, that sort of thing.'

'I don't know where you read such things, George. Not in the journals that I write for. However, it's a fair question. I'm not going there openly as a journalist. They admit private individuals to what they term a retreat, an opportunity to experience their way of life and to "nurture one's creativity," as they put it.'

'Subterfuge, eh?' Ambrose weighed in. 'Find out what goes on and spill the beans. Sounds like my cup of tea. How does one apply to attend this retreat? Just think, the two of us pretending to be arty types, while we're really there to uncover their murky secrets. Count me in.'

Verity rolled her eyes. 'Ambrose, you never disappoint. The thought of you pretending to be some precious aesthete while skulking around listening at doors. Fortunately for both us, that absurd state of affairs cannot arise. Applications for the next retreat are closed, so I'm informed, and I am one of only three persons invited to attend.'

'Is that a look of disapproval, Mortimer?' Verity asked, noting her brother's frown and the set of his shoulders, a sure sign of his displeasure.

'Hmm. Why do you feel impelled to undertake such an…' Mortimer shook his head in exasperation.

'Underhand, Mortimer? Is that the word you were about to utter?'

'You have no shortage of work. This series of articles on forgotten women you mentioned sounds most suitable.

Why must you always place yourself in awkward situations? What if these people discover you are not what you seem?'

Verity tossed her head. 'I hardly think they're the sort of people who would pose a danger if my purpose in being there were discovered, and I am more than capable of playing a part, as you well know. If I were discovered, they would simply ask me to leave. They're aesthetes, not East End ruffians.'

'I'm sure Verity knows what she's getting into,' Olivia interceded. 'It does seem a little ungracious to question her when she has kindly invited us into her new home. Come, Mortie, let's change the subject. I'm sure Verity would be only too glad to hear how Silvia is coming along.'

'Yes, I'd very much like that, Olivia.' Verity darted a look in her brother's direction. 'I will simply close the subject by saying that I'm leaving for Chase Manor on Wednesday next.'

Chapter 13

Verity consulted her watch. Fifteen minutes to Hereford. The engine's whistle sounded and, seconds later, the train rattled over a level crossing with farm carts standing in line, waiting for the gates to open.

The old gentleman sitting opposite her in the compartment awoke with a start, then settled back into a doze, snoring softly.

She felt for the letter in her handbag. It had arrived in the last post the previous day. She'd felt surprised and not a little indignant that George had sent a letter rather than coming to her in person. It was odd, but even now, after everything they'd been through together, George rarely seemed completely at ease in her company. Although he tried not to show it, there was always a degree of diffidence in his manner, if that was the right word. Wariness, then.

True, they came from different strata in society, but Verity had never treated him as anything other than her equal. They'd disagreed, even clashed heads on occasion, but that had only served to elevate George in her esteem. Mary had hinted more than once that George secretly carried a torch for Verity. In which case, it flared very dimly, for she had never sensed its glow.

Verity read the letter twice, then folded it and replaced it in her handbag. A letter indeed. She'd received formal reports and a telegram or two from him before. Terse and to the point, as would be expected with such forms of communication. But never a letter.

He was quite right. Any attempt to dissuade her, however well intentioned, would only make her more determined to press on. She would never permit a man to treat her with condescension. But that was not George's intention, she knew. And if she was honest with herself, there was comfort in the knowledge that he was waiting in the wings.

Two phrases stuck in her mind. *I will be thinking of you* and *Ever yours.* What should she make of them?

The train slowed. Open countryside gave way to houses. As they finally drew to a halt, Verity pulled down the compartment's window and gestured to a waiting porter. With her luggage loaded onto the porter's trolley, she passed through the ticket barrier. Trusting to the fact that her invitation had stated that a representative of the community would be there to meet her, she moved out into the station yard. Verity stood uncertainly looking around her for a moment, until she spotted a barouche, and a figure waving a handkerchief, stepping down from it and hurrying toward her.

'Miss Mallard – Verity.' Stella Miles came up briskly, pointing the porter to the waiting carriage. 'Welcome. Just think, a chance encounter in Liberty's and now here you are. I'm so glad you decided to attend our retreat. You'll love it. I simply can't wait to show you around.'

Stella paused and looked away. 'Do excuse me. There is another person who should have arrived on the London train. Now where can he have got to? Ah, I see him. Yoo-hoo!' Stella waved furiously at a young, bespectacled man with two suitcases at his feet and radiating an air of bemusement.

'Yoo-hoo!' Stella repeated, finally gaining his attention. For a moment she wondered whether he expected her to carry his luggage, but after a moment's indecision, he picked up his cases and walked towards her, shoulders bent under the unaccustomed weight.

'Mr Manning?'

'Yes, I'm Gregory Manning.' The young man confirmed in a clipped, high-pitched voice.

'Welcome to Chase Manor. I'm Stella Miles.'

Gregory put his suitcases down and shook the proffered hand. 'Pleased to meet you, Miss Miles.'

'Oh, it's Stella. We all go by our first names at Chase Manor, Gregory, and allow me to introduce Verity Mallard. She is also attending our retreat.'

He regarded Verity curiously through his pebble lenses for a moment and inclined his head. 'Miss Mallard.'

'Verity. I'm pleased to make your acquaintance, Gregory.'

'Now then, let's get aboard the carriage.' Stella led the way. 'It's only twenty minutes to the Manor.'

Gregory took up his burden and shuffled after Stella. Verity walked beside him, wondering whether she should offer to carry one of his cases, but that would be demeaning.

Her luggage was already stowed, with the porter standing beside the carriage, awaiting his tip. Touching the peak of his cap and muttering a 'thank you, ma'am,' he wheeled his trolley away.

'Cooper, put the gentleman's cases in the carriage,' Stella addressed the carriage driver. 'Quickly now, we're expected at the Manor by four-thirty.'

Not first names for everyone, thought Verity. The driver jumped down and busied himself with Gregory's luggage. Dressed in a worn dark suit, with patches on his elbows – Verity put his age at twenty-five. His dark hair and beard framed a face weathered by the outdoors, but still unlined. Not an artistic type, but a servant. Climbing back up onto the box seat, he flashed her a smile.

Stella kept up a steady stream of chatter on the journey, extolling the Chase Manor community and its leaders and speaking enthusiastically about her latest stained-glass creation.

'Oh, I forgot to mention that the third member of your little coterie on this retreat arrived this morning. Her name is Caroline Hislop. Quite an earnest young woman, she's an accomplished artist and well-versed in design and craft work.'

'Oh dear, my modest accomplishments will hardly bear comparison,' Verity remarked.

'I'm sure you'll discover talents you never realised you possessed,' Stella smiled encouragement.

As the carriage passed through the gates of the Chase Manor estate, Verity glanced at Gregory, sitting stiffly opposite her. All the way from the station, he hadn't uttered a word.

Chapter 14

Ambrose watched from beneath his umbrella, listening to the drumming of the rain on the fabric and flinching as a gust drove the rain sideways, peppering his cheek. It was his third day walking in Cavendish Square Gardens, observing the house.

Leaving Montagu Square on what he termed his morning constitutional, he'd spent an hour each morning in the park between nine-thirty and ten-thirty before taking refreshment at a nearby tea shop, then returning for a further hour.

Feeling a little like a love-struck youth and anxious lest his presence be thought suspicious and attract the attention of the park keeper, he circled the park, keeping a watchful eye for any sign of his quarry.

He recalled how he'd caught his breath the previous morning when she'd appeared, her figure framed in the doorway for a few fleeting moments before her husband joined her and escorted her to a waiting cab.

The shower petered out. Ambrose shook the water off his umbrella. According to his watch, it was time for morning tea. Turning to leave the park, he took a parting glance at the house – and turned back again.

She'd already descended the steps and was standing on the pavement, a parasol in one hand and a spaniel on a lead in the other. No sign of Sir Neville. Ambrose gulped. He'd spent days imagining this moment, but now that the prospect of speaking to her was in his grasp, he hesitated.

He saw her look up at the sky, deciding whether to brave the chance of another shower, then she stepped off the pavement, crossed the road and entered the park. Steeling himself, he stood at the edge of the path, wondering whether she'd recognise him. When, instead of circling the gardens in a clockwise fashion, she headed in the opposite direction, Ambrose felt relief for an instant, then followed, summoning up the courage to accost her.

She ambled, allowing the dog to sniff at trees, unaware of his presence. He slowed his pace, but her frequent halts brought him closer, despite himself. They approached the far side of the park, out of sight of her house.

A passing fox terrier, seemingly without an owner, bounded over, coming to a halt a foot from the spaniel and barking aggressively. Lady Ternan's pet retreated behind her skirts, which only emboldened the other dog.

'Shoo, get away,' she called out, poking ineffectually at the furry assailant with her parasol.

Ambrose's sudden appearance, thwacking the terrier on its rump with his umbrella, and shouting at it to be gone had the desired effect. The shocked cur yelped and raced away as fast as its legs would carry it. Lady Ternan's relief and gratitude showed in her face as she acknowledged her good Samaritan.

'Thank goodness you came along. Poor Bess was beside herself with fear. She's such a good-natured thing and no match for that awful creature. Do accept our thanks, Mr...?'

'Mallard, madam.'

Ambrose studied her face.

'We are very grateful to you, Mr... Did you say Mallard?' Her eyes signalled surprise and alarm.

'Violet, it's me, Ambrose.'

'Whatever do you mean? I am Lady Ternan. Clearly, you are under some misapprehension, sir. Now, Bess and I will be on our way.' She turned away, pulling at the dog's lead.

'Please, Violet, I only want a word, a moment of your time, nothing more. I think you owe me that.'

He watched as she retreated. In a fog of indecision, Ambrose struggled with conflicting emotions. Disappointment and annoyance on the one hand, but also relief. What good would come of crossing paths with Violet Mason again?

Reluctantly, he retraced his steps, berating himself as an old fool. Oblivious to the sound of footsteps on the gravel path, it took a gruff bark directly behind him to make him stop and look round.

Her eyes held his. 'Forgive me, Ambrose,' she whispered. 'Your sudden appearance unnerved me.' She looked around nervously. 'I must return home. My husband will be wondering what is keeping me. I promised I would be only a few minutes, just enough for Bess to get some fresh air.'

It was no pretence. Her anxiety showed on her face and in her voice.

'Then go. But promise you'll meet me again. For old times' sake. Please.'

She hesitated. 'He's away on business tomorrow. Here, at the same time.

Chapter 15

The carriage passed along an avenue of tall poplars, then into an open space flanked by meadows. Stella pointed; ahead, Verity saw the manor house. Gradually, its features revealed themselves. The building looked older than she'd expected. In weathered limestone, it had a long three-storeyed frontage and a gable roof incorporating several dormer windows. At its centre was the entrance, under a wide stone portico. The place she'd first seen in a photograph, with Oswald, Ursula and Dornford Lamont standing outside.

To her surprise, they turned off the road a furlong short of the house. A tall stone wall extended on either side of an open gateway. The carriage passed through it, revealing a small settlement arranged around a central pond. Verity noted rows of plain terraced cottages, two large stone barns, several outhouses, a sizeable wooden building having the appearance of a workshop with chimneys at either end, and several other structures.

Stella turned and smiled. 'Welcome to our Arcadia.'

The carriage continued on its way, skirting the pond. Half a dozen men and women stood watching as they passed, and faces appeared at cottage windows.

Still, they didn't stop.

Leaving the settlement, the carriage passed through a grove of trees.

If what they'd just seen was Arcadia, what on earth was this?

Verity surveyed the scene in wonder, as might a small child. Even Gregory Manning, who had said not a word since taking his place in the carriage, uttered a 'goodness me'.

The carriage drew to a halt outside a group of three quaint buildings arranged around a patch of lawn. The compact two-storied houses struck Verity as peculiar gothic fantasies. Each subtly different, they were a riot of fairy tale features. Steep sloping roofs of stone tiles, pointed arched windows, stone porches with elaborate tracery surrounding heavy oak doors with iron staple hinges and door handles, and, most curious of all, a series of earthenware plaques fixed at intervals upon the walls, colourfully glazed with images of woodland creatures – hares, deer, foxes, red squirrels, jays, swallows.

'Welcome to your accommodation,' Stella announced. 'We call them the Fairy Cottages.'

Cooper jumped down and opened the carriage door, offering a hand to assist his passengers in stepping down. Stella brushed it aside. Verity would normally have done the same, being naturally dismissive of any suggestion of dependence on a man. But seeing his simple, artless smile, she felt it would be churlish to follow suit, nodding her thanks as she stepped onto the gravel path before joining Stella outside the nearest house. Behind them, Gregory Manning managed to lose his footing, evading Cooper's attempt to catch him and sprawling onto the gravel, grazing the palms of his hands.

Verity picked up Gregory's spectacles and straw boater, which had become dislodged by his abrupt descent, while Cooper helped him to his feet.

'Good gracious, are you alright?' Stella watched anxiously while he brushed himself down and recovered his hat and glasses from Verity.

'Oh… y-yes, I think so. A foolish mishap, nothing to fret about,' Gregory muttered, rubbing his hands together to relieve the stinging of his palms. 'I should have watched where I was going, but *that* distracted me.'

Verity's glance followed his outstretched arm. How on earth had she missed it?

If the quaint houses seemed a fanciful indulgence, the sight she now beheld was surely a sign of an obsession bordering on madness.

On a patch of raised ground, framed on either side by stands of tall trees, a fantasy fortress, intriguing and wholly incongruous, glowed in the slanting sunlight of the late afternoon. Its central round tower topped with a conical slate roof, stood at the juncture of two stone wings, arranged at an angle to make an inverted V. A crenelated curtain wall with a stout wooden gate at its centre joined the ends of these buildings, enclosing a triangular central courtyard. From a flagpole at the apex of the tower, a pennant fluttered and, under the urging of a sustained wind gust, revealed a gold dragon against a field of pure white.

Tantalised by the sight, Verity gazed spellbound, imagining a fanfare and the gates opening to reveal a retinue of mounted knights in burnished armour, escorting ladies on palfreys wearing bright billowing robes and wimples on their heads. Even Gregory's self-conscious reserve couldn't mask a hint of childlike wonder. 'A veritable Camelot,' he murmured.

'Ha-ha!' Stella broke the spell. 'It always has this effect on our guests. I so look forward to seeing everyone's reactions when they see it. You might well call it Camelot, Gregory, but more of that later. It's called Myrddin's Keep, though there are some who refer to it as Thorpe's Folly. Now, let's turn to more practical matters for a moment.

'You, Verity, will be staying here,' Stella pointed to the nearest cottage. Above the door in crimson Celtic lettering was the name *Enid*. 'It's very comfortable and has everything you need. I trust you will have no objection to sharing with our other female guest. Caroline, has already made herself at home.

'No, not at all. I'll be very happy to.'

'And you, Gregory, will have possession of *Elaine*. Oh, that sounds rather indelicate, doesn't it? You'll be staying over there.' Stella pointed to the middle cottage.

'Cooper, put Miss Mallard's luggage inside, and then take Mr Manning across to *Elaine*. Gregory, I'll pop over after I've settled Verity in.'

A faint smell of violets greeted Verity as she followed Stella across the threshold.

'Come through to the parlour,' Stella said, indicating a doorway on her right.

The young woman sitting in an armchair put her book aside as Stella waved Verity towards her.

An earnest young woman, and an accomplished artist. That's how Stella had described Caroline on the journey from Hereford, giving Verity the mental image of a slight, bespectacled, bluestocking type, plain and plainly dressed.

'Caroline, this is Verity Mallard, your house companion during the retreat.' The woman who stepped forward

80

confidently could hardly have been more different from the person of Verity's imagination. In her tailored skirt of blue serge and black satin with matching bolero jacket, she would not have looked out of place in the smartest of London salons. Her immaculately coiffured auburn hair was held in place with tortoise-shell combs.

'Verity. I'm so pleased to make your acquaintance. I must say that I had formed an impression of someone… rather homespun, shall we say? But it seems we are quite alike. I don't know about you, but to me, the arts and crafts crowd can appear somewhat worthy.'

Earnest indeed? Forthright and brimming with confidence was more like it. A mirror image of herself, in character. Except that, for the purposes of her story, Verity would not be herself. She would take on the role of an acolyte, eager to fit into the community. She smiled, meeting Caroline's steady gaze. 'I must confess to having the same idea about you, but I'm pleased to find you as you are. I'm sure we will get along famously.'

Stella gave a diplomatic cough. 'Well, yes, I'm sure. Now then, let me acquaint you with how things are arranged here, Verity.'

'Oh, no need to go through it all again, Stella. I can pass on everything you told me to Verity. Isn't there another person you need to attend to? That young fellow who fell out of the carriage just now?'

'Oh. Well. If you like, Caroline.' Stella tossed her head and walked to the door. 'You'll be sure to tell Verity about tonight's dinner, won't you?'

'Of course, Stella.' Caroline grinned mischievously at Verity as Stella's footsteps retreated along the hallway.

Chapter 16

'Welcome, welcome, thrice welcome.' Oswald stood at the doorway of Chase Manor, arms outstretched. For the occasion, he'd elected to wear his best peasant smock, a purple affair with gold embroidery at the collar and cuffs, over sable trousers, tucked into calf-high fawn boots. To his right stood Ursula in a voluminous maroon cotton dress, its bodice emblazoned with a yellow rising sun motif; her hair, released from its usual long plait, framed her face, extending in a brown-grey curtain almost to her waist.

Following a step behind Stella, Verity and Caroline exchanged a brief glance, arching their eyebrows at one-another before composing their features. Gregory brought up the rear, blinking owlishly.

'Now, let me guess, you are Verity and you are Caroline.' Oswald pointed from one to the other. Before either of them could confirm her identity, he strode forward and hugged Verity, then repeated the performance with Caroline. As he only came up to their shoulders, the whole performance induced an urge to flinch, which both women managed to control, along with an equally powerful temptation to laugh out loud.

Gregory, however, did flinch when Oswald released Caroline and advanced on him, and took a step backwards. An awkward silence persisted for a few seconds until

Oswald gave a nervous laugh and slapped the young man on the shoulder.

'Ursula and I have the greatest pleasure in welcoming you to our wonderful community here at Chase Manor. Think of us as a family united in our love of art, beauty and, dare I say it, one another. We fervently hope that your time spent here will nurture you in both body and soul. Come inside now and meet some of our most prominent and accomplished members.' With a theatrical bow from Oswald and a curtsey from Ursula, they turned to lead the way into the house.

'Come in, come in.' Oswald stood gesturing at the dining-room door.

'I'll leave you now.' Stella whispered.

Inside, Verity recognised Dornford, clad much as she'd seen him at Arrowfield Hall, and, at his side, Elspeth, whose dress was decorated with motifs depicting the fable of the Fox and the Crow. However, it was the figure standing off to one side, leaning against the wall, that drew her attention. Aquinas Thorpe's tunic in sky blue, worn with a thin leather belt, extended to his calves, beneath which yellow stockings contrasted with red leather shoes. Emblazoned across his chest was the same gold dragon adorning the pennant above Myrddin's Keep. His dark eyes locked onto hers, his craggy features turning from a frown to a sardonic smile. Verity held his gaze until he shrugged and turned his attention to Caroline.

'May I…' Oswald's words of introduction were rendered redundant as Caroline took the initiative, crossing the room to stand face to face with Aquinas. 'I'm Caroline Hislop. Would I be correct in assuming you have some connection with Myrddin's Keep?' she said, pointing at the dragon motif.

Aquinas pushed himself away from the wall. 'I am Aquinas Thorpe and, may I say, I'm enchanted to make your acquaintance,' Aquinas attempted a courtly bow, hampered by the fact that Caroline stood a mere foot and a half in front of him.

'Ah, hence the term Thorpe's Folly.' Caroline turned away to introduce herself to Dornford and Elspeth.

Verity followed in her footsteps, bestowing a brief, 'How do you do,' on Aquinas.

Dornford's eyes darted to and from Caroline to Verity and back again, uncertain whom to address first. Elspeth took the initiative. 'I'm Elspeth, Caroline,' she began. 'Verity and I are already acquainted,' she continued, with a nod of recognition. 'I'm Dornford's fiancée. Come along, Dornford, do the honours.'

'Uh… yes, of course. I'm Oswald and Ursula's son, Caroline. I've been so looking forward to meeting you. Those watercolours you enclosed with your application were such delightful pieces. Elspeth and I have taken a special fancy to the floral painting. May we keep it?'

'Yes, of course you may and the other picture as well, if you wish.'

'Ah, no.' Aquinas crossed the room. 'I have laid claim to the Arthurian picture. Perhaps you would bestow it upon me as your favour?'

Caroline turned her head. 'Favour?'

'Yes, I use it in the chivalric sense. As a lady might bestow a scarf or some other keepsake to a knight.'

'Oh, I see. But doesn't that imply some measure of affection on the part of the lady?'

'Ah – we hold all ladies in the highest regard. Our code…'

'We? Our?' Caroline raised an eyebrow, relishing the change is Aquinas's demeanour. A few moments earlier, he'd displayed a hint of swagger, but now he shuffled uncertainly.

'Er…'

'He speaks of his little cohort of latter-day knights-errant, Caroline,' Elspeth interjected. 'The Order of the Golden Dragon. They're always looking for maidens to champion.'

Aquinas snorted and shot her a look of displeasure.

'I see. I'm all curiosity. You must sit next to me at dinner, Aquinas, and tell me all about it. And yes, of course you may keep my painting.' Caroline bestowed a dignity-restoring smile on him.

Unaccustomed to being less than the centre of attention, Verity consoled herself with the thought that as a journalist she'd struck a rich vein of material for her articles.

'Well, well,' Oswald clapped his hands. 'Now that we've made our introductions, let's be seated. There are place cards on the table. Dornford, you'll need to change places with Aquinas.'

Verity noted Dornford's momentary scowl at forfeiting his place next to Caroline.

After a few moments of shuffling past one another, everyone found their places. Oswald and Ursula occupied either end of the dining table. To Oswald's left, Caroline, Aquinas and Gregory sat side by side, and to his right sat Verity, Dornford and Elspeth.

'Nancy! Sally!' Gregory almost jumped out of his seat at Ursula's sudden ear-piercing exclamation.

Footsteps hurried along the passage and two women entered, the elder bearing a tureen, and the younger, little more than a girl, carrying a pile of soup bowls.

Verity saw a familial resemblance. Mother and daughter, no doubt. But the likeness went further, reminding her of the carriage driver, Cooper.

Having laid steaming bowls of what smelled like mushroom soup in front of the diners, the servants retreated.

'Ahem.' All eyes turned to Oswald.

'I should explain that it is not our custom to say grace. We make no assumptions as to the religious beliefs of our members, if indeed they have any. Such bounty as we enjoy comes from our joint endeavour, the fruit of our labours. Now, please…' Oswald picked up his spoon and set to.

Verity gingerly took a small spoonful. *Surprisingly good,* she conceded.

Oswald reached out and grasped the handle of a brown earthenware jug. 'This is our own cider. Please try some. There is also water, if you prefer it, in the white jugs.' Verity noted three pairs of brown and white jugs placed at intervals along the table.

'Cider, Verity?'

'Yes, thank you, Oswald.'

'And you, Caroline? We call it Chase Manor Original.'

'Please.'

Gregory rejected the offer of cider in favour of water. 'I rarely imbibe,' he whispered.

The others helped themselves, filling their glasses with the clear golden liquid.

Verity finished her soup and looked up. Everyone save Gregory had put their spoons down, and a few moments of awkward silence followed as he slowly spooned up the last of his soup, seemingly oblivious to his surroundings.

Aquinas watched from the corner of his eye and, as Gregory finally sat up, he turned to Caroline. 'May I…'

'One moment, Aquinas, before you start regaling Caroline with your tales of knightly quests and pageantry, why don't we allow our guests to tell us more about themselves?' Oswald beamed at Caroline.

'Oh, wasn't my letter of application sufficiently informative?'

'It certainly convinced us of your artistic talents.' Oswald leaned back, cradling a glass of cider in his hands. 'But what about you? Family? Attachments?'

Well, what can I say? Youngest of three sisters. Papa is a doctor. Mama died in a riding accident four years ago.' Pausing to allow the usual expressions of sympathy, Caroline cleared her throat and continued. 'Attachments, did you say, Oswald? Well, there's Gerald, of course.'

Verity couldn't be sure, but did Aquinas's shoulders slump just a little?

'But the engagement was a mistake. I'm afraid he took it rather badly, but *c'est la vie.*'

Aquinas sat upright and took a draught of cider. The sparkle in his eye did not escape Verity's attention.

'Do you have an idea of what you would like to accomplish during your retreat?' Elspeth enquired.

'I have it in mind to create a gesso wall panel. A triptych portraying the Fates, I have brought my sketches with me. I assume there would be no objection, would there?' Caroline looked enquiringly at Elspeth.

'None. It's an admirable idea. I believe you have undertaken similar work before?'

'Oh yes, in Glasgow, I had the good fortune to assist Margaret Macdonald and her sister Frances. So wonderfully talented, the pair of them.'

'But surely, Caroline, an Arthurian theme would present a better subject.'

Elspeth frowned at Aquinas's interruption.

'A triptych certainly, but one depicting Edith, Elaine and Guinevere. I can see it in my mind's eye – a wonderful artefact for Myrddin's Keep. You could work on it there.' Aquinas leaned closer to Caroline.

'Hmm. An intriguing idea, certainly. But I've quite made up my mind.' Caroline shifted in her seat, inclining away from Aquinas as subtly as she could.

'Excellent.' Elspeth seized the initiative. 'The Fates it is, and I have just the studio space for you at Sylvan Cottage. You'll be at the heart of the community rather than out at draughty old Myrddin's Keep.'

'But –'

Oswald held his hand up to quell Aquinas's protest. 'I think we must consider the matter settled. And if I'm not mistaken, it's time for our next course to be served.' He nodded to Ursula, who again bellowed to summon the servants.

Gregory managed not to flinch this time.

Sally rushed in and gathered up the soup bowls, piling them on the sideboard, then distributed dinner plates. Following behind, Nancy carried a stuffed saddle of lamb on a large carving dish. With the aroma of roast meat and herbs enveloping the dining room, Oswald started carving.

Next came bowls of buttered parsnips, boiled potatoes, carrots and runner beans.

Between mouthfuls, Verity turned to Dornford, intending to ask how the exhibition at Arrowfield Hall had turned out. Before she could speak, a finger prodded her elbow. 'Oh, Oswald, I'm sorry. Were you about to say something?'

For the next twenty minutes, Verity politely endured Oswald's recollection of a visit he'd made to Venice as a young man. Each time he took a mouthful of food, she hoped that his turgid recitation of palazzos and churches was done. But on he went.

Verity lent half an ear to him, nodding at intervals while also tuning in to the other conversations around the table.

Dornford and Aquinas vied for Caroline's attention, interrupting and speaking across one another. However, Dornford was compelled to depart the field of battle when Elspeth curtly intervened. 'For heaven's sake, Dornford, stop badgering the poor girl. Ursula and I are discussing arrangements for the wedding. Would it be too much to expect you to show an interest? It does concern you, you know.'

Left to suffer Aquinas's unchallenged attention, Caroline focused on her dinner. Amidst it all, Gregory picked silently at his food. Verity caught his eye and gave him a sympathetic smile, receiving only a blank look in return.

Sally remained on duty in the dining room after her mother returned to the kitchen. At a gesture from Aquinas, she replaced the empty cider jug in front of him with a full one.

When everyone had finished eating, she cleared the plates away. 'Pudding in ten minutes,' Ursula commanded.

'And now,' Oswald concealed a belch behind his napkin. 'It's your turn, Verity. What can you tell us about yourself?'

'Oh, I can't offer anything to match Caroline's talents, I'm afraid.'

'But you must have interests. You have an appreciation of the decorative arts, but what else should we know about Verity Mallard?'

Verity shrugged. 'Oh dear. Well, I adore the theatre. I have a friend who's an up-and-coming actress, as a matter of fact. Her name's Mary Phillips. Perhaps you've heard of her.'

'Who are your people, your family?'

Verity turned to face her questioner, taken aback a little by Ursula's forthrightness.

'I…' Verity reached for the water jug, pouring with a slight tremor. 'Excuse me,' she whispered. Acutely aware of being the focus of everyone's attention, she took a sip of water. 'I have the misfortune of having no close family. My parents passed away within two months of one-another. Father succumbed to pneumonia. It also killed my mother; not directly, but her heart was broken.' Verity took a lace handkerchief from her sleeve and dabbed at her eyes. 'That was five years ago. And… and George, my husband, left me twelve months ago,' she stifled a sob, 'drowned.'

Verity sat forlornly with her head bowed, while her dining companions made expressions of sympathy and condolence. *Did I just say George?* When she'd practised this very speech at home in readiness for being asked about her background, her husband's name was Albert. *How on earth did George pop into my head?*

'Oh, my dear lady, how ineffably sad to have suffered such a loss.' Oswald was all concern. Everyone looked on with mournful expressions.

Elspeth leaned across Dornford to squeeze her hand. 'Our hearts go out to you, Verity. Let us help heal the pain you must still carry within you.'

'Thank you, thank you all for your kind thoughts.' Verity blinked tears away and forced a smile. 'I feel certain that my stay among you will do me the world of good.'

Oswald cleared his throat. 'Ahem. Gregory, what can you tell us about yourself? I recall your letter of application mentioned that you are seeking perfection. A lofty ambition indeed and, much as I'm the first to extol the virtues of this wonderful community of ours, even I must admit that we have yet to achieve such a state.' Oswald chuckled and beamed at Gregory.

'Of course, perfection does not and cannot exist,' Gregory replied primly. 'It would be absurd to suggest so. I said I was a *seeker* after perfection. Is that not a goal that anyone possessing intellect and taste should set for themselves? I considered that this community and its ideals would support and nourish me in my endeavour. Was I mistaken?' Gregory fixed his owlish, bespectacled gaze on Oswald.

'Ha, what do you say to that, Oswald?' Aquinas drained his glass of cider and refilled it. 'Nourish me in my endeavour,' he pronounced theatrically, mimicking Gregory's tone and earning an angry look from the object of his derision.

'I say, there's no occasion to take that tone, Aquinas,' Dornford snapped. 'Our guest deserves to be treated with courtesy. Hardly chivalrous of you, is it.? Or is that the cider talking?'

Aquinas snorted and downed his cider, locking eyes with Dornford as he emptied the remaining contents of the jug into his glass.

'That's enough!' Ursula's forceful interjection reverberated around the room. 'In answer to your question, Gregory, you are not mistaken. Is there any particular way in which we might support you? Have you a project in mind?'

'I… well… not as such.'

'No matter. Oswald and I will take you under our wing. I think a spell in the pottery will serve as a suitable introduction to Chase Manor, don't you, husband?'

'Most certainly. Ah, here's our pudding. Excellent!'

Chapter 17

With no need of his umbrella, Ambrose leaned back on his bench, enjoying the warmth of the sun on his face. A distant clock chimed the half hour. Despite himself, he nervously stole a glance at his watch. Sitting upright, he straightened his tie and brushed a fallen leaf from his sleeve.

A pair of chattering nannies in identical grey uniforms passed by, pushing perambulators. Ambrose scanned the path to his right. A bonneted and caped figure rounded the corner. Could this be her? The absence of a pet spaniel made him doubt it, and the grey curls and stiff gait of the approaching lady confirmed that it was not Violet. For a moment, he worried that she might choose to share his bench, but she kept resolutely to the path.

Ten thirty-four. The path was empty, not a soul in sight. This was foolish. Why on earth was he anxious? If she didn't come, what then? Why, nothing. It hardly mattered, Ambrose reasoned, but the tension in his muscles and the throbbing in his temple said otherwise.

He saw the dog first, straining at its leash and earning a mild tug of rebuke. Had she seen him? He gave a tentative wave. Violet stopped twenty paces away. He waved again. She didn't move, but looked back the way she'd come. Ambrose feared she'd turn tail and return home, but she turned to face him and came briskly up to the bench.

Ambrose got to his feet. 'Thank you, Violet. Will you be seated?'

She nodded and joined him, tying Bella's lead to the arm of the bench. 'It's been a long time, Ambrose. You gave me such a shock yesterday. Why did you seek me out? What do you want?' Ambrose read suspicion, anger and something deeper in her eyes – fear.

'I… I never thought I would see you again. That day in Bombay when I saw the police taking you away, I'm ashamed to say I thought only of myself. I left India several years ago and, thanks to the kindness of relatives, I have a home in Oxfordshire. I saw your photograph in a newspaper and felt compelled to see you again. I want nothing from you, believe me. But knowing you were here in England, I couldn't put you out of my mind.'

'Oh,' Violet fiddled nervously with a silver brooch on her lapel.

'My presence distresses you, I'll go. I shouldn't have approached you. I'm sorry.' Ambrose got to his feet.

'No, please.' She clutched at his sleeve. 'I am not distressed. But when someone you'd not thought you'd ever see again suddenly appears before you, it's naturally disconcerting. Please. Stay.'

***

Heedless of his surroundings, Ambrose walked back to Montagu Square. Thankfully, Mortimer and Olivia were not at home. In the privacy of his bedroom, Ambrose relived each moment of his tête-à-tête.

Haltingly, she'd told him how her arrest had played out. 'Had I been prosecuted, a court case would have aired a great deal of dirty laundry. I will not name names, but at least two senior members of the judiciary would have faced disgrace. I was sent quietly on my way, with a one-way ticket to England.'

Ambrose reciprocated with a sanitised version of his remaining time on the subcontinent.

Ever the shrewd businesswoman, Violet had wisely remitted much of her earnings from The Saffron Salon and its sister establishments back to a London bank. So, by the time her ship berthed at Tilbury, she was ready to present herself as a recently widowed lady returning from India following the death of her well-to-do husband. After a brief period in widow's weeds, she emerged into society, restored and reinvented. 'I met Sir Neville through a cousin of his,' Violet explained. 'He'd lost his wife a year earlier. We have no illusions. It's hardly a love match, but we are both content.'

'I'm pleased for you,' Ambrose had responded.

She'd smiled. 'And I'm pleased to see you again, Ambrose.' She spoke with warmth. 'And I...' She looked away, frowning suddenly.

'What is it?'

She shook her head, untying Bella's lead and getting to her feet.

'Violet, what is the matter?' He stood and touched her arm.

'I can't tell you now,' she whispered. Ambrose felt her tremble. 'Tuesday, meet me here again. I'll not bring Bella. Perhaps we can find somewhere more private. I must go.'

Ambrose nodded and watched anxiously as she hurried away.

Chapter 18

'Sally, isn't it?' Verity addressed the young woman as she placed a tray on the breakfast table.

'Oh no, miss. Sally's my sister. I'm Tamsin. We do look much alike. Some people take us for twins, but she's a year and a bit older.' Tamsin busied herself arranging plates of poached eggs and buttered toast in front of Verity and Caroline. 'Sally's next door seeing to Mr Gregory's breakfast. I'll be back with your tea in a minute.'

'How did you sleep?' Verity took up her knife and fork.

'It took some time to drive last night's dinner out of my mind, but I eventually fell asleep. And you?'

'Much the same, I suppose. I don't know about you, Caroline, but this cottage makes one feel as though one's in a fairy tale. I half expected Rumpelstiltskin to appear, or to come downstairs and find the three bears sitting around this table.'

'Oh yes – or Prince Charming,' Caroline smirked. 'What on earth did you make of last night? I could hardly maintain a straight face with Aquinas literally breathing down my neck. Ghastly…' Caroline waited while Tamsin placed a pot of tea on the table. 'Ghastly man,' she continued when the maid had left the room.

'Yes, quite.' Verity nodded. 'And you also have an admirer in Dornford, by all appearances. I suspect Elspeth may have had sharp words with him afterwards.'

'Well, at least she helped to keep me out of Aquinas's clutches.'

Verity laughed. 'And to have you where she can keep an eye on you?'

'Ha, yes, of course. But…'

Verity looked up from her plate. 'But what?'

'I'm sorry. Here I am chattering away merrily, and all the time you're still grieving for your husband. It's most remiss of me.'

'Oh, Caroline. It's kind of you to sympathise, but there's nothing to be sorry about. I came here in part to leave such thoughts behind. Getting back to last night. What do you make of Oswald and Ursula?'

Caroline pushed her plate aside. 'Do you suppose they're quite… right?'

'Oswald's bonhomie didn't ring true, I must say.'

'And Ursula?'

'I'd say she rules the roost, wouldn't you?'

'Hmm. She's certainly forceful. I'm not sure what I expected them to be like, but it's difficult to conceive of them as utopian types. Do you think we've been mistaken in coming here?'

'It's a little too early to draw conclusions. From what I've seen so far, there are genuine artisans at work here. Let's see what today brings. At least you know what you'll be doing, Caroline – working on your triptych. I've no idea what lies in store for me.'

'Was that the front door?'

'Good morning. I do hope you slept well.' Elspeth swept into the room, followed by Stella with two garments draped over her arm. 'We're blessed with a fine day.' She took a seat at the table, leaving Stella standing near the door.

'Now then, Caroline, I'm so looking forward to seeing you at work. We'll go straight over to Sylvan Cottage as soon as we've finished here. Gregory is already at the pottery, and so it only remains to find a suitable activity for you, Verity.'

'Yes, I was only saying to Caroline that I wondered what I might be involved in, when you and Stella arrived.'

'You'll be with me,' Stella beamed at Verity. 'I need an assistant with my latest stained-glass creation. Will you join me?'

'Gladly. Will we also be working at Sylvan Cottage?'

'Oh no, not there. I have my own workshop – at Myrddin's Keep.'

Verity shot a glance at Caroline, whose wide-eyed expression mirrored her own misgivings.

'Excellent, that's settled,' Elspeth exclaimed. 'Now, before we set off, there are one or two items that you need to know. Although you both dined last evening at the Manor, that was a special event to welcome you here. We live very much as a community. Apart from breakfast, which you will continue to receive here, luncheon and supper are usually eaten communally in the refectory. You would have passed it yesterday. It's the smaller of the two stone barns near the pond.

'Then we come to the matter of dress. We women at Chase Manor wear simple smocks and gowns, such as these.' Elspeth pointed at Stella, whose outstretched arms supported two sack-like dresses, with high necks and long puffed sleeves. One in mauve, sporting a dandelion motif on the bodice; the other dyed yellow, with a cluster of acorns embroidered on it. Stella's own was of similar cut, and Elspeth's only differed in the richness and variety of its embroidery.

'I think they should fit,' said Stella. 'I thought the mauve for Caroline and the yellow for you, Verity. We can always make some alterations. Why don't you both go upstairs and put them on?'

Could they possibly be serious, or was this some silly jest? Verity's instinct was to laugh it off or take offence, but, like it or not, she must play her part.

Caroline had no such qualms. 'Whether they fit or not, is of no account.' She eyed the garments with obvious distaste. 'I will be wearing the clothes that I've brought with me. Nothing was stated in my letter of invitation about clothing, and I can assure you that had I been aware of any expectation I would wear *that*,' she pointed at the mauve dress, 'I should have declined the invitation.'

'But no one has refused before.' Stella looked beseechingly at Caroline. 'Besides, they are practical, and they show that we are all equal here, free of the dictates of fashion. Don't you see? Verity, you understand, I'm sure,' Stella smiled at Verity in anticipation.

'Um… yes. I'll go upstairs now.' Avoiding Caroline's shocked gaze, Verity took the yellow dress from Stella and left the parlour. Her cheeks burned with the thought of her Judas-like betrayal of her companion, but she stuck to her role.

Stung and surprised by Caroline's response, Stella turned a look of mute appeal on Elspeth.

'Stella's right. No one has refused before. Indeed, our guests have been only too willing to respect our customs and to abide by the spirit of our community.' Elspeth pursed her lips, taking the remaining dress from Stella and draping it over the back of a dining chair. 'I don't know what Oswald and Ursula will say. However, you've made your opinion on the matter very clear, Caroline. Please accompany me to Sylvan Cottage.'

Chapter 19

'Pass the salt cellar, would you?' Verity passed the object to Stella. At supper time the refectory hummed with conversation. Three long pine tables extended for most of the length of the building. Once a barn, the thick stone walls now encompassed the community's dining hall and kitchen.

Oswald sat at the head of the centre table. Ursula commanded the table on his left, and Dornford presided over the other. Verity counted over sixty people, their ages ranging from children of eight or nine to a sprinkling of septuagenarians. Stella had explained that younger children were fed separately.

Numbers were divided more or less equally between the sexes, the women wearing similar dresses, distinguished only by their colour and embroidered motifs. Most of the men wore working clothes and boots, such as might be found in any factory or workshop. Oswald, in his habitual Russian peasant garb, and Dornford in a dark velvet suit, were exceptions, but the most striking contrast was provided by Aquinas and his fellow members of the Order of The Golden Dragon. Seated together at the foot of the centre table, their medieval raiment spanned a rainbow palette of bold colour.

A cohort of young women and girls served the tables, rushing to and from the kitchen.

While Stella concentrated on her soup, Verity took stock of her immediate neighbours. The young women sitting opposite exchanged some initial pleasantries with her before turning their attention to their supper and whispering pieces of gossip to one-another. The young fellow on her right answered her greeting with a brief 'how-do,' then turned away to talk to the person on the other side of him.

Left to herself, Verity recalled the day's events.

That morning she'd reluctantly put on the yellow dress. It fitted, more or less. She'd looked at it in her bedroom mirror and shuddered. On returning to the parlour, she'd been relieved to find that Caroline and Elspeth had gone.

'Ah, I think it quite suits you,' Stella had said appraisingly. 'We change our dresses every three days. I'll bring you a fresh one. Now then, off to Myrddin's Keep we go.' Stella turned away, oblivious to Verity's look of distaste.

Ten minutes had brought them to the open gates of the mock castle. The courtyard beyond was empty save for two archery targets and a grey lurcher lying asleep near the entrance to the tower. Sensing their presence, the hound raised its head, emitting a low-pitched bark then loping across the yard to sit at Stella's feet. 'Good dog, Bran.' Stella stroked the dog's shaggy head. 'He's perfectly harmless.' Bran's dark eyes looked up appealingly at Verity. She obliged him with a pat.

All was quiet. Although it was past nine o'clock, no one appeared to be stirring. Verity surveyed the empty courtyard. The buildings on her right and left looked identical. Beneath pitched tiled roofs, their two storeys of blue-grey masonry connected the ends of the curtain wall to the central tower. Roofed timber galleries extended the length of the upper storeys, with a central staircase descending to the courtyard.

'Where is everyone?'

'They're not renowned for early rising. I imagine most of them are breakfasting in there,' Stella nodded toward the tower. 'Come, we'll go to my workshop.'

Verity found herself in a room bounded by high walls with narrow arched doors connecting it to its neighbours. High on the far wall, a row of semicircular curved windows let the daylight in. A heavy timber workbench occupied the centre of the space, and leaning against the walls were various finished examples of Stella's craft.

'Here's my latest commission.' Stella led Verity to the bench. 'It's a depiction of St George and the Dragon, as I mentioned to you in the carriage yesterday. I've hardly started yet, but the cartoon shows the design. It has several panels, you see, to fit a gothic-style window.'

Verity inspected the cartoon, and some completed sections of the work filled with pieces of glass in rich reds, greens and blues arranged within a framework of lead strips. 'It looks awfully intricate, Stella. However did you learn to do this?'

'You could say it runs in the family. My father designed windows for Heaton, Butler, and Bayne. Have you heard of them?'

Verity shook her head.

'They have a studio in Covent Garden. I loved to watch my father at work there when I was a girl. He allowed me to assist him and, when I showed promise, I was offered employment in my own right.'

'And what path led you from there to this place?'

Stella frowned. 'Oh… that's a story for another time.'

'I'm sorry. I didn't mean to pry.'

'No, no, there's no need to apologise. But we must get on. This window will hardly make itself. Now then, about this commission –'

The door to the courtyard creaked. 'Such a wonderful bright morning, made brighter yet by two such glorious exemplars of the female virtues.' Aquinas stood framed in the doorway for a moment, then bowed with a flourish before swaggering into the room. In his wake walked a young woman.

Despite Aquinas's typically flamboyant garb, it was his companion who held Verity's attention. She seemed somehow familiar. Slender, blue-eyed and pale, with her light chestnut hair tied back loosely. Her close-fitting ivory dress, delicate gold embroidery on the cuffs and along the hem of the skirt, was the very antithesis of Stella and Verity's uninspiring gowns. A thin circlet of silver resting on her forehead gave her a faintly regal look, Verity thought. But why did she seem familiar? Someone Verity knew? No, now she had it; not a person, but a painting. Was it a Burne-Jones or perhaps a Millais? An idealised image of medieval beauty and purity.

'Oh, it's you, Aquinas,' Stella said flatly. 'Verity is kindly assisting me with this,' she added, pointing to the cartoon.

'So I see. How fortunate that you will be spending time with us at Myrddin's Keep, Verity. I had no opportunity to speak with you at dinner last night, but now we can become better acquainted. It will be my pleasure to show you around my demesne.' Aquinas stood so close to Verity that she felt his breath on her cheek. It had taken tremendous self-control on her part to refrain from confronting his crude attempt at intimidation. 'Won't you introduce me to your companion?' she asked, stepping deftly to one side.

'Eh… oh, this is Lavinia,' Aquinas didn't attempt to conceal his annoyance.

'Good morning, Lavinia, I'm Ver…'

'No time for that now,' Aquinas growled. 'Come on,' he muttered to Lavinia, who nodded to Verity and turned on her heel, following Aquinas out into the courtyard.

Lost for words, Verity looked at Stella.

'I'm so sorry, Verity. He can be a brute. I thought he might have had the good grace to leave us alone. He owes me that much. Anyway, you did the right thing.'

'It was not wholly unexpected, Stella. His behaviour last night gave me a glimpse of his character. I can assure you I am perfectly capable of dealing with the likes of Aquinas Thorpe.'

Despite its unpleasant beginning, the morning had passed pleasantly enough to begin with. Verity did her best to help, passing prepared pieces of coloured glass to Stella, who carefully arranged them into patterns and held them in place with strips of lead.

Mid-morning, Stella called a halt. 'Tea?'

Against the back wall were a stone sink, a narrow deal table with two rickety chairs, and a dresser stocked with crockery. A copper kettle stood on a portable stove nearby. While Stella bustled about filling the kettle, lighting the stove and putting out the tea things, Verity, attracted by sounds coming from outside, drifted over to the door. The noise swelled as she opened it. The courtyard was now alive with movement and voices: loud, raucous, male.

In the centre of the space, two young men of similar build and height skirted each other warily, their burnished helmets and the longswords they brandished flashing in the sunlight. Their knee-length surcoats told them apart, one in plain light green, the other quartered in crimson and white.

The combatants were silent, watchful. The source of the clamour came from the gallery of the opposite building, where a group of similarly clad men whistled and hollered, urging the swordsmen on. A few paces apart, two young women wearing dresses like Lavinia's, leaned on the balustrade. Each clutched a scarf – one crimson and white, the other green.

A jarring clash of metal on metal brought Verity's attention back to the combatants, their swords reverberating as a swinging cut by green was blocked by his opponent. They remained breast to breast, their blades locked between them until crimson and white broke away, hefting his sword menacingly, then thrusting point first at green, who parried and pirouetted to his left to take up his guard once more. Verity watched as they circled, clashing, parting and clashing again. To her, it resembled a dance rather than a fight, choreography, not combat, and she wondered how long they would keep at it. On the point of going back indoors to join Stella, she was taken by surprise when green feinted, then with a roar of belligerence, pressed home his attack, thwacking his opponent on the helmet with the flat of his sword.

'A kill! A kill!' the men in the gallery roared. 'Piers! Piers!' Green acknowledged them, holding his sword aloft.

His vanquished opponent had fallen to his knees, holding his helmeted head in his hands. Green, without a backward look, crossed the courtyard, removing his helmet to reveal a head of thick, dark hair, and ascended to the gallery. The men clapped him on the shoulder and shouted their congratulations as he passed through them to embrace the young woman holding his favour.

Verity's eyes moved to the other woman standing forlornly, head bowed, but showing no sign of coming to her defeated champion's aid.

He remained on his knees with his sword lying at his side. Slowly and painfully, he loosened the helmet's strap and took it off. His shoulder length fair hair fell forward, veiling his face. Verity crossed the courtyard at a run to kneel in front of him. 'Are you badly hurt? Can you stand?' She thought he hadn't heard and was about to repeat herself when he raised his head.

'Oh… who?'

She read confusion in his eyes.

'I'm Verity, let me help you up.' She extended her hand.

'No, you shouldn't…'

'What do you mean?'

'Women are not… are not permitted.' The fellow rose shakily to his feet and turned away, following in the footsteps of his opponent.

Hoots of derision rose from the men in the gallery, accompanied by threatening gestures. Thinking at first that they were directed at the vanquished swordsman, Verity was alarmed to realise that she was the object of their displeasure.

'Verity, come back inside,' Stella stood in the doorway beckoning furiously.

Curbing her instinct to march across the courtyard and confront her abusers, Verity returned to the studio.

Stella closed the door behind her, muting the whistles and cat-calls.

'Oh dear,' said Stella, shamefaced. 'I should have warned you not to go out there when they are indulging themselves in their ridiculous knightly pursuits, as they call them. Knightly, indeed! They're no more than lumpen fools playacting. To think that they purport to live according to the rules of chivalry. Silly nonsense.' Stella shook her head. 'Come, I've poured the tea and there's some shortbread.'

Verity joined her at the table. 'Why are they permitted to behave in such a fashion?'

'If you mean, why doesn't Aquinas, as their leader, exert some discipline? Ha – they behave boorishly because that is precisely how Aquinas conducts himself. You saw that for yourself.'

'Do Oswald and Ursula condone this sort of thing?'

Stella shrugged.

Verity sipped her tea in silence.

'Do try some,' Stella proffered a plate of shortbread. 'I'll show you how to cut the glass into shape later.'

Although sensitive to her companion's attempt to change the subject, Verity spoke her mind. 'You called this place – Chase Manor – *our Arcadia* when we arrived here yesterday. I remember the genuine delight you expressed in being part of this community when we first met in Liberty's and again at your exhibition at Arrowfield Hall. Yet, here you are putting up with the likes of Aquinas and his crew.'

Stella frowned. Verity wondered whether she'd gone too far and considered apologising.

'I do find joy here,' Stella whispered. 'It's complicated. Please don't press me on the matter. Perhaps when we are better acquainted, I'll say more.'

***

Verity put her recollections aside and returned her attention to the present. One of the women sitting across the supper table was asking where she came from. She replied and asked some questions of her own. While part of her mind was engaged in commonplace conversation, she allowed her eyes to rove around the refectory.

The Arthurians were in full voice. Apart from Aquinas, she counted eight of them. Men, that is. And three young women – Lavinia, and the two who had stood on the gallery that morning. Huddled together at the foot of the table, they sat eating in silence while the men buzzed with coarse, excitable banter, loud exclamations and back-slapping, Aquinas very much to the fore.

Her eyes moved beyond them, searching until she saw Caroline sitting at the far table amidst a group of men, deep in conversation with one of them. Verity tried to catch her eye. She waved when Caroline looked in her direction and received a cheery wave in reply.

By sheer ill-luck, her wave also caught the attention of another. Aquinas, in the act of draining his mug of cider, happened also to be looking in Caroline's direction. Assuming at first glance that she was waving at him, he quickly realised that her gaze was fixed on someone behind him. He jerked his head around, spilling cider on his doublet and scowled at the sight of Verity.

For an instant, she feared he might approach her, but mercifully, he turned away, brushing at the spillage on his clothing.

Chapter 20

Verity appeared at the parlour door. 'Ah, there you are, Caroline. I'd thought we would walk back from supper together, but all of a sudden you'd disappeared.' She took off her bonnet and put it on the table.

Unaware of its occupant, she stepped toward the armchair facing Caroline's seat near the inglenook. 'Oh, goodness, Gregory, I didn't see you there. No, please don't get up. I'll sit here at the table.'

Gregory hesitated, bent awkwardly half-way between standing and resuming his seat, goggling from Caroline to Verity and back again. Finally, he made his decision. Straightening, he wished the ladies goodnight, bowed and walked stiffly to the door.

'Don't forget now, Gregory. Tomorrow evening, after supper. A round of whist. We can't have you sitting all alone,' Caroline called after him.

Verity occupied the armchair. 'Why on earth –?'

Caroline forestalled her. 'I simply couldn't pass up the opportunity.'

'Opportunity?'

'I saw Gregory leaving the refectory. I'd spotted him earlier at Ursula's table, looking lost and uncomfortable. The poor man almost jumped out of his skin when I came up behind him and took his arm.'

'Oh dear. Whatever must he have thought?'

'At first, it was just the shock of my sneaking up on him. But he clearly struggles with any form of social discourse, especially with the opposite sex.'

'Yet you persuaded him to come here? He looked like a hunted hare when I entered. Cornered by two women. What a fearful situation for him.'

'I actually managed to get a few words out of him. Despite his acute shyness, I sense a soul who craves human company.'

'Did he speak about his day? How did Ursula put it? "Oswald and I will take you under our wing," or something along those lines.'

'He did, a little. I asked him about the pottery. It seems that he spent most of the day watching Oswald fashioning some earthenware jugs. "They're most solicitous," he said, meaning Oswald and Ursula. "Most anxious to learn about my family and so on".'

'Hmm,' Verity mused. 'I had an unpleasant experience at Myrddin's Keep this morning, but I would rather that than spend a whole day in Oswald and Ursula's company.'

'An unpleasant experience at Myrddin's Keep? The mind boggles. You must enlighten me before my imagination runs riot.'

Chapter 21

While Sundays were universally acknowledged as a day of leisure at Chase Manor, Saturdays were a matter of choice. Some attended to their craft, while others favoured sport. Arnold Wright had formed a football team from the men at the furniture workshop, playing fixtures against the nearby villages. In summer, it was cricket. Visits to Monk's Fallow and further afield were also popular. Elspeth and several of the women had just departed for a shopping expedition to Hereford.

Dornford found his parents at the kitchen table. 'Nancy said you wished to see me.'

Ursula pointed to a seat. 'A difficulty has arisen. Show him, Oswald.'

Dornford took the letter from his father. 'From Wales?'

Oswald nodded. 'From Maynard. Read it.'

Dornford scanned the extravagant penmanship, so characteristic of the writer's mercurial nature. Two paragraphs, blunt and to the point. 'Oh.' Dornford shook his head. The letter dropped from his fingers. 'Dead?'

'Yes, it's a calamity. Your mother and I are at a loss. Maynard should never have allowed this to happen. Slipped out, for goodness' sake.'

'And then slipped trying to cross the stream, by the sound of it,' Ursula laughed mirthlessly. 'We have nature to thank.'

Dornford eyed his mother uncomprehendingly. 'Whatever do you mean?'

'You've never been there. It's a grim, unforgiving place. Imagine if she'd got away. It's a serious blow, no mistake, but it could have been so much worse. I curse the desolation when I'm there, but it can be a blessing in disguise.'

'Maynard says he's dealt with the… body.' Dornford shuddered inwardly. 'So, what is there to be concerned about?'

'First of all, there's the fact that he'd not yet got her to sign, so we are denied her fortune.' Ursula took a deep breath. 'Then…'

'Then what?'

'Better that you tell him, Oswald. Then you can explain what must be done to recover from the position that you have put us in.' Ursula willed herself to contain the scream of rage rising in her throat. 'I'm going outside to feed the chickens. Dear God, Oswald, there are times when I swear I could…'

Oswald tensed, screwing his eyes shut until Ursula's footsteps receded and the kitchen door slammed shut behind her.

'Pa? What is it?'

Oswald cleared his throat. 'I've lost money, Dornford. A considerable amount. An investment. Copper mine in Chile.'

'Investment?' Dornford scoffed. 'What in God's name do you know about investment? Honestly, Pa, what possessed you?'

'It did well at first. Good returns. Really.' Oswald squirmed in his chair, avoiding his son's glare. 'So… I doubled –'

'Hah!' The table shuddered as Dornford slammed his fist down.

Oswald whimpered, covering his face with his hands.

Dornford eyed him silently for a few moments. 'Pa.' Dornford dropped his voice to a whisper. 'Look at me. Please, Pa.'

Oswald dropped his hands. A tear formed and slid down his cheek as he turned to face his son.

'You didn't think of this investment on your own, did you?'

Oswald shook his head.

'Who?' Dornford mouthed the question.

Oswald swallowed hard. The word formed in his mouth unsaid. With a shudder, he forced it past his lips. 'Aquinas.'

***

'Hand the basket over first.' Caroline reached across the stile as Gregory balanced precariously on the other side.

'Just a moment,' Gregory puffed with the exertion of lifting the picnic basket, until, with Verity lending a steadying hand, he managed to hand it to Caroline.

'Over you come then,' Caroline stood back as he swung one leg over, then stopped uncertainly astride the stile. 'Now the other leg,' Caroline encouraged.

Despite catching his heel, Gregory maintained his balance, stepping down onto the grass with his dignity intact.

Verity hitched up her skirt and followed. 'There's the perfect place,' she indicated, pointing to a spot at the river's edge in the shade of a willow tree.

Over a few hands of whist the previous evening, the two women had done their best to breach Gregory's stiff reserve. He'd yielded little information at first, but eventually they learnt that he'd been born on his family's country estate in Lincolnshire. 'I remember little of it. I was sent to a preparatory school in Epsom at seven, then to Harrow. My parents established themselves at their house in London, and the estate is leased. Of course, it's mine now. Now that they've both… passed away.'

'Oh, Gregory, how sad for you,' Verity had smiled consolingly. 'I too have lost both my parents.'

'We are an odd family. We *were* an odd family, I mean. I have no close living relatives. How unusual is that?'

As though the disclosure of so much information had been too much for him, Gregory had relapsed into diffidence, focussing his attention on the cards and meeting any further attempts to draw him out with monosyllables or blank stares.

Reluctant to press him further, Caroline and Verity kept to small talk while dealing and playing their hands. Gregory made no attempt to join in, but seemed content to play in companionable silence.

When the clock on the mantelpiece struck ten, he had wished them goodnight. 'Good night, Gregory, thank you for your company,' Verity rose to show him out.

'Yes, good night,' Caroline echoed. 'Oh, by the way, would you care to join us for a picnic tomorrow afternoon? Weather permitting, of course. Meet here at noon?'

Gregory stood stock still, fixing his spectacled gaze on Caroline. To Verity, it appeared as though some internal struggle was taking place behind those thick lenses. A simple decision to anyone else seemed to require a tremendous effort in Gregory's case.

'Uh... noon? Here at noon. Yes... th-thank you,' Gregory had stammered, allowing Verity to lead him down the passage to the front door.

***

'Come along, let's get the rug down, Verity marched to the spot she'd pointed out and spread the blanket she'd brought from the cottage. 'Gregory, put the basket down here and let's see what Tamsin's found for us. Hmm – a cottage loaf, some butter. What's this? Ah, a pork pie, some slices of ham. Hard-boiled eggs. A pot of mustard. Then, we have...' Verity held the object up to her nose. 'Cheese – Cheshire by the smell.'

'And to wash it all down...' Caroline swung a bulky carpet bag from her shoulder and set it down gently. 'Two bottles of cider and a bottle of lemonade, if you'd prefer that, Gregory.'

'Come, Gregory, sit down here.' Verity patted the blanket. Obeying, he sat with legs outstretched, fanning himself with his boater while the women set about arranging the picnic.

'Make yourself useful, would you, Gregory, and pour some drinks,' Caroline said over her shoulder as she cut some slices of bread.

'I say, would you mind if I had some of the cider?'

'Cider? Of course not. We'll all have some. Pour away.'

Apart from the unwelcome attentions of a bumblebee, which seemed to take a particular pleasure in stoking Gregory's phobia about stinging insects (or indeed insects of all kinds) the picnic was a success. Such clouds as there were failed to prevent the sun from making a decent showing. A soft breeze ruffled the surface of the river, and the three picnickers felt themselves a world away from Chase Manor.

Later, Verity and Caroline strolled along the bank, leaving Gregory lying with his head propped up on the picnic basket, his boater shielding his pink cheeks from the sun.

The cider had taken its effect. His chest rose and fell rhythmically. But before it made his eyelids heavy, it had loosened his tongue.

'Goodness, the poor chap's had quite a time of it with one thing and another,' Verity held her hand out to assist Caroline in negotiating a fallen tree branch near the water's edge.

'He's just the type to suffer from bullying. Harrow was clearly a great ordeal for him.' Caroline reached down to disentangle her skirt from a twig.

'Then both parents gone within the space of a month.' Verity shook her head. 'No wonder he came down from Cambridge with only a third. From the look on his face, that seemed to cause him more anguish than his bereavements.'

'Hmm. Perhaps we should have dissuaded him from drinking cider. I feel rather guilty. Won't he be mortified when he realises how much he told us about himself?'

'Perhaps. But he's a grown man. He has to make his way in the world as best he can.'

'Well, the money should help, surely. Sole heir. Country estate. House in Mayfair. The world's his oyster, Verity, if he would only realise it.'

'Yes. Well, let's change the subject. What about tomorrow? What on earth can we find to do around here on Sundays?'

'Oh, I intended to mention it to you earlier. I have accepted an invitation. Tomorrow afternoon.' Caroline grinned sheepishly. 'Promise you won't laugh.'

'Why on earth would I laugh?'

'It's a lecture in the barn, you know, the meeting hall.'

'A lecture? Something on the finer points of marquetry, or embroidery, that sort of thing?'

'Er, not exactly. The title of the lecture is *Socialism - the way forward.*'

'Oh, I see. No laughing matter then. All very worthy, I'm sure. Not the antidote to an otherwise dull Sunday afternoon. I hadn't thought of you as an ardent socialist, Caroline.'

'I'm not. If you must know, it's the speaker rather than the subject that interests me.'

'Now, I'm all ears.'

'I met him over supper. His name's Arnold Wright.'

'Ah, yes, I saw you conversing with a man. Working type, rather than one of Oswald's aesthetes.'

'He's a master woodworker. And I can tell you he has a greater appreciation for artistry in manufacture than Oswald will ever have. I've seen his work. It's exquisite. Just because a man speaks plainly and spurns affectation, doesn't mean he has no finer feelings, you know.'

Verity held up her hands. 'Far be it from me to suggest such a thing, Caroline. I can see that he's made quite the impression on you.'

'Yes, I won't deny it,' Caroline smiled. 'Come with me tomorrow. Meet Arnold for yourself.'

Verity pulled a face. 'Will it be a long lecture? Those benches in the barn look rather unyielding.'

'Then bring a cushion, Miss Delicate,' Caroline scoffed.

'Very well, I give in. I'll come. Now it's time to wake Gregory and pack up the picnic things.' Verity turned and marched back along the river bank with Caroline's whoop of triumph ringing in her ears.

Surprisingly, Gregory negotiated the stile with ease on their return journey. Skirting the edge of a meadow that would bring them within sight of their cottages, the trio stopped at Caroline's urging to pick some hedgerow flowers. 'I'll make some drawings for you both, if you like.' Placing her specimens carefully in the picnic basket, she turned to the others. 'Did you hear me? I… oh, we have company, do we?'

Verity prayed that the two approaching riders would pass them by. Although the sturdy hunters they rode didn't quite match Verity's image of medieval destriers, they were caparisoned for the joust, in colours matching their riders' surcoats.

One she recognised as the green knight from the courtyard at Myrddin's Keep. Piers – that was the name. To her dismay, the other horseman revealed himself to be Aquinas Thorpe, both horse and rider in purple, emblazoned with the golden dragon.

At their side ran Bran. Verity held her breath, willing the riders to continue on their path. They drew level fifty yards away, unaware of the onlookers. Not so Bran. With a gruff bark, he veered towards them, covering the ground in broad strides to come to a halt at Verity's feet, tail wagging and eyes pleading for a pat.

Verity obliged, maintaining a wary eye on the riders, who kept to their course. Her attempt to shoo the dog away only sent it toward Caroline. She, in turn, ruffled its shaggy head and tried to urge it quietly away.

Pleased with the attention he was receiving, Bran transferred his attention to Gregory.

His shriek of disgust when the dog licked his hand set Bran barking. To Verity's dismay, the clamour attracted the attention of the horsemen, who turned their mounts and closed in at a canter.

Caroline took Verity's arm. They stood defiantly, determined not to flinch as the horses bore down on them, showing no sign of pulling up, until, at the last moment, they wheeled to left and right, slowing to a walk and circling back to stand so close to the two women that they felt the horses' breath on their faces.

'Ah, the Lady Caroline.' Aquinas bowed in the saddle. 'How gratifying that our paths should cross again. I was only remarking to Piers here last night what a welcome addition you make to our community. Out and about with your friend, eh?' Aquinas gave Verity a sour look. 'Such a dull way to spend the afternoon. I know, why not let me whisk you away to Myrddin's Keep. There's room up here. I promise I'll keep a good firm hold on you.' Aquinas extended a gauntleted hand to Caroline.

'We are returning to our cottage. Please remove your horses from our path.' Caroline stooped to pick up the picnic basket. 'Gregory, come along. We're going back now.'

'So, you would rather this little fellow's company than mine?' Aquinas affected an air of wounded pride. 'Why, he's so insubstantial that I hadn't noticed him skulking there by the hedge. Let me take a closer look.' He turned his horse's head and skirted around Caroline.

Gregory edged away at his approach. 'G-go away, Thorpe.'

'Oh, it has a voice, does it?' Aquinas reined in his mount. '*G-go away, Thorpe,*' he mimicked in a mincing tone. 'Dash it, Piers, the fellow means business,' he called over his shoulder. 'What do you think we should do? Beat a hasty retreat?'

Piers urged his horse forward, grinning. 'Hmm, I know, I'll challenge him to a duel. You can tie both my hands behind my back to even up the odds. What do you say, Hercules? Would you fight me to defend the honour of the women?'

'Leave Gregory alone, you brute.'

Aquinas turned in the saddle.

'Ah, the Mallard woman. And what will you do about it? Peck me to death?'

'This!' Verity thwacked a fallen branch she'd plucked from the hedgerow hard on his horse's rump.

Frantically trying to gather the reins, and with one foot scrabbling to find its stirrup, Aquinas swayed and bounced in the saddle as his startled mount galloped away.

'Go!' she snarled at Piers, brandishing the branch.

To her relief, he galloped off without a word.

Out in the middle of the field, he caught up with Aquinas and grasped his horse's bridle, bringing it to a halt.

'Now, we're for it.' Caroline said.

'We'll have to make a dash for the stile. Put the hedge between us and them. Let's hope Gregory can keep up.'

A hundred yards distant, the two horsemen argued. The sound of raised voices floated across the meadow. Arms gesticulated. And then, with a shake of his fist, Aquinas turned away.

'Are they?' Caroline grasped Verity's arm tightly.

'Yes, they're going. Come Gregory. Oh dear, look, Caroline.'

Their companion sat on the grass with his head in his hands. Next to him, regarding him with concern, sat Bran.

'Go along, Bran, follow your master,' Verity urged.

The dog merely wagged its tail.

'Go on, you silly dog. Shoo.'

Verity was about to repeat herself when a shrill whistle had Bran pricking up his ears. For a moment he hesitated, looking appealingly at Verity until a second piercing whistle sent him haring away.

Chapter 22

'Are there any more questions?' Arnold Wright scanned the audience for raised hands.

Verity fervently hoped not. After an hour and a half of lecturing, which despite its impassioned delivery, failed to convince her of the merits of the dictatorship of the proletariat, class consciousness, historical materialism and a host of other isms peppered throughout Arnold's speech, she yearned to step outside for some fresh air.

She wasn't unsympathetic to the notion that working people should derive greater benefit from the value of their labour, and she held no objections to trade unionism, as such. But oh, what a dry topic.

Clearly, her fellow audience members had no such qualms, eagerly asking question after question. Most of them, she noticed, were men in Sunday best suits, holding their cloth caps or balancing bowler hats on their knees. Among the sprinkling of women in attendance, Verity was surprised to spot Tamsin, sitting next to her brother Seth. There were hardly any of what Verity regarded as the aesthetic types in the community and none of the Arthurians.

Thank goodness she'd brought a cushion, but even that was proving insufficient against the unyielding oak bench beneath her.

Two more questions followed, receiving lengthy responses from Arnold. Verity felt her eyelids drooping.

'Would you care to borrow my watch, Arnold?' The words reverberated around the barn, jolting Verity awake. 'It's well past four o'clock, high time you and your socialists made way. Of course, you're welcome to stay and join our poetry reading circle. Who knows, you might find it soothing after all that impenetrable Karl Marx guff.'

Surrounded by a group of young women, including Stella and Elspeth, Dornford struck a haughty pose, brushing his hair from his eyes with a theatrical flourish.

'That's it for now, brothers and sisters. We'll convene again next Sunday. Thank you for your attendance.' Arnold stepped down from the lectern, stopping to shake hands and chat, showing no sign of acknowledging Dornford and his followers.

Outside, Caroline took Verity by the hand and steered her in Arnold's direction.

'Arnold, Yoo-hoo. It's Caroline. Wonderful lecture.'

'What's that?' Arnold turned round. 'Oh, yes, Caroline. Thank you so much for coming along. And to you too, Miss…'

'Verity. Verity Mallard. Caroline and I are both here on retreat.'

'Pleased to meet you, Verity. Caroline mentioned you at supper the other night. Do I see another supporter of the cause?'

'Cause? Oh, you mean socialism. I won't pretend to have leanings in that direction. But I have strong opinions on votes for women.'

Arnold smiled. 'Well, we have that in common. Look, I can't stop to talk now, but perhaps the three of us can get together at supper. I'll save places for you.'

Chapter 23

'Thank you, Tamsin,' Verity spoke up as the girl cleared the breakfast dishes away. 'Could I ask a favour of you?'

'Favour, miss?'

Verity pointed to the envelope lying on the tablecloth. 'This letter.'

'Oh, I'm sure that Miss Stella would be the person to speak to about letters.'

'I see. It's just that I thought if you were planning to visit the nearest village, Monk's Fallow, isn't it? You might drop this into the post-box. I'd rather not bother Stella with such a small matter, knowing how busy she is, and here's a little something for your trouble.' Verity lifted the letter to reveal a half-crown piece.

Tamsin eyed the coin warily. 'Well…'

'Yes, Tamsin?'

'My brother Seth goes into the village on Mondays. I could ask him to take it with him today, I s'pose.'

Verity smiled, bending to retrieve her handbag, and withdrawing her purse. 'Here's something for Seth as well,' she said, placing a second half-crown on the table.

Tamsin blinked. 'Thank you, thanks very much, Miss Verity,' she gabbled, scooping the letter and coins into the pocket of her pinafore before turning for the door with her tray of dirty dishes.

'Oh, and one thing more.'

Tamsin halted mid-stride and turned her head.

'Let's keep this to ourselves, shall we?'

'Yes, miss,' Tamsin nodded and continued on her way to the scullery.

Verity replaced her purse, acutely aware of Caroline's amused gaze. 'Yes, Caroline?'

'Oh, nothing at all, Verity. No explanation is necessary.' Caroline adopted a serious expression, quite at odds with the sparkle in her eyes. 'Please don't enlighten me; I much prefer wild conjecture.'

'No doubt various lurid possibilities are arising in your mind. Would it disappoint you to know that my letter concerns a perfectly ordinary matter of business?'

'Yet you wish to keep its existence a secret?'

Verity shrugged.

'Oh, don't misunderstand me,' Caroline leaned across the table, 'in view of what we've seen of this place over the weekend, I would be reluctant to place any correspondence of mine in the hands of a member of the Chase Manor community. Stella's pleasant enough, but…'

'Quite. Arnold was most enlightening about certain aspects of this community last night at supper. There's no love lost between him and the Lamonts, that's plain. By the way, I hope I wasn't playing gooseberry. I'd say he has more than a passing regard for you.'

'Oh, there's the door; Stella and Elspeth come to conduct us to our labours.' Caroline's eyes twinkled. 'He's asked me to take a stroll with him.'

Chapter 24

A pot of tea for two, please,' Ambrose told the waitress.

'I wondered if you'd come,' he said to Violet as the waitress scurried away. 'You were in such a state of agitation when we spoke in the park. It's been playing on my mind ever since.'

Violet forced a smile. 'I had second thoughts, I admit. I still can't get over the shock of seeing you again. Bombay seems like a dream to me now, as though I were never really that person. In some ways, it pains me to be reminded of it.' She looked away, watching the rain steaming down the window. 'But not every memory hurts.' Violet met his eyes. 'I have always thought of you fondly, Ambrose,' she said, her smile no longer forced but full of warmth.

Ambrose nodded. 'We had good times. And look at you now. Lady Ternan. A new life. It warms my heart. Truly. But the other day you…'

Ambrose fell silent while the waitress placed a silver teapot and a jug of milk on the table.

'The other day, I let the burden that I carry get the better of me. I should have controlled my feelings, but I'm really at my wit's end.' Violet's hand shook as she poured tea into Ambrose's cup and then her own.

'You must share it. A burden shared and all that. I'll do whatever is in my power to help. For old times' sake, eh?'

Violet avoided his gaze, adding milk to her tea and stirring. When she looked up, Ambrose saw tears forming and offered her the handkerchief from his breast pocket.

She mouthed a silent thank you, and dabbed at her eyes. Composing herself, she handed the handkerchief back. 'Do you know anything about my husband Neville?'

'Matter of fact, I do. Looked him up in *Who's Who.*'

'Then you know that he's an MP.'

'Yes, and I read about his business interests. You've married a rich and influential man.'

'Yes, and such men have enemies.'

'Politics is an unforgiving business.'

Violet bit her lip. 'Of course. But there is one person in particular. A fellow Member of Parliament. That person is determined to damage my husband's reputation.'

'May I ask why?'

'Oh, it's a long-standing grudge. Neville and he were directors of one of the railway companies. Neville discovered that the fellow was engaged in dishonest dealings and had him voted off the board. His name is Roderick Mounsden.'

'Do you have any idea how Mr Mounsden intends to damage your husband's reputation?'

Violet dropped her voice to a whisper. 'Through me, Ambrose. He knows.'

'Ah… Bombay?'

'Yes. The Saffron Salon and what went on upstairs,' Violet hissed. 'He wants to shame Neville through me.'

'So he's threatened your husband, has he?'

'No, he's threatened me.'

Ambrose shook his head, reached into his coat pocket and withdrew a silver cigarette case. 'Do you mind? I rarely indulge, but I feel in need of a smoke.'

'No, not at all.' Violet turned her attention to the window while Ambrose lit his cigarette. The rain had stopped, but the sky remained leaden with the threat of a new shower at any moment.

'Do you mean that he has yet to approach your husband?'

'Yes. He says he will do so unless…'

The look on her face betrayed what was on her mind.

'The blackguard.' Ambrose's raised voice drew curious looks from the occupants of nearby tables. 'Forgive me, Violet, the very thought makes my blood boil.'

'I may as well say it plainly. He wants me to sleep with him as the price for his silence. It's perfectly repugnant. And I've no doubt that were he to get his way, he'd still go ahead and publicly disclose my past, once he'd tired of me. I'd kill myself first.'

'No!' Ambrose retorted emphatically, but in a whisper. 'There must be a way to deal with this. I'll not stand by and see you used in this way. How did he approach you?'

Violet gave a humourless laugh. 'He accosted me in the park as I was walking Bella. Just near the spot where you came upon me the other day.'

'When was that?'

'A week ago. I have until the twenty-third of the month to respond. I am to write to him at the House of Commons.'

'Then we have ten days.'

Chapter 25

It was a productive morning. George Benson had tracked down Lord and Lady Wheelgrave's wayward younger daughter to an address in Primrose Hill. After observing her comings and goings for two days, he'd discovered the identity of her male escort, a ne'er-do-well and one-time subaltern named Desmond Farrar. A quick note to His Lordship, and a handsome cheque would be winging its way to him.

After collecting the post from his pigeonhole on the ground floor, he ascended to his third-floor office with a spring in his step. The unexpected appearance of a man coming in the opposite direction resulted in a mild collision on the second-floor landing.

'I'm so sorry.' George reached out to steady the figure leaning precariously over the banister. 'Good Lord – Ambrose!'

'Oh, my dear chap, there you are. I waited outside your office for half an hour in the hope you'd turn up.'

'Well, come on up. A glass of scotch will steady your nerves, and you can tell me all about it.'

George dropped the mail on the desk and waved Ambrose to a chair. 'A dash of soda, if my memory serves?'

'Oh, yes, just a small dash.' Ambrose sat and looked around the room. 'You've decorated this place since I was last here. No more peeling paint, I see, and is this a new carpet?'

'Here you are.' George handed a glass to Ambrose and took a seat behind his desk. 'Business has been good lately. I thought I'd spruce this place up. Now then, to what do I owe the pleasure?'

Ambrose took a bracing sip of whisky. 'I'm here to seek your help, George. It's a sticky business, I'm afraid. Concerns a lady.'

'You'd better explain.'

'You recall that address you found for me?'

'Address? Oh, yes. Lady Ternan, wasn't it?'

George nursed his glass and settled back in his seat as Ambrose recounted his meeting with Violet and all that had ensued.

Ambrose finished his tale.

'Does it seem likely?'

'What do you mean?' Ambrose asked.

'Wouldn't this Roderick Mounsden be sullying his own reputation by disclosing that he had been a party to adultery? Is the man married?'

'According to Violet, he's a widower of several years' standing.'

'Hmm, so she's convinced he'd go through with it?'

'For heaven's sake, George, the poor woman's desperate. I've come here to seek your help, not play twenty questions.' Ambrose threw his hands up.

'Of course I'll help, old man. But I can't guarantee to come up with something. You know, find a skeleton in his cupboard; something to threaten him with. Not in a few days, at any rate.'

'I can pay you, George. I've got a bit put aside.'

'No, Ambrose. Comrades help one another. You'd do the same for me. I'll do my best. All I'm saying is, there may be nothing we can use against him.'

Ambrose nodded. 'I know you'll do your best, dear friend. Thank you.'

Chapter 26

'Oh, it's you, Mr Benson.' Nel sat behind the counter, polishing silverware as George entered the pawnshop. 'Alfie and Dick are out on business, if you was wanting to see them. Some pub, they said.'

'Ah, I should have known. Old habits. And how are you finding things here?'

'Oh, the shop's doing quite well, thanks for asking, now that those King brothers are out of our hair.'

A twenty-minute cab ride brought George to Covent Garden and the familiar interior of The Lamb and Flag.

From the doorway of the pub's back room, George spied Alfie in his usual place in the far corner, with Dick sitting next to him. Facing them across the table, and with his back to George, a shabbily dressed man hunched forward, gesticulating as he talked.

Alfie's lips moved in response, resulting in increasingly excitable gestures. The argument was cut short when Alfie caught sight of George and waved. The man turned round, affording George a look at his pinched, stubble-lined face. *I'll bet his nickname's Ferret*, he thought as the fellow swore and rose from his seat, muttering as he sidled past on his way out.

George took his place. 'Friend of yours?'

'Nah, that was Weasel Watkins.'

George chuckled.

'What's funny, guv?'

'Oh nothing. He didn't look too happy.'

'That's 'cos I gave him a good rollicking. Tried to palm me off with some old tat. I can tell the difference between paste and real diamonds a mile off. Don't take kindly to geezers trying to pull a fast one. Anyway, never mind him. What brings you in here, Mr Benson?'

'There's someone I'd like you to keep tabs on. Can you spare a few days?'

'Ooh, now then, that's a bit of a tall order. Normally, we'd say yes, of course, but it's a bit tricky right now. Ain't it, Dick?' Alfie nudged his brother.

'Eh?'

'With that job we've got coming up.' Dick felt Alfie kick him under the table.

'Oh yes, that's right. That job. Of course.'

'Job?' George asked.

Dick hesitated. 'You tell him, Alfie.'

Alfie leaned forward conspiratorially. 'Well-to-do family, guv, fallen on hard times. Pawning the family jewels. Dick and me's got to do a valuation. Long job.'

'Oh, congratulations.' George glanced at Dick, who quickly looked away, biting his lip.

'Yes, we're calling at their London house tomorrow,' Alfie grinned. 'You may know it.'

'Really. Where is it?'

'Big place down the end of The Mall. Can't miss it.' Alfie's grin spread from ear to ear. Dick spluttered, shoulders shaking with the laughter he could no longer stifle.

'Sorry, guv, couldn't resist pulling your leg.' Alfie apologised, slapping his brother on the back. 'Come on, Dick, pull yourself together.'

'Hilarious, Alfie,' George smiled indulgently. 'Now you've had your joke, how about it?'

'Yeah, all right, we can do a few days. What's it about?'

'Have you heard the name Roderick Mounsden?'

Alfie and Dick shook their heads.

'He's an MP and a nasty piece of work. I want to know where he goes and what he gets up to.'

'What's he done then?'

'It's more a case of what he might do, Alfie. I'm sorry, but I can't tell you more. This is his address.' George slipped a piece of paper across the table. 'Usual drill. See where he goes, who he talks to. Anything he gets up to that he shouldn't.'

***

George wanted his supper. A couple of pints with Alfie and Dick had left him in need of food to mop up the alcohol. Shuffling some papers into his desk drawer, he caught sight of the small pile of mail he'd collected earlier in the day, which Ambrose's predicament had put out of his mind until now.

Two invoices. An overdue cheque from one of his clients. George put them to one side and mechanically opened the next envelope. The handwriting put all thought of food out of his mind.

Dear George,

Thank you for your letter. I will admit to being touched by your words. As you say, it

137

would be futile to attempt to dissuade me from pursuing my story, but I sincerely appreciate your concern and that you have my interests at heart.

It has only been a few days since I arrived, but I must say that this place brims over with possibilities. If I can't discover something sensational to print, I may as well throw away my fountain pen.

I told you that only three individuals have been invited to attend the retreat. I could not ask for a better companion than the other female in the trio. Her name is Caroline Hislop. She's twenty-two, a most accomplished artist, and quite like me in character. Yes, George, imagine that.

The other member of our group is quite the opposite. The young man is called Gregory Manning. He's painfully shy and retiring, and I do believe that he would be content to lock himself away from the world as long as he was surrounded by books and works of art. Nevertheless, Caroline and I are doing what we can to draw him out of his shell.

Honestly, George, you'd never credit the cast of distinctly unusual characters that make up the community here. The manor and estate belong to a couple named Oswald and Ursula Lamont. They affect a bohemian air, and

Oswald in particular is fond of airy, idealistic expressions. They have a vain and fatuous son, Dornford, who is engaged to be married to a surprisingly level-headed woman called Elspeth. Indeed, it seems to me that Ursula and Elspeth are the real decision makers here.

And then we go from the unusual to the absurd. A band of grown men masquerading as Knights of the Round Table in a mock castle, led by a pretentious and objectionable bag of wind going by the name of Aquinas Thorpe. There, I think that goes some way to expressing my contempt for the man, though I could go on.

Now, it would be remiss of me to tar the entire community with the same brush. Most of the people here are pretty decent types, genuine artists and artisans who seem to get along despite the eccentricity surrounding them.

Only last evening at supper, I encountered as down to earth a person as you could hope to meet. Arnold Wright is a master woodworker. I saw some of his furniture at the exhibition I attended in Highgate, and I doubt you'd find anything finer. Once one makes allowances for his socialism, he very much comes across as the voice of reason, and it was through him that I discovered a most intriguing piece of information.

It appears that Chase Manor has a sister community. It's shrouded in mystery. And from time to time, community members are chosen to go there. It's deemed a great privilege, apparently. It's called The Blessed Plot. Truly, would you credit it? Mind you, Arnold considers it a lot of tommyrot. It's just a way of disguising the fact that some people can't wait to get away from Chase Manor, he says.

Well, George, I think you'll agree that I'll have more than enough material to hand to write a thoroughly riveting article in due course. And I can assure you that Caroline and I are more than equal to dealing with the inflated egos surrounding us.

Farewell for the present. Caroline and I are expecting Gregory Manning for a game of whist. Yesterday, we made a little progress in breaking down his reserve. I'm sure there must be more to him than meets the eye.

Your true friend,

Verity

P.S. Should you wish to write to me, address your correspondence post restante to the post office at Monk's Fallow.

He read it three times. Twice to absorb her news and form a mental image of the place and the people she'd mentioned. In his third reading, George sought to gauge her feelings. Not about Chase Manor. Those were perfectly plain. *Dear George.* A normal salutation: there was nothing to be construed from it. *I will admit to being touched by your words.* George fancied a glimmer of encouragement in that. *You have my interests at heart.* A second glimmer. The rest was chatty and confiding, but no more than would be expressed to any close acquaintance. He dwelt over the valediction. *Your true friend.* Yes, more intimate than a plain *Yours* or *Yours sincerely*, but not, *Ever yours*, as he had written.

'Don't be a damned fool, George,' he muttered, folding the letter and placing it is his desk drawer. At least there was no sign of any danger to her in what she'd written. And she'd all but invited him to write to her. *Now then, supper awaits*, he thought as he locked his office door behind him and descended the stairs with a slight spring in his step.

Chapter 27

It had been a long day. Alfie spent the morning kicking his heels outside Roderick Mounsden's address in Mayfair. Then, when Dick took over at midday, he'd crossed the city to Whitechapel. He felt guilty saddling Nel with looking after the pawnshop most of the time. Not that she complained, but Alfie knew he should do more to help. He sent her off shopping, slipping a couple of quid into her purse.

Yesterday had been a waste of time. Neither he nor Dick saw hide nor hair of Mounsden. Surely he'd emerge soon.

Parliament wasn't sitting, so at least there would be no need to traipse down to Westminster after him. But if all he did was sit at home, there'd be nothing to report to George Benson.

Dick was relieved to see Alfie at six. 'Still no sign of him,' he reported.

'Alright, you'd better be getting along,' Alfie gave his brother a knowing wink. 'That Gwennie Morris ain't the sort of gel that likes to be kept waiting.'

Thankful for the stone horse trough near the street corner, Alfie perched on the edge to take the weight off his feet, eyeing Mounsden's front door fifty yards away. After a fruitless half hour, he got up and paced up the street, crossing the road at the end and walking back down on the other side.

He was about to repeat the process when the sight of a police constable coming his way prompted a change of plan. Ever wary of attracting the attention of the rozzers, he casually disappeared around the corner. A furtive glance behind revealed the unwelcome sight of the constable following in his footsteps, leaving Alfie with no option other than to duck through the open doorway of Grosvenor Chapel. The final chords of the weekly organ recital sounded shortly after he sidled into an empty pew at the back. As the audience shuffled out into the aisle, Alfie kept his head down in an attitude of prayer as the church emptied.

The place fell quiet. Deeming it safe to go back outside, Alfie froze at the sight of a pair of boots at the end of his pew. Heart racing, he lifted his head, suppressing the oath forming on his tongue as he realised that the austere figure looking down on him wore a black cassock, not a policeman's uniform.

'Are you troubled, my son?' the priest spoke softly. 'I saw you in prayer and sensed something might be amiss. You are not a member of the congregation, but all are welcome in God's house. Whatever ails you, the power of prayer will bring you peace. Let us pray together.'

Alfie had no choice but to slide along the pew as the priest moved in. No churchgoer himself, Alfie felt intimidated and somehow guilty in the presence of clergy, as though they might read his thoughts. It was nonsense, of course, but he couldn't help it. His unease grew at the thought that the priest might be expecting him to pray out loud. Instead, the man knelt on an embroidered hassock and raised his palms, praying in a whisper. Alfie adopted the same posture, silently moving his lips and cursing inwardly at the thought that Roderick Mounsden might choose this very moment to leave his house.

Please God, let this chap stop, he thought, wondering if that counted as a prayer. If so, it worked. Rising stiffly to his feet, the priest turned and patted Alfie's shoulder. 'There, my son, rest here awhile in God's grace.' Alfie smiled weakly. The priest advanced down the aisle. Before he was halfway to the altar, Alfie was outside, dashing back to his vantage point at the horse trough.

Having caught his breath, he resumed his vigil. Not knowing when he'd have a chance to eat anything, he felt in his jacket pocket for the packet of sandwiches Nel had made for him. He was halfway through a round of tongue and piccalilli when Mounsden's front door opened. Hastily stuffing the remaining sandwiches back into his pocket, he got to his feet.

With a furtive glance up and down the street, a young woman emerged and walked briskly away towards Grosvenor Square.

Alfie chuckled. Dolly Parker, eh? No wonder he hadn't seen her plying her wares around Covent Garden lately. 'Moved up west, eh, Dolly?' he muttered to himself.

Half past seven. Alfie clicked his fob watch shut and dropped it into his waistcoat pocket. Perching on the edge of the horse trough had given him pins and needles. Stamping his feet, he decided it was time to take another walk up and down the street. He'd hardly started when a movement in the corner of his eye brought him to an abrupt stop. He waited for the man to turn away before crossing the road and falling in a few steps behind. There was no mistaking the heavily moustachioed face he'd glimpsed between the collar of the fellow's frock coat and his topper.

Alert for any sign that Mounsden might summon a cab, Alfie kept pace. Ten minutes later, they crossed New Bond Street. Shortly after, Alfie dodged through the heavy traffic in Regent Street, losing sight of his quarry for a few heart-stopping seconds. He might have lost him altogether had Mounsden not stopped to purchase a buttonhole carnation from a street vendor before striking off into the heart of Soho.

'Blimey, not Stan's,' Alfie scratched his head, watching Roderick Mounsden pass through the side door of a dingy second-hand bookshop in Beak Street, receiving a nod of recognition from the doorman. 'Well, I'm blowed, Stan's of all places?' Alfie shook his head and followed, knowing full well that the door led not to the shop but down a flight of steps to a notorious drinking and gambling den run by the redoubtable Stanley Tolley, ex guardsman, bare-knuckle boxer, and occasional guest at several of Her Majesty's Prisons.

'Oi, oi. Watcher Alfie. 'Aven't seen you round these parts for a while.' The doorman's pock-marked face broke into a grin.

'Just passing, Tommy. Thought I'd stop by to wet me whistle and say hello to Stan. How is the old bruiser?'

'Bit touchy on account of the toothache. I offered to bring a pair of pliers along, but e's not too keen.' Tommy chuckled and held the door open. 'In you go then.'

Although he'd not frequented Stan's for nigh on two years, its odour of smoke, spilt ale and the cloying mustiness of a space untroubled by the passage of fresh air seemed all too familiar, filling his nostrils and seeping into his clothes.

At the foot of the dimly lit stairs, Alfie emerged into the Front Room, as everyone referred to the area containing a long bar counter along one wall with tables and chairs placed haphazardly around the floor.

Stan sat at his usual corner table with a scantily clad woman on either side. Alfie tipped his bowler as he passed by on his way to the bar, receiving a grunt and a wave from Stan, who had a bottle of French brandy at his elbow. One of the women rose from her seat, parting her scarlet lips in a smile.

'No, no, love. Just having a quick drink,' Alfie waved her away, earning a fierce scowl in return.

'What'll it be?' the barman put aside the glass he'd been polishing with a dishcloth. 'Pint of best,' Alfie replied, looking around the room and seeing no sign of Mounsden. 'Ta,' he pushed two pennies across the bar in exchange for his beer. 'Looks a bit quiet in here tonight.'

The barman resumed his polishing. 'It'll liven up when the theatres close. The back room's quite busy, though,' he said, nodding towards the curtained doorway at the far end of the bar. 'Three or four card schools. Fancy a game yourself?'

'Dunno. Not sure me luck's in. No harm in going through and having a look, though.'

Stepping through the curtain, Alfie couldn't suppress a cough. The air inside the back room was even thicker with smoke. A couple of heads turned to look, then returned to focus on their hands.

Five of the six card tables were in use. Alfie had no need to guess what was being played. Poker was the only choice at Stan's. The players' drinks were serviced by a small bar to the right of the curtained door. He nodded to the young barmaid behind the counter and perched on a stool at the bar. Alfie was perplexed to see no sign of Mounsden until he realised that the figure sitting with his back to him at the closest table was his quarry. Divested of coat and hat, he was in the act of dealing.

Four players shared Mounsden's table. Alfie only recognised one. Sidney Fisher, who sat directly opposite Mounsden, owned a grocer's shop in Dean Street. Originally a porter at Leadenhall Market, he'd done well for himself by 'sheer hard work and a good head for the mathematicals,' as he liked to put it. In contrast with Sidney's impressive girth, the figure to his left was a beanpole of a man – balding, with chiselled features and black gimlet eyes. The player on Sidney's right looked as out of place in Stan's back room as Mounsden himself. Sporting evening dress, he had a military air about him, sitting bolt upright and studying the cards with a fierce concentration. The last player, a young fellow of twenty-five or so by Alfie's reckoning, affected an air of studied indifference, lolling in his chair with feet outstretched, a cigarette between his lips.

Alfie finished his pint and ordered another. He was half-way through it before it struck him. Looking over Mounsden's shoulder, Alfie watched him deal. It was the grip that first aroused his interest. Mounsden's left hand held the pack with the index finger extended behind the cards and protruding over the top edge of the pack while the other fingers and the thumb compressed the deck from either side, causing the cards to bow slightly. Alfie recognised the *mechanic's grip*. Not that of the casual player, but the method adopted by a professional dealer – or a card sharp.

It took Alfie back to his childhood. Davey Roper was a drinking mate of his father's. Alfie had always looked forward to Friday nights when his dad finished work at the docks. Just before his old mum dished up their supper, the door knocker would sound, and Alfie would race down the passage to let Davey in. After they'd eaten, he'd beg Davey to show him some tricks. Out would come a pack of cards. First of all there'd be 'find the lady'. Every week, Alfie convinced himself that this time he'd do it. But no matter how hard he concentrated, the Queen of Hearts eluded him. It frustrated him to the point of tears, but then Davey would disarm him by deftly manipulating the pack. Shuffling the cards with dazzling dexterity and showing off card-sharping techniques. Alfie learned about culling and stacking to organise cards within a pack by sleight of hand. Or palming cards, which Davey called *hand-mucking*. When Davey and his dad left for the boozer on the corner, Alfie would try to emulate his teacher.

If Mounsden was cheating, he was damned good at it. Gradually, Alfie watched the winnings at Mounsden's elbow grow. Despite his *good head for the mathematicals,* Sidney Fisher was not doing well. Scooping up his few remaining coins, he was the first to get up and leave.

His immediate neighbour, the young man, was more fortunate, winning two hands in a row with a pair of queens and a straight.

Three hands later, the military type threw in his hand with a snort of disgust. 'Better things to do than waste my time here,' he growled. 'Good night to you, Mounsden,' he added, ignoring the other two players and disappearing through the curtained door.

With only three players remaining, Alfie sensed a growing air of tension. The young fellow had dropped his languid attitude, leaning over his cards and concentrating with a furrowed brow. He won the next hand with two pairs.

The end came within three hands. Losing to Mounsden, ace high to a pair, he went down in the next game to the beanpole, by three sevens to a straight. The next hand, with Mounsden dealing, turned into a tense three-way tussle with a steadily growing stake. Alfie watched as the young fellow made a poor job of concealing his emotions, his left leg fidgeting rhythmically under the table. Mounsden was first to fold, dealing the cards as the others played cat and mouse. The young fellow's agitation spread to his face, beads of sweat forming on his brow and glowing cheeks. Finally, calling – his hands trembled as he revealed a king-high straight. Beanpole permitted himself the thinnest of smiles, watching the young fellow's scarlet cheeks turn to chalk as he contemplated his opponent's full house.

'Bad luck, old man,' Mounsden offered sympathetically, pushing back his chair. 'That's me for tonight.' Pocketing his winnings, he got to his feet. 'Better luck next time,' he called after the chastened young fellow as he left the room.

Alfie finished his beer and retired to the front room. Intending to follow Mounsden when he left, he took a seat at an empty table and pretended to tie one of his bootlaces.

Mounsden emerged, smoothing his hair.

'Hoy!' Alfie looked up abruptly at the sound of Stan's booming bass, startled lest the outburst was directed at him. 'Mr M,' Stan continued, beckoning to Mounsden with one hand and brandishing a brandy bottle in the other.

Mounsden turned in Stan's direction. 'Not tonight, Stan.'

'Nah, come on over. Got something you need to hear. Come through,' Stan pointed to a door in the wall behind him and got to his feet, shooing away his female companions.

Mounsden shrugged. 'Five minutes, then.'

Alfie watched the door close behind them. Five minutes, eh? He wondered whether to stay where he was or wait outside. Deserted by Stan, the two women at his table rose and approached a chap standing at the bar. Keen not to attract their attention, Alfie shifted in his seat. He'd assumed that beanpole had stayed to play some more poker, but there he was, crossing the room and making for the stairs to the street.

Turning away from the bar, one of Stan's women eyed the room. Despite his earlier rebuff, she headed towards him, swaying her hips suggestively. 'Damn,' Alfie muttered under his breath. That did it. He'd have to wait outside. Avoiding eye contact, he rose and made for the stairs. Halfway up, the unmistakable reek of Thames fog infiltrated his nostrils. The doorman was barely visible as he emerged onto the street, shrouded in a swirling blanket of choking soot and mist. The street lamps were unequal to the murk, casting the faintest of glows.

Alfie covered his mouth and nose with his muffler. *A real pea-souper, and no mistake,* he thought. *Sorry, Mr Benson, but I'm not hanging around in this for no one.*

Disorientated, but trusting in his innate knowledge of London's streets to find his way, he turned for home.

'There you are, Mounsden.' The reedy, disembodied voice came from behind Alfie's left shoulder. 'I thought I'd never find you in this fog. I can hardly see my hand in front of my face. It was a good night, though. Where should we go to share the winnings?'

Alfie reached into his pocket.

'That young fool. Loved wiping the smile off his face,' the voice continued.

Alfie's match flared.

Beanpole's eerily lit features flickered into view.

'Oh. It's not…' Beanpole's face contorted in surprise. Then, he was gone. Alfie dropped the match and listened to the man's footsteps echoing on the cobbles, growing fainter.

Chapter 28

'So, the Honourable Roderick Mounsden MP cheats at cards.' George leaned his elbows on the table.

'It threw me a bit when it was that other geezer that cleaned out the young bloke. But they was in cahoots, see.' Alfie took a long drag of his Woodbine. 'He was fiddling those cards for sure, and they must have been signalling to each other somehow.'

'Hard to prove anything, though.'

'Well, what do you want me and Dick to do now, guv? We know what he does at Stan's, but maybe there's something else? Want us to keep watching him?'

'Yes, if you would. Let's say two more days.'

George left Alfie in The Lamb and Flag. He'd promised to keep Ambrose informed, but hesitated to call on him with nothing more useful than the card-sharping business. Give it another day or two, he thought.

***

'I wondered if you'd come. I would not have blamed you if you'd washed your hands of the whole business.'

Ambrose looked crestfallen.

'I'm sorry. Forgive me. I'm truly grateful for your support. It's more than I deserve. Is there any …?'

'I have an associate,' Ambrose began, 'no, not merely an associate, but a dear friend. A private investigator named George Benson. He's working to discover anything that we can use against Mounsden.'

'Oh, I see. And has he discovered anything?'

'He will inform me as soon as he does. He's entirely trustworthy and diligent.'

Bella whimpered, growing restless. 'She's keen to continue her walk. Would it be an imposition to meet me here in the park again tomorrow? Even if there's no news from your Mr Benson, it would be a comfort to see a friendly face.'

'But of course.'

'Come along then, Bella.'

Ambrose remained on the bench, watching Violet and the dog for a few moments before rising and setting off in the opposite direction.

He'd no idea what compelled him to stop and look back.

Violet stood at the edge of the path facing a looming figure blocking her way. Her fear was obvious, even at a distance. Bella lay quivering at her feet.

From twenty paces away, Ambrose broke into an ungainly trot on seeing the man grip Violet roughly by the wrist.

'S-stop,' he panted. 'You, sir, stop that!'

The man glanced in his direction, then turned back to Violet, increasing the pressure on her wrist until she cried out in pain. As Ambrose finally reached the pair, puffing heavily, her assailant pulled Violet towards him and bent to whisper in her ear before turning on his heel.

'Are you alright, my dear?'

Violet shivered violently, rubbing her wrist. 'Mounsden,' she whispered, on the verge of tears.

Fuelled by rage, Ambrose marched off in pursuit. 'Mounsden, you blackguard. Stop and face me.'

The man turned back. Broad shouldered and a head taller than Ambrose, a scowl of annoyance crossed his face. 'Who the devil are you, sir?'

'A gentleman who will not stand by and watch a defenceless woman being assaulted.'

'You'll mind your own damned business if you know what's good for you.' Mounsden advanced menacingly. 'Now clear off,' he added, prodding Ambrose's chest with his forefinger.

'I insist that you apologise to the lady at once. You are a dis –'

Ambrose's jaw took the full force of Mounsden's fist. Dropping to his knees, he keeled over, scraping his cheek on the gravel, and lay still, vaguely aware of Violet's scream and Mounsden's receding footsteps.

Fighting the urge to vomit and giddy with double vision, he staggered to the nearest park bench, with Violet supporting him.

'Is he alright? Looks as though he's had a nasty turn.'

Violet stopped dabbing at Ambrose's cheek with her handkerchief. 'Yes, he's had a bit of a fall. I expect he'll be alright presently.'

The park-keeper looked doubtful. 'You never know with an old gentleman like that. Why, the shock might be the death of him. My old uncle, he tripped over his own doorstep. Up he gets, saying he's as right as rain, and five minutes later he drops down stone dead. I said to the missus –'

'I'm feeling a lot better,' Ambrose interrupted weakly. 'Thank you for your concern. It's nothing but a bit of a scratch.'

'Well, if you're quite sure, sir. You just sit there for as long as you want. No sense in moving until –'

'Thank you. Quite sure. This lady is taking good care of me.' Ambrose forced a smile.

'Very good, sir, madam.' The park-keeper touched the peak of his cap and walked away.

'Oh, Ambrose, this is all my fault. I should never have involved you. You must keep away. Tell your private investigator that I no longer require his assistance. Please, Ambrose, it's too dangerous.'

Ambrose touched his cheek tentatively and winced. 'How long is it since we met in India? Twenty-five, no, twenty-six years. I've done a lot of things in my life, Violet, good things and some I'm not proud of. But I've never allowed myself to be intimidated. Old indeed, damned impertinence. You'll just have to believe me when I say that George Benson and I have dealt with far worse than Mounsden. So there can be no question of my stepping away.'

'But what if…'

'Mounsden has made a grave mistake. I have allies, resourceful allies. I promise you that brute will regret crossing swords with Ambrose Mallard. What did he threaten you with just now?'

'He reminded me I have seven days in which to acquiesce to his…' Violet shuddered. 'Or he'll carry out his threat to expose my past.'

Ambrose thought for a moment. 'It would be premature for us to meet tomorrow, and I think it best if you refrain from walking Bella here for the present.'

'But Bella must have her exercise. And what reason would I give for not walking her?'

'Hmm, say you have sprained your ankle. Could a servant walk her instead?'

'Oh, Kate could do so, I suppose. Bella takes to her. But when will I hear from you, Ambrose? This whole situation is pure torture.'

'Does your husband read your mail?'

'No, certainly not.'

'Then I'll write to you.' Ambrose clasped her hand. 'Trust me. And remember to limp.'

***

'Come in.' George looked up from his desk. 'Ah, Mortimer and… good Lord, Ambrose, your face. What happened? Take a seat, please. But first things first.'

George poured three generous measures of scotch and soda. 'Now then. Fire away.'

Ambrose recounted his encounter with Mounsden.

'Struck you? In broad daylight?' George shook his head and turned to Mortimer. 'Would you credit it?'

'What I find hard to credit is that the two of you have embarked on this business without so much as a by your leave. Had it not been for the fact that Ambrose could not conceal his injury when he returned to Montagu Square this morning, I dare say I'd be none the wiser. For Ambrose to embark on some quixotic folly hardly comes as a surprise. But for you, George, to go along with it and not think to inform me is profoundly disappointing,' Mortimer declared.

'But, my dear chap, George was just –'

Mortimer cut Ambrose off. 'It was bad enough hearing about your tawdry past in Bombay –'

'Stop!' George got to his feet. 'You're not lording around your estate now, Mortimer. You are in my office, and you'll do me the courtesy of speaking in a civil manner. Far from acting quixotically, Ambrose is surely doing what any gentleman would do when a lady finds herself at the mercy of a vile creature like Mounsden. If you have come here with the intention of preventing me from doing my damndest to protect the lady's honour, then you should leave.'

Mortimer locked eyes with George and downed his scotch.

'You do me an injustice, George. Yes, it's true that Ambrose has acted from the noblest of motives, and I apologise for speaking sharply just now. But why did neither of you seek my help in this matter? Do you suppose that because I'm now married, I've ceased to care about my old friends? Does our past comradeship count for nothing?'

George sat down. 'I – yes, if I'm honest with myself, I *had* thought of you in that way. You have Olivia, Sylvia, and the estate to consider. You're not the free agent you were, Mortimer.

'He's right, old chap.' Ambrose patted Mortimer's arm.

'Thank you, Ambrose. I should have held my tongue. I'm truly sorry to have spoken so disrespectfully to you.'

'Think nothing of it. I was in the wrong.'

Mortimer blew out his cheeks. 'Let me start again. Ambrose, George – Mounsden must be stopped. The fact is, I know the man. Not well, certainly, but enough to know that he's a deeply unpleasant character. You see, he's a member of my club – The Unicorn.

'Of course I haven't attended the place much lately, what with being in the country, but I've popped in since coming up to town.'

'How much have you told Mortimer, Ambrose?'

'Uh, Mortimer knows about my past association with Violet, Lady Ternan, and Mounsden's threats. And of course, I explained that you had offered to help. To try to find a chink in the fellow's armour.'

George nodded. 'I've had him followed. Alfie and Dick have volunteered their services. We've discovered something about his habits, but whether it amounts to a chink in his armour, as you put it, is another matter.'

George refilled their glasses and repeated Alfie's account of Mounsden's visit to Stan's place.

'It seems that among his other dubious talents, Mounsden cheats at cards,' he said in conclusion, 'but it's not something we can prove.'

'You mean that the threat of a public accusation of cheating might dissuade him from threatening Lady Ternan?'

'Precisely, Mortimer. He's a public figure. A Member of Parliament.'

Mortimer nodded. 'I gather his name is being talked about as a future Home Secretary. Perhaps there is a way.'

George arched his eyebrows. 'Go on.'

Chapter 29

'How much more satisfying to have a foursome for whist,' Caroline shut the door behind Arnold and led him along the hallway to the parlour. 'Have you visited this cottage before?'

'Oh, yes. Most of the furniture comes from my workshop.' Arnold ducked his head and entered. 'Good evening, Verity. I'm sorry I wasn't able to speak with you at supper.'

'Oh, no need to apologise. As you might have noticed, Stella and some of her friends had me surrounded. They have taken it upon themselves to try to persuade me to become a permanent member of the community.'

'Now then. I don't believe you've met Gregory.' Caroline slipped her arm through Arnold's.

'No, I've seen you around and about, but we've not actually met, have we? How do you do, Gregory.' Arnold extended his hand.

'Ah.' Gregory rose awkwardly from his seat. 'Likewise. Most pleased to make your acquaintance.' He shook Arnold's hand, cheeks reddening at being the centre of attention.

'Shall we be seated? Arnold and I will play against you, Verity, and Gregory. Then we'll swap partners after ten hands. Is that acceptable to everyone? Oh, by the way,

Arnold has contributed a bottle of rather decent port. Such a welcome change from cider, if I may say so. And there's ginger beer for you, Gregory.'

An hour and a half passed pleasantly. 'There – the last trick to Gregory and me.' Caroline collected the cards and put the pack to one side.

'You were saying earlier that you are being asked to stay on here.' Arnold turned to Verity.

'That's right.'

'And will you?'

Verity smiled. 'I've been non-committal. Stella tells me I'm a great help to her with her stained-glass work. And I suppose I'm picking up some of the techniques. But I really see this as an interesting interlude. Nothing more. Between the four of us, I will be returning to London when the three weeks are over.'

'Elspeth is urging me to stay as well,' Caroline volunteered.

'Well, that hardly comes as a surprise. You are a genuine artist. Just what the community needs.' Verity exclaimed. 'And what have you decided?'

'I think I may stay on for a while.' Caroline blushed, glancing sideways at Arnold.

'Good. I'm pleased for you both.' Verity grinned as Caroline turned a deeper shade of scarlet.

'And you, Gregory. What have Oswald and Ursula got in store for you?'

Gregory shrugged. Interrupted in the act of polishing his spectacles, he squinted myopically. 'Um, I don't know.'

'Have they said anything to you about staying on?' Verity persisted.

Gregory put his spectacles back on and shook his head.

Verity gave Caroline a despairing look.

'Are they teaching you anything, Gregory?' Arnold took up the baton. 'You've been at the pottery studio since you arrived here, haven't you?'

'Oh, I've tried my hand. All fingers and thumbs – but not in a good way.' Gregory looked around to see if anyone had reacted to his attempt at a witticism. 'You know, throwing pots on the wheel – fingers and…' He trailed off and studied his feet.

Caroline broke the awkward silence. 'What will you do then, Gregory? When the retreat is over? Is it back home to London?'

Gregory lifted his head. 'They said something.'

'Who? Do you mean Oswald and Ursula?'

Gregory nodded. 'And Dornford.'

'What did they say?' Caroline felt like an angler trying to coax a reluctant salmon to shore, fearing that the line might go slack at any moment.

'I'd finished loading the kiln. The kitchen door was open, and I'd stopped to wipe my feet in the porch. It was muddy crossing from the studio, so…'

Caroline resisted the urge to hurry him along.

'Very muddy, actually. It was most fortunate that I didn't slip. Do you remember we had that heavy shower?'

Caroline bit her tongue.

'Uh, where was I? Oh, yes. They were speaking. Of course, it's not the done thing to eavesdrop, but I could have sworn they mentioned my name.'

'They were talking about you.'

'That was what I assumed. Then it went quiet for a few moments. And then Ursula said, "That's the answer. The Blessed Plot shall have a new resident". And they all laughed. I didn't want them to think I'd been listening, so I went back along the path, then turned back and whistled loudly as I approached.'

The thought of Gregory whistling loudly struck both Verity and Caroline as wildly out of character, but they said nothing.

'When I wiped my feet and entered the kitchen, it was empty.'

'The Blessed Plot? Isn't that the place you mentioned to Verity and me the other night, Arnold?' asked Caroline.

Arnold snorted. 'It's a sham. Oswald and Ursula maintain that there's some sister community, to which the most committed members of Chase Manor may gain admission. It's a figment of their imagination. A convenient way of explaining why occasionally someone leaves without warning. It's because some people can't stomach Oswald and Ursula and all their nonsense, if you ask me.'

'Yes, that was what you said before, Arnold.' Verity furrowed her brow. 'But it occurred to me that in a community of this size, people must come and go quite regularly. Yet from what I understand only a very few are said to have gone to this Blessed Plot.'

Arnold shrugged. 'I still say it's a fraud. Just like those two and that son of theirs.'

'Hmm. Perhaps you're right. But if it turns out there is such a place, where is it, I wonder?'

Gregory got to his feet. 'I must go. Thank you, Caroline, Verity, and you, of course, Arnold. I'm quite fatigued.'

'You look rather tired, I must say, Gregory,' Verity said sympathetically. 'Shall I see you out?'

'No, thank you.'

'Shall we have a nightcap? There's still plenty of port left.' Caroline pointed to the bottle.

Verity nodded and watched Arnold fill their glasses.

'Tell me, Arnold?'

'Hmm.' Arnold put the bottle down. 'What would you like to know?'

'Well, you've made it plain what you think of the Lamonts. What is your opinion of Aquinas Thorpe?'

Arnold threw his head back and laughed. 'Ah, what can I say? A grown man playing at Knights of the Round Table. But,' his face grew serious, 'we keep out of each other's way. You should as well.'

'Too late for that, I'm afraid. Caroline and I have both had the misfortune to meet him, although it's me he seems to have taken a particular dislike to.'

'Keep away from the man. I mean it, both of you.'

'Oh, Arnold, you needn't worry as far as I'm concerned,' Caroline squeezed his arm. 'Our paths haven't crossed since last weekend. It's not so easy for Verity.'

'Stella's stained-glass workshop is at Myrddin's Keep. We do our best to avoid Aquinas and his band of so-called knights.'

'Privileged louts, all of them,' Arnold said contemptuously.

'Overgrown schoolboys, that's how I think of them. But what about the women?' Verity asked. 'Why on earth do they associate with Aquinas and his ilk?'

Arnold shrugged. 'Aquinas will go too far one day. If either of you feels threatened, you must tell me.'

Chapter 30

George had to hand it to Mortimer. After their fractious meeting in George's office, Mortimer had devoted himself to the plan that he'd outlined. Within forty-eight hours, George found himself in the familiar surroundings of Mortimer's townhouse in Montagu Square.

'Please take a seat,' Mortimer greeted him as he appeared at the door of the dining room.

Ambrose, already seated at the table, waved and beckoned him in.

George waited for Mortimer to commence proceedings.

'Just one moment.' Mortimer held a hand to his ear. 'Ah, here she comes.'

Sweeping into the room with a warm smile of greeting, Olivia took a seat next to George.

'I've asked Olivia to join us. Indeed, having tended to Ambrose's injuries and hearing how they came about, she insisted on playing a part in thwarting Mounsden.'

'It horrifies me to think of what Lady Ternan must be going through,' Olivia said forcefully.

'I spent yesterday afternoon and evening at the Unicorn Club,' Mortimer began. 'As a member of long standing, I'm well acquainted with its officeholders. The Chairman, Sir Nicholas Godber, is a retired judge. I had the honour of appearing at the bar before him on a couple of occasions.

To cut a long story short, I have the agreement of Sir Nicholas and the governing committee to pursue the following course of action.'

George listened intently.

'It will be Tuesday evening,' Mortimer said in conclusion. 'As Sir Nicholas put it, "that is when Mr Mounsden usually graces the club with his presence". He has a routine. Scotch and sodas in the Morning Room, that's the club bar, then to the Blue Room, which is set aside for cards on Tuesdays and Thursdays.

'I need hardly point out that it's a touchy subject. Accusations of cheating against a public figure must be handled with great delicacy. We all remember the Tranby Croft business.'

George remembered it all too well. It was a scandal of sensational proportions. In September 1890, Bertie, or more correctly Edward, Prince of Wales, was among the guests attending a house party at Tranby Croft, a country house in Yorkshire. In the evenings, Bertie played baccarat with several of the male guests, among whom was Sir William Gordon-Cumming, a lieutenant colonel in the Scots Guards and a member of Bertie's social circle, known as the Marlborough House set.

Accusations emerged that Gordon-Cumming cheated by surreptitiously adding to his stake after a winning hand had been declared. Despite attempts, in which Bertie was personally involved, to deal with the matter privately, Gordon-Cumming sued his principal accusers for slander and the matter proceeded to court, with Bertie being summoned as a witness. The judge found against Gordon-Cumming, sparking a storm of controversy. He was dismissed from the army and became a social outcast.

∗∗∗

George looked at himself in the mirror. He'd not had occasion to wear evening dress since attending the theatre to watch Mary Phillips and Anna Jesenska in *Hedda Gabler*. He gave a last tweak to his bow tie and headed for the door. Twenty minutes later, he alighted from a hansom cab outside the Unicorn Club on St James's Street.

'Ah, yes, Mr Benson, Sir Mortimer Mallard is awaiting you.' The concierge clicked his fingers to summon a young footman. 'Convey this gentleman to the Committee Room.'

George followed the servant up the central staircase and along a corridor on the first floor. Opening a door at the far end, the footman stood aside for George to enter.

'Come on in, old man.' Mortimer stood in front of a marble fireplace next to a tall, clean-shaven man with sparse white hair and a patrician bearing.

'Sir,' Mortimer turned to his companion, 'allow me to introduce my good friend and associate, Mr George Benson.'

'Sir Nicholas Godber,' the man inclined his head, 'a pleasure to make your acquaintance, Mr Benson.'

George returned the gesture. 'Sir Nicholas.'

'Let us be seated.'

Sir Nicholas placed himself at the head of the highly polished committee table, with George and Mortimer on either side.

He spoke with authority, sitting stiffly with a straight back as though presiding over a court of law. 'The Blue Room opens for card play in,' he glanced at the clock on the mantelpiece, 'thirty-five minutes, at eight p.m. Mr

Mounsden is taking refreshment in the drawing room. He arrived twenty minutes ago with a guest.'

Mortimer caught George's eye and gave a nod of encouragement.'

'Would his guest be a thin, sharp-featured fellow going bald?'

'I believe so, according to our concierge. That description corresponds with the man he was playing cards with at an establishment in Soho, I understand.'

'That's correct, Sir Nicholas, my associate witnessed them.'

'Ah, indeed, your associate. That would be a Mr Alfred Cotton?'

'Yes, sir.' George looked questioningly at Mortimer. 'Shouldn't Alfie be here by now?'

Mortimer grinned. 'Alfie, you can come out now.'

George followed Mortimer's gaze. Emerging from behind a screen in the corner of the room, a figure in blue and grey servant's livery stepped self-consciously over to the table.

'How do I look, Mr Benson?'

Conscious of Sir Nicholas's austere presence, George resisted the urge to laugh. 'My word, Alfie. You almost had me fooled.'

'Mr Cotton has kindly agreed to wear the club's livery so that he may observe the card play without raising suspicion. There will be two servants in attendance in the Blue Room. Never fear, Mr Cotton, if any of the members require drinks and so forth, Draper will attend to it. You need only remain unobtrusively in the background and keep an eagle eye on Mr Mounsden and his guest.' Sir Nicholas bestowed an avuncular smile on Alfie.

'Club rules allow cards to be played on Tuesday and Thursday evenings.' Sir Nicholas continued. 'The only game permitted is *vingt-et-un*. Tables are set for four players and, it goes without saying, that members are expected to behave with decorum. We do not set limits on stakes, but there is a tacit understanding that members will not gamble to excess. Cheating by a member or guest is rightly considered unthinkable. There, it only remains for everyone to act according to plan.'

'One thing, sir,' George asked. 'Have any members expressed concerns about Mounsden? Having played cards with him, I mean.'

Sir Nicholas sniffed. 'No, Mr Benson, if that had been the case, I would have dealt with it swiftly and decisively. My enquiries tell me that Mounsden is a seasoned card player who does very well, but no one has accused him of cheating. His guest has accompanied him on several occasions and it seems he often prospers at Mounsden's expense.'

'That's it, of course.' Mortimer exclaimed. 'They are in this together.'

***

'Good evening, Mounsden.'

Roderick Mounsden stopped in the Blue Room doorway and turned to face the speaker. 'Oh, it's you, Mallard. Didn't realise you had a liking for cards.'

'I'm not much of a player, but my guest, George here, enjoys a game, so I brought him up to see if we might join a table.'

Mounsden gave George an appraising look. 'Hmm. Mr Lorimer and I could accommodate you.'

'Roland Lorimer,' Mounsden's companion nodded to George and Mortimer.

'Very well, Mounsden, Mr Lorimer, it seems we have a game on our hands.' Mortimer smiled. 'Lead on.'

***

Mounsden snapped his fingers.

Draper left his station in the corner of the Blue Room and approached.

'Yes, sir?'

Mounsden pointed to the empty glass at his elbow. 'Scotch and soda.'

'Of course, sir.' Draper produced a silver tray from the crook of his arm and placed the glass on it. 'May I get anything for you, gentlemen?'

After a chorus of no thankyous, he bowed and left the room.

'Still happy to play?' Mounsden turned to Mortimer. 'You and your guest don't seem to be having much luck.'

'Hmm – our fortunes may change. A few more hands. What do you say, George?'

George considered the dwindling stack of counters at his elbow. 'A few more,' he nodded, glancing sideways to where Alfie stood.

'Lady luck is a fickle mistress. Your deal, Mallard,' Mounsden sat back and felt in his pocket for his silver cigarette case. 'Dash it, left it downstairs.'

For a split second, Alfie wondered who on earth Mounsden was waving to. 'You – you man.' Mounsden gestured impatiently.

The absence of Draper left him with no choice. With a nod of recognition, he adopted what he hoped would pass as the measured gait of a club servant.

'Step lively, damn it.'

Fearing that his cockney accent would betray him, Alfie managed a garbled, 'Yus, sir.'

Mounsden blinked, muttering 'damned servants' and shaking his head. 'Left my cigarette case in the Morning Room. Silver, with my monogram. Pop off and get it and tell that other fellow to hurry up with my drink while you're at it. Don't know what this club is coming to,' he added, turning to pick up his cards.

Alfie mumbled another 'Yus, sir,' looking over Mounsden's shoulder at George and scratching the bridge of his nose. Receiving a similar signal in return, he pivoted on his heel and walked away, passing Draper with Mounsden's scotch in the doorway.

Two hands later, Mortimer and George watched as Lorimer scooped up his winnings, arranging their losing counters together with Mounsden's into a neat pile.

'Well Lorimer, looks as though you've taken my luck as well as Mallard's and Benson's,' Mounsden said gruffly, turning to finish the glass of scotch sitting next to a still healthy pile of counters at his elbow.

'Your cigarette case.'

Mounsden swivelled in his chair to face not Alfie but Sir Nicholas Godber.

'Please excuse this intrusion, gentlemen. Far be it from me to interrupt your game. I merely wished to extend an invitation to join me and members of the committee for a drink. It's a courtesy we extend to our members from time to time, and of course, your guests are most welcome to accompany you. Shall we say in five minutes, in the Committee Room?'

'Delighted, Sir Nicholas,' Mortimer piped up.

'And you, Mr Mounsden?'

'Uh, yes. We will need to settle our tally. Lorimer here has had the devil's luck tonight.'

'Of course. I'm sure you gentlemen can see to that afterwards.'

***

'Brandy, scotch, sherry?'

Draper listened to their drinks orders and walked over to the sideboard to pour them.

'For the benefit of our guests, I am the club Chairman, and with me are two members of our committee, Sir Kenelm Digby and Lord Martlet. Please be seated,' Sir Nicholas announced.

The two men sitting across the committee table nodded acknowledgement.

Sir Kenelm was known to Mounsden, having occupied the post of Permanent Secretary at the Home Office since 1895. He knew Lord Martlet only by reputation, as a crusty and irascible member of the House of Lords, and a close friend of the prime minister.

Draper set their drinks on the table and left the room.

'An enjoyable game?' Sir Nicholas raised his sherry glass, sniffed and took a sip.

Mortimer and George shook their heads ruefully.

'Mr Lorimer here had the run of the cards,' Mortimer gestured in Lorimer's direction, 'And Mounsden fared quite well, all things considered. I feel rather guilty bringing

171

George here as my guest, only to have him leave with a considerably lighter wallet.'

'Congratulations to you, Mr Lorimer. Fortune has smiled upon you, it seems.' Sir Nicholas stretched his arms, hands clasped, over the committee table. 'You must tell us your secret.'

Lorimer glanced sideways at Mounsden. 'Uh, secret? Oh, just luck.' Despite himself, he could not prevent his voice from quavering.

'Of course, Mr Lorimer.' Sir Nicholas smiled briefly. 'Hmm, do you know, I have the strangest feeling that I've met you before. Can't think where.'

Under the gaze of the three committee members, Lorimer quailed. Not trusting himself to speak, he shrugged, praying for the conversation to take a different turn.

'Forgive my curiosity, my dear chap. Don't mean to pry. Terrible habit of mine, I'm afraid.' Sir Nicholas looked away, taking up his glass.

The tension gripping Lorimer's rib cage like a vice, eased.

Sir Nicholas sat back, pensively sipping his sherry.

Mounsden looked up at the committee room clock. 'Love to stay and chat, but I have another engagement. If you'll excuse me, Godber, I'll step outside with these gentlemen and settle up, then I must be on my way.'

'Got it!' Sir Nicholas put his glass down. 'I know where I've seen you before, Lorimer. I would have appeared quite different to you then. Not talking to you across a table as we are doing now, but looking down from the bench as I pronounced sentence upon you.' Sir Nicholas paused, noting Lorimer's expression of wide-eyed panic and

Mounsden's involuntary clenching of his fists. 'Without my wig and robes, I would naturally look different to you.'

'What the devil –'

Sir Nicholas held up his hand to silence Mounsden's outburst. 'Roland Thomas Lorimer. Yes, I recall the case well. You were convicted on several counts of obtaining money by deception. Oh yes, several unfortunate people lost their meagre life savings thanks to you. What was your sentence, Lorimer?'

Lorimer shook his head violently. 'No, not me.' His voice, brittle at best, emerged as little more than a squeak.

Sir Nicholas gave a dry laugh. 'Let me refresh your memory. I sentenced you to five years' hard labour.'

Lorimer bowed his head, shrinking into himself.

'The purpose of such a sentence is to punish the criminal. But it should also serve to make the transgressor see the error of his ways and to correct that error. Have you corrected your error, Lorimer? Am I to believe that you, as a friend of the Honourable Nigel Mounsden MP, are now a reformed character, an upstanding citizen?'

'This is intolerable.' Mounsden jumped to his feet, eyes blazing.

'Sit down, man, if you know what's good for you.'

Mounsden blinked, caught off guard by the harsh, gravelly voice of Lord Martlet.

'Resume your seat, Mounsden,' the urbane but forceful tone of Sir Kenelm Digby weighed in.

He sat.

'Mr Lorimer,' Sir Nicholas continued. 'You will answer me. Have you reformed?'

Lorimer nodded, not daring to look up.

Sir Nicholas raised his voice. 'Mr Cotton. Will you please join us?'

Changed back into his normal clothes, Alfie emerged from behind the screen in the corner.

Mounsden shot him a look of anger and puzzlement as it dawned on him that he was looking at the man he'd browbeaten as a club servant. Lorimer kept his head down.

'Mr Cotton. Please describe what you saw in the Blue Room earlier this evening.'

'Well, sir, I watched these two gentlemen, Mr Lorimer and Mr Mounsden, playing cards.'

'And they were playing *vingt et un* with Sir Mortimer Mallard and Mr George Benson?'

'Yes, pontoon, as I call it.'

'And what did you observe in particular?' Sir Nicholas hooked his thumbs into his lapels, recalling the stance he'd so often adopted in the past as a cross-examining barrister.

'That gentleman,' Alfie pointed at Mounsden, 'was up to all sorts with them cards.'

'Could you be more specific, Mr Cotton? What, precisely, was Mr Mounsden "up to" as you put it?'

'He was peeking. That's getting a look at the top card before dealing. Then there was palming and mucking. That means hiding a card in your palm then swapping it for another card. He's good at it. You'd never know unless you knew about sharping. When he's shuffling and dealing, he can do whatever he likes with them cards.'

'Poppycock!' Mounsden slammed his fist on the table. 'Do you seriously believe the word of this, this… East End guttersnipe?'

'Keep a civil tongue in your head, Mounsden.' Martlet's eyes blazed with unconcealed contempt.

'And they was signalling too.' Alfie continued, keeping a wary eye on Mounsden.

'Really, Mr Cotton,' Sir Nicholas continued. 'And what form did this signalling take?'

'He,' Alfie pointed at Mounsden, 'likes to shift his counters about. Stacking them one way, then another. He fiddled around with them every hand. Not obvious, but I clocked him alright. Then he,' Alfie turned to look at Lorimer, 'he fidgets. You know, rubs his nose, taps his fingers on the table, bites his lip, that sort of thing.'

'Damn it all.' Mounsden turned to Mortimer. 'Mallard, tell them. You didn't see anything of the sort. You and your guest played for over an hour, and did either of you raise any objection? No, of course you didn't, because there was nothing to object to, was there?'

'On the contrary, Mounsden, if Mr Cotton informs me that you have been cheating, I have every confidence in him.'

'Why? Do you know the blighter? What the deuce is going on here, Mallard? You'd be well advised not to cross me, sir.' Mounsden puffed out his chest threateningly.

Mortimer thought of Verity. When faced with aggressive or overbearing individuals, she had a knack of asserting herself without resorting to verbal retaliation. A studied pause, an imperious gaze. She could stare down belligerence with ease. Mortimer ignored Mounsden's challenge. Reaching for his cigarette case, he took his time, selecting a cigarette, tapping it on the case, then fishing in his pocket for a matchbox and striking a light. Mounsden watched him with mounting rage, judging by the colour of his cheeks. Mortimer drew on his cigarette as he shook out the match, then exhaled a long plume of smoke through his nose.

'Mr Cotton is a good friend of mine and a man of the utmost integrity. Rather than issuing crude threats, Mounsden, you would do well to sit and listen while I tell you why Mr Cotton was invited to be here this evening. You made a fatal mistake when you assaulted a relative of mine. A mistake that has led directly to your unmasking as the cheat and coward that you are.'

Mounsden narrowed his eyes, brows furrowed in thought. Mortimer sensed his uncertainty and pressed on.

'My relative, Ambrose Mallard, came to the defence of a lady whom you, sir, were manhandling. There, I see from your expression that you recognise the incident to which I refer. On Friday last, in Cavendish Square Gardens. The lady's name needn't be mentioned here: Sir Nicholas, Sir Digby and Lord Martlet know to whom I am referring. Mr Mallard, your senior by many years, was violently set upon by you and sustained painful injuries. And don't be misled for one moment into thinking that we don't know why you were there. It was to threaten her honour.'

'Disgraceful.' Lord Martlet fumed.

'I knew you were a cheat before this evening, and tonight was my opportunity to unmask you.'

'Nonsense.' Mounsden scoffed.

'Oh no, not nonsense. Do you deny that you attended a tawdry drinking den named Stan's in Soho where you and Lorimer played poker? Take another look at Mr Cotton, Mounsden. You didn't notice him then, but he observed you and saw you cheating.'

'Pah. Stuff and nonsense. I don't frequent such places.'

'Stan wouldn't take it kindly if he knew that.' Alfie shifted his position to stand in front of Mounsden. 'He's a rogue himself right enough, but he'd be very unhappy at someone taking advantage on his premises and I wouldn't want to make Stan unhappy, not for all the tea in China, I wouldn't.'

'Don't you dare threaten me, you –'

'And what about you, Mr Lorimer?' Sir Nicholas interjected. 'Would you want to risk running afoul of this Stan? You do not have any advantages of social standing, do you? An ex-convict, an accomplice in card sharping, and heaven knows what other disreputable activities. Don't look to Mr Mounsden for protection. He will cast you aside like a used cigar stub if he has no further use for you. Your card is marked, if you'll excuse the pun. I will have no hesitation in asking the police to investigate you. And I can assure you that such an investigation would be most thorough, your life turned upside down; and what would they find, I wonder?'

Lorimer's head jerked up. 'I'm not taking the blame. He's the one you should be threatening with the police.' Bristling with indignation, he inclined his head at Mounsden. 'I didn't want to carry on after the first few times, but he insisted.'

'Are you saying you participated in cheating at cards at Mr Mounsden's instigation and that you have continued to do so at his urging?'

'Urging? If you call violence to my person *urging*, then yes.' Lorimer pulled up his left sleeve, exposing the underside of his forearm. 'That's what a naked gas flame can do.'

Sir Nicholas wrinkled his nose in disgust. 'I see. Well. Mr Lorimer, if you wish to avoid the attentions of the police and to protect yourself from Mr Mounsden, you must cooperate and do precisely as we tell you.'

'Damned fool,' Mounsden hissed.

'Sir Nicholas, if I may, it is time to bring matters to a head.' Sir Kenelm Digby rose to his feet, his calm, measured tones contrasting with Sir Nicholas's courtroom theatricality. 'You must understand two things, Mounsden. Unless you desist in your thoroughly vile harassment of the lady alluded to by Sir Mortimer, you will be exposed as a card cheat. Your political career, or what is left of it – for I can tell you now that any hopes you may harbour of achieving high office in the government are dashed – will be over. You will become an outcast, a pariah shunned by decent society. What is more, there is every reason to believe that a prosecution could be brought against you in the courts.

'The second thing you must understand is that you are no longer welcome at this club. If you do as we direct you tonight, you may avoid public disgrace. The committee will not formally renounce your membership. However, you will on no account attempt to enter these premises. Should you fail to heed my warning, you will be escorted outside in a most ignominious fashion.'

'Damn it, Digby. Is this how you treat a fellow gentleman?'

'You have lost the right to be considered a gentleman.'

Mounsden got to his feet and took a step towards the door.

'Remain where you are; I have not finished,' spoken softly but with iron authority, Sir Kenelm's words had the desired effect.

Sir Kenelm indicated a sheet of paper lying on the table.

Mounsden bent over the document, resting on his clenched fists. He spoke without raising his head. 'You cannot expect –'

Sit Kenelm cut him off. 'Sign now, or *this* letter will be presented to Sir Edward Bradford,' he said, placing another sheet of paper on the table.

At the sound of the Metropolitan Police Commissioner's name, Mounsden looked up. Under the implacable gaze of the committee members, he took the fountain pen held out to him by Sir Kenelm, signed and left the room without another word.

'And now, Mr Lorimer, before you leave, you will write an affidavit in Sir Nicholas's presence detailing your involvement with Mr Mounsden. If all is well, it will never see the light of day. However, should Mounsden renege on the undertaking he has provided, you can expect to find the police at your door.

Chapter 31

Ambrose got to his feet at the sight of Violet entering the tea shop. Her smile illuminated her face as though the years had rolled away and she was once again the vivacious proprietress of The Saffron Salon.

'My dear, I've ordered a pot of tea. Would you like something to eat, a pastry perhaps?'

Violet sat, smoothing her skirt nervously. 'Oh, I couldn't eat a thing, thank you, Ambrose. The relief – I can't begin to describe the relief, the weight you've taken off my shoulders. When I read your letter yesterday, I… how shall I put it? It was as though I'd taken wing. Most extraordinary and so unexpected. Not that I had no faith in you, Ambrose, but the prospect of being free from his threats seemed so distant.'

Ambrose's reply had to wait while the waitress delivered their tea.

'He's been discredited. I was about to say shamed, but it's obvious the man has no shame. Nothing will appear in public, but he has been left in no doubt that if he puts a foot wrong, he'll face utter ruin. I only wish I'd been there to see it.'

'Please convey my thanks to your friends. You mentioned a George Benson?'

'Yes, a man I'd stake my life on. We also have my relative Sir Mortimer Mallard to thank and, last but not least, one Alfie Cotton. Salt of the earth. A wonderful chap.'

Violet nodded. 'Something else rather marvellous has happened.'

'Yes?'

'I told him.'

Ambrose blinked. 'Who did you tell? Tell what exactly?'

'My husband. He knows about my life in Bombay. The Saffron Salon. Everything.'

'Heavens. Everything?'

Violet grinned. 'Not quite everything. Not about us. He – he was wonderful, quite wonderful.'

'You mean he forgives… no, no, I don't mean that. He *accepts* your past?'

'I married you for who you are,' he said. 'We all have a past. What you were is of no account.'

'Oh, Violet.' Ambrose reached across the table to squeeze her gloved hand. 'What a thoroughly decent fellow. I should like to shake his hand.'

'I think it best that the two of you do not meet. I would have to explain how I know you.'

'Of course.'

'I have something for you.' Violet slipped her hand from Ambrose's grasp.

He watched her reach for her handbag and retrieve a small box covered in red leather.

'Open it,' she whispered, placing it on the table.

Ambrose drew it to him, hesitating for a moment before lifting the lid. 'Oh, my dear,' his voice trembled at the sight of a pair of gold cufflinks engraved with the initials A and

V intertwined. Unable to say more, he gazed at the cufflinks, running a finger over the engraved initials, heedless of the tears forming in the corners of his eyes.

'Here.' Violet offered her lace handkerchief.

'Ah, oh dear, making rather a spectacle of myself.' Ambrose dabbed at his eyes. 'Thank you, thank you from the bottom of my heart,' he began, blinking the tears away. 'I… oh.'

Violet was already halfway to the door.

'But what about your tea?' he called out weakly.

As the door closed behind her, Ambrose held her handkerchief to his nose for a moment before tucking it into his jacket pocket.

Chapter 32

'I find it hard to believe that you'll be leaving us in a few days.'

Verity pushed her plate aside. 'I know, Caroline. Somehow, this last week has simply flown by. Yes, I shall be returning to London. I've learned enough here to realise that stained glass is not my forte. Mind you, Stella has encouraged me to stay on. It's kind of her, for she would manage perfectly well without me. Perhaps it's more a question of having someone to talk to. Anyway, you two are settled.'

Caroline stole a glance at Arnold, sitting next to her at the refectory table. 'My triptych is almost finished. Arnold and I are planning a joint venture. Furniture of our own design incorporating decorative panels, which I will produce. We have sketches. Would you like to see them?'

'Most certainly.'

'As it's Friday, I thought we could get together after supper. Cards again, and I'll show you the sketches then. They're back at the cottage. And of course, Gregory must see them too. Hasn't he come out of his shell these past few days?' Caroline craned her neck, looking around the room. 'Can't see him. Can you spot him, Arnold?'

Arnold got to his feet. 'Hmm, no. Not on this table nor the others. Perhaps he's left, returned to his cottage.'

'I suppose he must have done.' Verity mused. 'I hope there's nothing amiss. I would have thought he'd at least say hello, now that he's one of us, as it were.'

'Yes, it's strange… '

Interrupted mid-sentence by a raucous clamour, Caroline looked over her shoulder. 'Oh, I might have guessed,' she sighed, shaking her head.

'You have him, Oliver.'

'Come on, Piers, hold hard, man. He's tiring.'

Around the foot of the middle refectory table, directly behind Caroline and Arnold, a throng of Arthurians gathered around two of their number. Sitting opposite one another, their elbows on the table and right hands clasped together, the men's faces were contorted in a contest of strength.

Caroline turned away. Conversation was impossible against the din of voices accompanied by the rhythmic stamping of feet as the Arthurian men urged the two arm-wrestlers on. Nearby, their female companions stood apart, murmuring to one another.

Verity pulled a face in sympathy with Caroline, sitting up to look over her friend's shoulder at the spectacle beyond. A gap between two of the standing spectators gave her a view of the two contenders. Piers had his back to her. She recognised his opponent as the man Piers had defeated in the courtyard at Myrddin's Keep – his fair hair glued to his cheeks with sweat, teeth clenched in a desperate rictus grin.

Their arms quivered. Exhortations from their supporters grew louder and more insistent: *'Piers! Oliver!'*

Almost imperceptibly, one gained the ascendency. The knotted muscles in Piers's neck bulged. Little by little,

Oliver's arm gave way. More beads of sweat sprouted at his temple, running down his face and into his eyes.

'Ha, you've got him now.' One voice rang out above all the others. Aquinas stood at the end of the table, mug of cider in hand. 'Finish it, man,' he roared.

Verity looked away for a moment. The spectacle drew the attention of everyone in the refectory. She noticed some were leaving, casting distasteful glances at the commotion and shaking their heads. Others, men mostly, stood on benches to gain a view.

Caroline leaned closer to Arnold, who put a protective arm around her. 'Let's go,' she mouthed.

Verity nodded, stooping to retrieve her handbag from the floor at her feet.

A sudden howl of animal rage, from the midst of the Arthurians, brought her to her feet, bobbing her head to see what was happening.

Eyes wild with triumph, Oliver's right hand pinioned Piers's arm to the table. Then, with a contemptuous snarl, he pulled away, leaving his opponent leaning awkwardly on his side before sitting up and rubbing his shoulder.

Oliver's supporters surrounded him, cheering and whistling. One of them handed him a jug of cider, which he lifted to his lips and drained, spilling the liquid over his doublet.

Aquinas's scowl showed his displeasure. Turning away he came face to face with Caroline and Arnold as they made to leave.

'What's this?' The scowl turned to a leer. 'Well, I never. There I was thinking you were a lady, Caroline, and now I see you with this common working man. Been filling your head with socialism or some such nonsense, I'll be bound.' Aquinas took a step closer.

Caroline winced at the reek of cider on his breath. 'Please go back to your friends. You're obviously drunk.'

'Ha, the little lady commands me, does she?' Aquinas swayed. 'Why don't you come and join us?' Piers could do with some consolation. Come, I'll sit you on his lap.'

'Stop making a damned fool of yourself.' Arnold shielded Caroline. 'Go back to Myrddin's Keep and take your rabble with you.'

Aquinas blinked. 'Did you hear that?' he called over his shoulder. 'That sounds very much like a challenge to me. This fellow has the temerity to challenge the Seigneur of Myrddin's Keep. What shall we do with him?'

'Throw him in the pond,' a voice piped up, followed by a chorus of laughter.

'Come on then. To me, my good knights.' Aquinas threw his cider mug to one side, eyes gleaming.

'Caroline, go home now with Verity,' Arnold whispered.

'Stop this at once!' In a voice more forceful than a regiment of sergeant-majors, Ursula came stumping through the refectory, interposing herself between Aquinas and Arnold.

'Take your brutes and get out – and your doxies too,' Ursula faced Aquinas, legs splayed and hands on hips. 'You are not welcome here. You will confine yourselves to Myrddin's Keep for the next week.'

Aquinas appeared dumbstruck. Grumbles of discontent could be heard from his supporters.

'Oswald!' Ursula shrieked. 'Come here at once and exert your authority.'

Like a frozen tableau, no one spoke until Oswald could be heard threading his way through the onlookers. 'Excuse me. Can I squeeze through? Thank you.'

Ursula fumed, tapping her foot until Oswald emerged red-faced at her side.

'Oh, what was that commotion about?'

'For heaven's sake, are you deaf? It's them.' Ursula pointed at the gaggle of Arthurians. 'Not satisfied with behaving like barbarians among themselves, they're trying to pick a fight with Arnold.'

Oswald glanced at Arnold. 'What on earth did you say to them? Not more of your socialist sermonising, I hope?'

'What?' Arnold rolled his eyes.

'It had nothing to do with Arnold.' All eyes turned to Verity. Stepping up onto the bench and then onto the refectory table, she towered over the scene. 'Ursula knows full well who is at fault here, Aquinas and his motley collection of ill-bred oafs. This man, who masquerades as a champion of chivalry, has insulted Caroline and threatened Arnold for no reason. Don't look at me in that way, Oswald. Everyone here knows that these so-called Arthurians are a law unto themselves. Why on earth are they tolerated?'

'Ho, ho. A veritable Boadicea.' Aquinas strutted up and down, drawing laughter and ribald comments from his supporters. 'Well then, my dear Oswald, why are we tolerated? Would you care to enlighten everyone?'

'Dear God.' Ursula left Oswald's side, taking Aquinas by the arm and drawing him forcefully away to the corner of the barn. Oswald hesitated before following in their wake.

Out of earshot, the three conferred in furious whispers under the bemused gaze of the onlookers, until Aquinas broke away. 'Come, knights. Come, Guineveres. We are leaving. But let no one be in any doubt – we will return. No one impugns the honour of the Order of the Golden Dragon.'

***

'What a night.' Oswald slumped onto a chair at the kitchen table. 'I'll get along to Myrddin's Keep tomorrow and smooth things over with Aquinas. You know how he gets when he's been drinking. He'll be more amenable in the morning.'

'Oh, yes, Oswald, of course. That's your answer to everything, isn't it?' Ursula marched over to the oak dresser occupying one wall of the kitchen, reaching up to the top shelf for the bottle of brandy kept there.

'Do you think that's wise, dear?'

Ursula gritted her teeth. Selecting a glass, she placed it and the bottle on the table.

Oswald watched her pour a large measure, gulp half of it while still standing, then drag out a chair and plump herself into it.

'Now, of all times. At least Dornford wasn't there. You know how he loathes Aquinas at the best of times.' Ursula sighed.

'Elspeth wasn't best pleased at his departure.'

'Then again, retiring to Sylvan Cottage complaining of a headache, meant she didn't witness tonight's performance.' Ursula took another gulp of brandy. 'Elspeth knows what's at stake here, even if she pretends to be morally superior to the rest of us.'

'Let's hope the journey went well. It's the first time Dornford has escorted anyone. I'll feel happier when he's safely back home. Do you mind if I join you?' Oswald eyed the bottle of brandy.

Ursula jerked her head. 'Fetch a glass. He has to learn. At least his charge was compliant when they left.'

'Meek as a lamb,' Oswald poured himself a brandy. 'A toast. To the Blessed Plot.'

'The Blessed Plot. And let's hope all goes to plan this time.' Ursula drained her glass. 'So, it appears that Caroline and Arnold are walking out together.'

'Hmm. Well, I suppose there's no harm in that. It might provide Arnold with a distraction. Blunt his revolutionary zeal, as it were. And as she's staying in our community, we'll benefit from her artistic flair. She undoubtedly has talent.'

'Granted, Oswald. However, she still refuses to embrace our ways fully. Insisting on wearing the clothes she brought with her conveys a regrettably independent attitude.'

'Perhaps she'll mellow.'

'Then there's Verity. I gather she will be returning to London. I can't say I'll be sorry to see her depart.'

Oswald nodded. 'It's not as though she's shown any great aptitude. Artistically, I mean. Stella sings her praises, but that's because she appreciates the company. It will be a pity to lose a woman with a fortune, however.'

'Oh, don't delude yourself, Oswald. She's not Blessed Plot material. There's something about her that doesn't ring true. The grieving widow seeking solace through art, and so on. You saw how she acted this evening, the way she tore into Aquinas.'

'Yes, a formidable performance indeed.'

Ursula reached for the brandy bottle.

'Another, dear? It's not like you.'

'What will they think when they find out?'

'About Gregory? What's there to think about? Gregory has been called away urgently because his father is gravely ill. That's what they'll be told. Elspeth can call on them in the morning.'

Chapter 33

'It all happened in such a rush, I simply hadn't the opportunity to tell you earlier. It's not as if it came as a great surprise to him, poor man, but to hear that your only living relative is at death's door is nevertheless unnerving. Dornford accompanied him to Hereford Station. It's such a shame.' Elspeth got up from the breakfast table. 'I must fly. Terribly sorry to drop the news on you so unceremoniously.'

'Did Dornford say how Gregory was when he left him?'

'Oh, Dornford had some other business to attend to. He simply saw Gregory onto the London train and went straight on to his destination from Hereford. He's not expected back until sometime next week.' Elspeth sidled towards the door. 'Must go.'

Verity and Caroline listened for her footsteps in the passage and the click of the latch as she left the cottage. Verity saw her own incredulity mirrored in Caroline's expression.

'It can't be,' Caroline began. 'Gregory's parents are dead. We both heard him say so. He wouldn't have lied to us, would he?'

'He wouldn't have it in him. Something very disturbing is going on here, Caroline, and I intend to find out what it is.'

'How? How can you?'

'Can I clear away the breakfast things?' Tamsin bustled in from the kitchen, tray in hand.

'Yes, thank you, Tamsin. We've just been told that Gregory has gone. Did you know?'

'Well, Miss Verity, me and Sally heard it from our brother. Seth took Mr Gregory and Mr Dornford to Hereford Station in the carriage.'

'Really? What time did they leave?'

'Sometime in the morning, I think. Now, Mr Gregory was here at breakfast time. Sally said he was his usual self. A bit quiet, but then he were always a bit quiet.' Tamsin held her chin, concentrating. 'I remember now. Seth arrived back at the farm at midday, so I suppose they must have left not long after eleven.'

'Did Seth say anything about Gregory? How he seemed?'

'He did say that Mr Gregory must have taken the news about his father really hard. Mr Dornford had to hold him steady and help him into the carriage, then out again at the other end.'

'So Dornford saw him off at the station and went on somewhere else, I understand?'

'Somewhere else? I dunno about that.' Tamsin rubbed her chin again. 'Seth carried their luggage onto the platform. I thought they were catching the same train.'

'Did Seth tell you that they caught the same train, or did you just assume that they must have done?' Verity asked.

Tamsin shook her head. 'Oh, I can't be sure. Maybe I just thought it. Is it important?'

'Would you ask Seth to call here? At ten thirty. I will have a letter for him to take to the post office. It must go today.' Verity opened her purse and produced two half-crowns. 'You can leave the dishes, Tamsin. Caroline and I will see to them.'

Tamsin scooped up the coins. 'I'll be getting along then.'

'Thank you. And remember, no one else must know. Is that clear?'

'Yes, Miss Verity.'

Caroline could hardly contain herself. 'Another letter? You must tell me what's on your mind.'

'Very well. This afternoon, I will suddenly succumb to an indisposition.'

'Oh, are you not feeling well?'

'Perfectly well. The indisposition will be a ruse. A gastric upset, I fancy. It will prevent me from going to supper in the refectory.'

'To what end?'

Verity smiled. 'I shall use the opportunity to visit the Manor.'

Caroline rolled her eyes. 'Visit? A visit is undertaken when residents are at home. Ursula and Oswald will be in the refectory, and Dornford is away. Who are you visiting?'

'All right, let's speak plainly. I will slip into the Manor while no one is there and conduct a search. We know what Elspeth told us isn't true. And from what Tamsin said just now, it sounds as though Dornford and Gregory have gone somewhere together.'

'London?'

Verity shrugged. 'Wherever they've gone, we need to find out. Gregory's having to be helped into the carriage? Doesn't that seem suspicious? He can't have been suffering from grief, and even though he can be rather clumsy, I don't see why he'd need Dornford to steady him. I'll come right out with it, Caroline. I'm worried that Gregory will come to harm. I think he may have been taken away against his will.'

'In heaven's name, why?'

'It's obvious, isn't it? What else could be behind it but money? Gregory is the sole heir to his family's fortune. Somehow they mean to deprive him of it?'

'They? Dornford and Elspeth, you mean?'

'Not on their own. Ursula and Oswald must be behind it.'

'If you find out where Gregory has been taken, what then?'

'Then I will need the assistance of a friend of mine. Hence the letter.'

***

Enveloped in a sable cloak borrowed from Caroline, Verity followed a woodland path, emerging near the pottery. The shadow of the manor house fell across the garden at the rear, spreading as the sun went down. With barely a half-hour of daylight remaining, she crossed swiftly to the back door.

Secure in the knowledge that no one in the community locked their doors, she lifted the latch and entered the kitchen. On her only previous visit, when she, Caroline, and Gregory were invited to dinner on their first night, she'd entered by the front door. She recalled that they'd been led along a passage past other rooms before reaching the dining room, which lay adjacent to the kitchen near the main staircase.

A cursory inspection of the kitchen revealed nothing of interest. Two doors led off it. The first gave access to a scullery and pantry. Opening the other, Verity found herself in the manor's central passageway, with the staircase on her right. To her left, she recognised the entrance to the dining room. Beyond it was a large reception room, overlooking the lawns at the front of the house.

Turning back along the passage, the first room she tried looked like a combined drawing room and library. Verity pressed on. Almost hidden off a narrow corridor leading past the staircase, a baize curtain concealed another door. The view within reminded her of the estate office at Thorneycroft. Beneath a single window stood a heavy oak roll-top desk. Along the walls on either side of the room, two matching cabinets rose from floor to ceiling with cupboards and drawers below, and pigeon-holed shelves above. But whereas Thorneycroft's estate office was a model of orderliness, here chaos reigned. Ledgers and piles of documents lay scattered about or stuffed into pigeonholes in no apparent order. She swiftly examined the cupboards and drawers, finding only more disorder.

In her mind, it had all seemed so much simpler. Seth had given her a real spark of hope. Arriving at the cottage that morning, cloth cap in hand, he'd shuffled into the parlour at Verity's invitation, fidgeting nervously in his seat at the breakfast table. Verity forced herself to summon up some small talk to try to put him at his ease. Somehow, the subject of cricket arose. Verity was at a loss to remember how that came about, but it had the desired effect. A stalwart of the Monk's Fallow village cricket team, Seth's eyes lit up with reminiscences of past innings. After regaling her with recollections of a county match he'd watched between Herefordshire and Kent, Verity had gently but firmly brought the conversation around to Gregory's departure.

'How did Gregory seem to you, Seth?'

'He was… how shall I say? In a trance. That's the word. Like his mind was somewhere else.'

'Did he speak?'

'Not a word. He just sat there in his overcoat with the collar pulled up and his hat pulled down on his head. You could hardly see his face.'

'What did Dornford tell you?'

'Well, miss, he took me aside when we'd settled Mr Gregory in the carriage and told me he'd received bad news about Mr Gregory's father. "At death's door", he said. He kept his voice down, not wanting to cause more upset to Mr Gregory. "I'll put him on the London train, then I'm going off on business. I won't need you to bring me back".'

'Did he tell you where he was going?'

'No.' Seth bit his lip, giving Verity a sideways glance.

'Yes, Seth. Go on, there's more, isn't there?'

'Well, when we arrived at Hereford Station, I helped to get Mr Gregory inside. We sat him in the waiting room. Then I went to get their luggage from the carriage.' Seth hesitated. 'I don't know as I should be telling you all this, miss.'

'No, I understand. I don't want you to get into trouble. But, you see, I think Mr Gregory might be in some danger. You needn't worry that any of this will get back to Dornford or his parents.' Verity leaned closer. 'You can trust me, Seth, I promise.'

Verity held her breath, reluctant to press him further.

'Hmm.' Seth straightened his back and turned to meet her eyes. 'When I brought the suitcases into the station, Mr Dornford was at the ticket counter. I put the bags down and waited. I wasn't trying to eavesdrop or nothing, miss.' Seth looked away sheepishly.

'No, Seth, I'm sure you weren't, but you couldn't help overhearing, is that it?'

Seth nodded. 'I expected that he'd buy a ticket to London for Mr Gregory and one to wherever he was travelling to. If I'm honest, I was a bit, you know, curious.'

Verity smiled. 'Curious to learn where he was going on business.'

'Yes. But when he spoke to the ticket clerk, he asked for two tickets to some funny sounding place. Not London, I'm sure of that.'

'What was the name of this funny sounding place?'

'It didn't sound like a place in England.' Seth pulled a face. 'They have lots of strange sounding places in Wales. Could be somewhere in Wales, I thought.'

'Could you say it for me?'

Seth shook his head.

'What letter did it start with? Can you tell me that?'

'It were a word starting with a, like you'd say a in apple. Ab, that's how it started, then I dunno - *Abrist. Abrist* something. Best I can do. When Mr Dornford reached for his wallet to pay, I moved away. I didn't want to look like I was listening.

'No, I see. Is there anything else you can tell me?'

Seth shrugged. 'I took the bags to the waiting room and left.'

'Very well. You've been a great help, Seth. Thank you. If you'll wait here for a few minutes, I'll go and finish a letter I was writing, then I'd like you to take it straight over to the post office at Monk's Fallow.'

'Right you are, miss.'

Verity rose and seated herself at an escritoire near the window.

'Oh, there's something else, miss.'

Verity put her pen down. 'Yes?'

'That funny name. I think I've heard it before. When I took the mistress, Mrs Valentine, and Miss Swain to the station a couple of months back. I could swear that I heard the mistress ask for tickets to… that place.'

'Who is Miss Swain?'

'Oh, she was chosen. For the Blessed Plot. A great honour, they say. The mistress was taking her.'

***

'Curse this mess.' Verity stopped rummaging through the cabinets and turned her attention to the desk. A bundle of papers revealed nothing save some bills for art supplies. She moved them aside and tried opening the roll-top. Locked. Frantically, she searched the two desk drawers. The sight of a bundle of keys nestled among assorted detritus in the right-hand drawer ignited a flash of hope. Two minutes later, with the light failing fast, she conceded defeat, flinging the keys back into the drawer in exasperation.

As if to mock her, a framed photograph of Oswald and Ursula, gazing sternly at the camera, stood on top of the desk. There was no point in remaining. Verity turned, took one step towards the door, and halted. Had she seen it or imagined it? The inscription on the photograph. Not the one of the Lamonts. The one next to it. An outdoor scene showing a house, set in a gaunt landscape under lowering skies. A grim-looking place, she thought, and unremarkable save for one thing. Someone had added a handwritten inscription at the base of the photograph. Verity leaned closer. She'd not imagined it – *The Blessed Plot.*

Verity stood back. Somewhere in Wales. Somewhere amidst bare hills and sparse, wind-blasted trees. But where?

She turned away, shaking her head. Out in the passage, the last vestiges of light shone through a fanlight above the front door, illuminating a patch of wall between the kitchen and the dining room. There it was again, captured in oils; the house in the photograph formed the subject of a landscape in a gilt frame, hanging on the passage wall. The scene was painted from a different angle to that in the photograph, but it was clearly the same place; the painter's brush strokes emphasised the unforgiving nature of the landscape more dramatically than any photograph. Verity studied the house itself. A farmhouse, perhaps? Two storeys of dark grey stonework studded with small narrow windows under a slate roof, with squat brick chimneys at either end. Something about it made Verity shudder.

The painting was unsigned. She inspected the rectangular plaque fixed to the bottom of the frame.

Nant-y-Geifr Farm

Devil's Bridge

Intent on memorising the words, Verity failed to notice the sound of voices until the crunch of footsteps on gravel approaching the front door grew too loud to miss. Mere seconds before Oswald and Ursula crossed the threshold, she flitted through the kitchen and stepped out into the night.

***

'Ah, here she comes.' Caroline detached herself from Arnold's embrace.

'Oh, back from supper already?' Verity swept into the parlour, removing her cloak. 'Thank you for lending it to me, Caroline,' she said, draping it over the back of a chair. 'Not interrupting anything, am I?'

'Well, we hadn't expected you quite so soon.' Caroline grinned at Arnold. 'But never mind. I'm all ears.'

'Has she told you what I've been up to, Arnold?' Verity sat and tucked a wayward strand of hair into place.

'You suspect that Gregory has been taken somewhere. It all sounds a bit fantastic. You're sure that he hasn't just gone back home to London?'

'I'm certain of it. You're fond of saying that The Blessed Plot doesn't really exist, aren't you, Arnold? And I can understand why, but it's an actual place, and that's where Gregory has been taken.'

'Where is this place, then? Have you found that out?'

'Yes, and no. I have a name, but I don't yet know the precise location. Now then, you two, I have a plan to find Gregory. A friend of mine named George Benson will be in Monk's Fallow on Wednesday. He's a private investigator. He will have the job of finding Gregory. However, that is only part of my plan. This whole place, the Chase Manor Community, is based on a falsehood. Oswald and Ursula present themselves as benefactors, selfless patrons who wish only to nurture a community of artists and artisans. If I'm correct, their motives are sinister

200

rather than benign. They look for vulnerable people to exploit. Gregory fits the bill to a tee: impressionable, retiring, with no close family, and a sizeable fortune. Granted, this community is successful to a degree, given the talents of folk such as yourselves, but Oswald and Ursula want far more than can be provided by honest endeavour.'

Arnold nodded. 'You won't get an argument from me.'

'Nor me,' Caroline agreed. 'But you said that finding Gregory is only part of your plan?'

'Quite right. The reason I've decided to remain here is to expose the Lamonts for the frauds they are, and to see that Aquinas gets his just deserts while I'm at it. And I will need your assistance. What do you say?'

'Of course,' Caroline responded with enthusiasm. 'We'll be happy to do so, won't we, Arnold?'

'Hmm.'

Verity frowned. 'You sound uncertain, Arnold. Do you have reservations?'

'I'm as keen as you are to expose the Lamonts, but have you considered what that would mean for this community? The people whose livelihoods depend on it. Genuine folk like my fellow woodworkers. If the Lamonts are brought down, they'll suffer too.'

'You're right, of course. I realise that there may be unfortunate consequences. However, if the Lamonts are engaged in serious criminal acts, they must be brought to light. We can't sit back and allow them to continue. We'd be complicit. It's regrettable that innocent parties may suffer, but what would you have me do?'

Arnold shrugged. 'I know. Let's hope that something can be salvaged.'

Chapter 34

Stella frowned at Verity's sudden appearance at her door. 'Oh, it's you. I thought you were preparing to leave us.'

'Not until Wednesday, Stella. Would you spare me a few minutes?'

Stella softened. 'Yes, of course, please come in. I was intending to go to Myrddin's Keep, but I can't summon up the enthusiasm to work today.'

Verity followed her into the parlour of the cottage she shared with two other young women.

'The others are out,' Stella explained. 'What was it you wanted?'

'I've been thinking, Stella.'

'I see. And how does that concern me?'

'I thought you should be the first to know. I've decided to stay. For a little while longer, at any rate.'

'Stay? Why, that's wonderful.' Stella took Verity's hand. 'I felt sure that you would come to appreciate our way of life here. But then you said you were leaving, and my heart sank. I… no, it doesn't matter.' Stella turned her face away.

'Tell me. What were you about to say?'.

'I felt so alone.'

'Look at me, Stella. That first day, when you took me to Myrddin's Keep. I asked how you could love this place despite Aquinas's contemptible behaviour toward you. You said you found joy here but wouldn't say more.'

Stella nodded but avoided Verity's gaze.

'You will think me mad to use a word like joy when I tell you what binds me to this place, yet it is the only thing that has an echo of joy in my life. Apart from my friendship with you.'

'An echo of joy? What do you mean?'

'Come with me.' Stella withdrew her hand. Taking a shawl from the hallstand by the door, she led Verity outside.

She hurried along, head bowed, drawing her shawl tightly around her shoulders. After passing the furniture workshop, Stella took a path unfamiliar to Verity. Shrubs grew densely on either side until they entered a clearing. At its centre stood a house of honey-coloured stone, larger than any of the cottages in the community and almost half the size of Chase Manor. Railings surrounded a neat front garden with rose bushes along the path leading to the front door.

Stella stopped ten paces short of the garden gate, twirling a strand of hair nervously in her fingers.

'What is this place?' Verity whispered.

Stella gave her an anguished look and turned away. For several minutes, she remained staring at the house as though rooted to the spot. 'Come,' she said at last, leading the way through the garden and up to the front door.

Stella hesitated once more. Verity watched the rise and fall of her shoulders as she took deep breaths and placed her hand on the door knocker. Three forceful raps reverberated. Stella put all her strength into it, slamming the knocker violently against the door, her entire body shaking with the effort. Crying with frustration, Stella continued her assault upon the door until, suddenly, it was wrenched open from within.

'For heaven's sake… oh, it's you.' The woman in the doorway stood, hands on hips, scowling at Stella. Middle-aged, in a plain black dress with a white pinafore, she had the air of a hospital matron. After giving Verity a brief look of disapproval, she turned her attention back to Stella. 'Whatever possessed you to come here without a by your leave? You know you are only permitted to visit once a month by prior arrangement. You must leave now.'

Stella spoke through gritted teeth. 'I must see him now, Millicent. I *will* see him now, do you hear?'

'Impossible.' The woman planted herself firmly in the entrance.

Stella said later that she never knew where she found the strength, but with a sharp cry of rage, she launched herself, forcing a passage into the house, leaving her adversary clinging to the door handle to remain upright. Verity seized the moment and stepped nimbly past the woman before she could recover.

Heedless of the protestations behind her, Stella led Verity into the house, along the hallway, through a sitting room and out into a glass conservatory. Without stopping, Stella went through a door opening to the rear garden. 'Come on, quickly,' she called over her shoulder.

Verity followed her outside. There was more to the house than she realised, for close behind it was another building, long and low, in similar stonework, with a paved yard. And there, in groups of two, three or more, were children. Verity counted sixteen boys and girls, ranging from infants to twelve or thirteen years of age. At the school door, for that was clearly the purpose of the building, a pair of young women supervised their charges.

Stella turned, beckoning Verity to her side. Her eyes, no longer clouded with anguish, shone. 'There, look, there he is.' She pointed to two young boys, one fair, the other with a mass of dark curls, throwing a ball to each other.

'Jeremy,' Stella called out, waving. Then louder, 'Jeremy.'

The dark-haired lad halted in the act of throwing and turned, a smile of childish delight on his face.

'Mother,' he yelled, flinging the ball back to his companion and scampering across the playground.

'Stop at once, boy!'

Verity started violently, her ears ringing. Directly behind her, stood Millicent, her face like thunder.

'Janet, take the boy inside now,' she bellowed.

Confused and frightened, Jeremy stood, unable to move, until one of the teachers took him by the arm, marching the weeping boy into the school while the other children watched open-mouthed.

'No!' Stella raced across the schoolyard only to have the door slammed in her face. Frantically, she turned the door-handle, but to no avail. 'Go away, Stella,' the teacher's voice came from inside. 'I've locked the door.'

Stella rattled the handle, calling her son's name until she became hoarse, then slumped onto the doorstep, head in hands, sobbing.

Grappling with twin urges – to berate the woman standing at her shoulder and to rush to Stella's aid – Verity reluctantly succumbed to the latter. Stella's sobs gradually subsided. With Verity's support, she got to her feet and allowed herself to be led back across the playground.

Millicent stood imperiously in their path, arms folded, contempt etched on her face.

Verity ignored her and guided Stella back the way they'd come, through the house and along the shrub-lined path.

Back in her cottage, Stella sat mutely in the parlour. Under Verity's concerned gaze, she sought to compose herself until she felt able to speak. 'Now,' her voice was barely a whisper, 'now, you've seen the source of my joy… and my despair.'

'Jeremy is your son?'

Stella nodded. 'My son. Mine. Not his. He shall not have him.'

'Do you mean Jeremy's father?'

Stella laughed bitterly. 'Father? He fathered him. But he's no father. That such a sweet soul could come from that… fiend.'

'Who? Who is he?'

Stella snorted. 'Do you need to ask? Aquinas. And I'll save you the trouble of enquiring how. He forced himself on me. One day in my studio at Myrddin's Keep. I'd only arrived at Chase Manor a month earlier and, oh, he was such a gentleman at first. He offered me the studio, praised my work and acted so solicitously. The mask soon fell away. It didn't take long for me to realise what he wanted. To become one of his Guineveres, as he calls them. A plaything to be used and cast aside. I did my best to avoid him, thinking he'd turn his attention elsewhere. And then…'

'But why isn't Jeremy living here with you? Why are you kept from him?'

'It's Aquinas's doing, with Oswald and Ursula's connivance. The children in our community attend that school. Millicent is the headmistress. Jailer would be a more apt title.'

'Do you mean that the children are kept there against their will, Stella?'

'Most of them live with their parents or parent, but all must attend the school. We do not adhere to convention here. Most of our children are born out of wedlock, as the saying goes. It involves no stigma.'

'Then where does Jeremy live? Surely not with Aquinas. There are no children at Myrddin's Keep.'

'Jeremy lives in that house. He and two others. Myrtle is an orphan, and Olwen is another of Aquinas's offspring. Her mother has left the community. I don't doubt that Aquinas would like me to leave.' Stella's eyes flashed. 'I'll never desert my son.'

'Stella, I don't understand you. When we first met in London, you extolled the virtues of this place. It was no act; your feelings were genuine. When you referred to Chase Manor as Arcadia, I saw the look in your eyes. You meant it. How can you think that?'

Stella rose and stood at the window with her back to Verity. 'You'll think me foolish. I am foolish, yet it can't be helped.'

'You needn't tell me if it causes you distress.'

'It causes me distress to keep my feelings bottled up, Verity. I must tell someone, or I shall burst. Laugh at me if you will. I'm in love with Dornford. There, can you imagine anything more ridiculous?'

'Ah.'

Stella tossed her head. 'You may well say, ah. That one syllable communicates the absurdity of the matter most eloquently. Stella loves a man who is engaged to another.

A man whose parents are complicit in separating her from her son. Could anything be more hopeless and ill-conceived?'

Chapter 35

'Oh, it's you, Elspeth. Oswald's just taken some pots to the kiln.' Ursula wiped her hands and turned away from the potter's wheel. 'You look flushed; have you been exerting yourself?'

'I've just come from Stella's. Verity was with her, and I thought I should let you know straight away.'

'Know what?'

'She wants to stay. She no longer wishes to leave on Wednesday.'

'Who wishes to stay?' Oswald appeared at the studio door.

'Verity, Oswald. It seems she is taken with our way of life. That's how she put it to me.'

'Hmm. I must say, it surprises me. What does she think she will do if she stays?'

'She professes a desire to work in stained glass. Stella says she has displayed an aptitude in the craft and seems keen to support her.'

Oswald rubbed his chin. 'Are we to believe that she would make a commitment to become part of our community? Turn her back on her smart life in London?'

'She does realise that she'll have to make a substantial financial contribution, doesn't she?' Ursula gave Elspeth a searching look. 'You have told her that?'

'Of course.' Elspeth responded, reaching into her sleeve. 'Voila,' she added, waving a slip of paper. 'A cheque for £80, no less.'

Oswald's eyes lit up 'Well, I believe that settles it.'

'Bring it here, will you?' Ursula reached for the cheque. 'A useful sum, to begin with. Yet…'

'Yet what, my dear?' Oswald bent to examine the cheque over his wife's shoulder.

'Yet, I'm not convinced that our Verity Mallard is what she purports to be, Oswald. Don't let this cheque cloud your judgement. We must maintain an air of scepticism where she is concerned. Perhaps my suspicions will prove to be unfounded; we must wait and see.'

'Very well, and if all goes to plan in Wales, we will not have need of her money,' Oswald grinned.

'Have you heard from Dornford?' Elspeth asked. 'Will he be returning soon? With the wedding only a month away, there is much to do. I do hope he won't be there too much longer?'

Ursula forestalled Oswald's reply. 'Dornford has been instructed to wait there until the matter is settled. I cannot understand why you should be concerned about arrangements for the wedding; the only contribution required of Dornford is to be there on the day. You and I will manage all arrangements, which is as it should be.'

'But I miss him, Ursula. He is my fiancée, after all.' Elspeth crossed her arms defiantly.

'Oh, for goodness' sake – '

An insistent tapping diverted Ursula from berating her prospective daughter-in-law.

'It's Millicent.' Oswald beckoned to the figure standing on the other side of the studio door. 'To what do we owe the pleasure?'

'There will be no pleasure derived from what I have come here to tell you.' Millicent looked unwaveringly at Oswald, her face a mask of disapproval. 'This morning, I was subjected to a… I can only refer to it as an assault. An assault on my person and an assault upon the good order of the school.'

'My word, Millicent,' Oswald took a step back. 'What on earth happened?'

'Stella brazenly forced her way in despite my denying her entry. Marched clean through the house, if you please, and approached her… approached Jeremy.'

'Indeed? What on earth possessed her? Stella is always so amenable.'

'Perhaps it was the influence of the person accompanying her. I believe she is here on retreat. Stella called her Verity. Perhaps she has encouraged Stella to behave in such an outrageous fashion.'

'Oh, I see. But I can't think what possible motive Verity would have.' Oswald turned to Elspeth. 'You've just come from them. Did they say anything to you about this incident?'

'No, Stella did appear rather subdued, but they said nothing about it to me. However, if you want my opinion, she's been treated appallingly. Being kept from her son other than when *she* permits it,' Elspeth glared at Millicent. 'It's unjust.'

Millicent stiffened. 'Is my authority to be questioned? Let me remind you, Oswald, Ursula, that I govern the school in accordance with your instructions. And I carry out those instructions to the letter. To the letter, I tell you.' Had Millicent the ability to breathe fire, Elspeth would already have been reduced to a pile of ashes. Instead, she confined herself to a malevolent glance in that direction. 'Perhaps the boy should be sent to live with his father.'

'What!' Elspeth exclaimed, moving to stand squarely between Oswald and Millicent. 'No, Oswald, that would be cruel.'

'Enough!' All eyes turned to Ursula. 'I've heard quite enough. Millicent, you will return to the school. You are quite right to inform us of this unfortunate event, but you must leave it to Oswald and me to decide what needs to be done. Elspeth, you can leave as well. I've heard more than enough of your opinions.'

'But…' A single look from Ursula quelled Elspeth. Turning on her heel, she followed Millicent out of the studio.

'What now?' Oswald asked. 'It would be cruel to send the boy to Aquinas.'

'I don't know. This is a distraction we do not need. Leave the matter be for now. It bears out what I was saying earlier.'

'What do you mean, dear?'

'About Verity Mallard. We must be on our guard.'

Chapter 36

'You needn't have done this.' George took his seat opposite Ambrose. More accustomed to dining at the corner chop-house near his office, the opulence of Rules in Covent Garden made him uneasy.

'Nonsense, my dear chap. I never deny myself the opportunity to dine here when I'm in town, and what could be better than to share a dinner with my good friend, George Benson.' Ambrose nodded to the hovering waiter, who proceeded to fill two champagne glasses.

'Pol Roger, one of the better vintages,' Ambrose beamed at George and raised his glass. 'To Violet.'

George echoed the toast and put the glass to his lips. *One of the better vintages* seemed like faint praise; he'd never tasted better.

'How's your appetite, George? Hearty, I hope.' Ambrose perused the menu. 'The oysters are first class. Then, the pheasant's wonderful, but so is the beef. Oh, and they do a magnificent venison pie. I always have difficulty making up my mind.'

'I'll be guided by you, Ambrose; it all looks good to me.' George put his menu aside.

'Very well. You'll not regret it. A dozen oysters to set the scene, then roast beef. We'll have a bottle of hock and a decent claret to wash it all down. Marvellous. This is the life, George.' Ambrose patted his stomach in anticipation.

The waiter made suitably approving comments at their choices and departed for the kitchen.

'Now then, George, humour me. Tell me again what happened at the Unicorn Club. I wish to savour every moment of Mounsden's comeuppance.'

George complied, faithfully recounting Mounsden's descent from arrogant bluster to ignominious retreat.

Ambrose had difficulty containing his glee, earning disapproving looks from an elderly couple at a neighbouring table.

The empty oyster shells were removed and duly replaced with two plates of roast beef, with roast potatoes, carrots, French beans and parsnips, accompanied with rich dark gravy and horseradish sauce.

Between mouthfuls, Ambrose kept George entertained with tales of his time in India. Had anyone else spun such fanciful stories, George would have been inclined to dismiss them as fantasies or gross exaggerations, but where Ambrose was concerned, he thought that they were all too true.

It wasn't until a bowl of apple crumble and custard had taken the same route as the roast beef that George, having undone the buttons of his waistcoat, produced the letter. He'd thought twice about confiding in Ambrose, but knew full well that his friend would be mortally offended had George kept it from him. In any case, he had to admit that he was loath to act alone, and Ambrose, despite his eccentricities, had proved the staunchest of allies in the past.

Without a word, he slid the envelope across the starched white tablecloth. Caught in the act of draining a glass of hock, Ambrose raised his eyebrows at the sight of Verity's handwriting. George watched in silence as he extracted the letter and read it.

Dear George,

I will keep this letter brief. I need your help. I can see you now, reading these words and shaking your head. What on earth has she become involved in this time, you'll be thinking, although I wouldn't blame you for expressing yourself rather more bluntly than that!

You'll recall my saying that Chase Manor has a sister community called The Blessed Plot, and that community members are chosen to go there from time to time. Far from being blessed, I have reason to think that it is a most sinister place and that Gregory Manning, the shy young man I mentioned to you, has been taken there against his will. I've discovered that The Blessed Plot is in Wales, a farmhouse near somewhere named Devil's Bridge, which is hardly comforting. But in the absence of a gazetteer, I'm unable to determine its location.

George, I need you close at hand. Forgive me for presuming upon your good nature once again, but there is an inn at the nearest village. The Wheatsheaf at Monk's Fallow. I will call on you there on Wednesday morning.

Your true friend,
Verity

P.S. I admit I've let myself in for more than I bargained for, so you needn't point it out to me when we meet.

Ambrose folded the letter and replaced it in the envelope. 'We must leave tomorrow. Don't waste your breath trying to dissuade me. I'm coming with you. I'm utterly determined, George. I'll go alone if necessary. I —'

'Of course you must come.'

'I won't be fobbed off. Don't you think… oh, you want me to come?'

George nodded. 'If you would be so kind, Ambrose.'

Chapter 37

'Thank you again, Seth.' Verity climbed down from the wagon.

'My pleasure, Miss Mallard, I'm sorry I couldn't bring you in the carriage. Mr Lamont has gone off somewhere in it.'

'No matter. Are you sure you don't mind waiting here?'

'I've got some supplies to pick up, miss, so it en't no bother. I'll be back here in a couple of hours, if that suits.'

'Perfectly.' Verity turned and entered the Wheatsheaf Inn.

'Good morning.' Verity's cheery greeting echoed around the public bar, drawing suspicious glances from two wizened old men on a settle in the corner with tankards of ale in front of them.

Undaunted, she crossed to the unattended bar. 'Hello, is anyone there?'

Receiving no reply, she listened for any signs of approaching footsteps, but heard only some unintelligible mutterings from the drinkers in the corner. Preparing to call out again, the appearance of a bald head followed by a broad pair of shoulders and a torso of impressive girth rising behind the bar struck her as both unexpected and comical.

'Did I hear someone calling? I was down in the cellar,' the man said, finally standing upright. 'Oh, it was you, was it, madam?'

'Yes, it was, Mr …?'

'Lambert, madam. I'm the landlord.'

'Good morning, Mr Lambert. I believe you have a gentleman from London staying here?'

'Ah, would you be Miss Mallard? They said you would be calling.'

'They? Is there more than one?'

'Yes. A Mr Benson and… now what was the name of the other gentleman.? Oh, yes. Same name as you – Mallard.'

'Indeed, and where might I find them?'

'They're in my private room for guests. It's this way, if you'll follow me.'

Lambert waddled out from behind the bar. Verity followed his expansive posterior through the taproom and down a passage to a door at the far end. Mallard? Could George have brought Mortimer? She hoped not. He was bound to disapprove, and there'd be a scene.

'Here we are.' Lambert opened the door and stepped back to allow Verity to squeeze past. 'Please ring the bell if you want anything,' he added, before returning to the bar.

'Verity!' Ambrose crossed the room in three broad strides, arms outstretched.

Momentarily crushed in his enthusiastic embrace, Verity smiled weakly over his shoulder at George.

'Aha, the look on your face.' Ambrose released her and stepped back, grinning broadly. 'I'll wager you weren't expecting to see me.'

Verity paused to take a breath. 'No, I wasn't, but if it's any consolation, Ambrose, I'm glad it's you and not Mortimer. When the landlord said there was a Mr Mallard here, I had premonitions of my brother coming to lecture me and demand that I return to London forthwith.'

Ambrose winced and turned to look at George. 'Will you tell her?'

'Tell me what?'

George gave a half-smile. 'Good morning, Verity. It's good to see you.'

'Tell me what?' Verity repeated with a hint of irritation.

'Mortimer *would* have come had not Ambrose and I moved heaven and earth to dissuade him. And there is also Olivia to thank for making him see sense.'

'I wrote to *you*, George. This has nothing to do with Mortimer. Why on earth did you involve him?' Anger overtook irritation. Verity's eyes blazed.

'What would you have me do, Verity? Mortimer's your nearest relative. He cares for you as a brother should. He can be a little overbearing at times, I grant you, but his motives are beyond reproach. Think of everything he's done in the past. What we've all done together.' George struggled to keep calm. How many times had he weathered Verity's petulance?

Her retort was as icy as her stare. 'If that's all you can say, you can return to London this instant. I have no need of you. Just... go.'

George dug his nails into his palms, all but overwhelmed with seething anger. Damn the woman. Once he said what was in his mind, there'd be no turning back.

'George, listen to me.'

Ambrose's words were almost lost in the fog of rage clouding George's mind. A gentle tug on his sleeve made him dimly conscious of his friend gazing earnestly at him.

'George. Let me speak to Verity. Leave us for a few minutes, would you? Go and sit in the bar. Come along, my dear chap.'

Ambrose steered George towards the door. Verity stood stock still, jaw clenched, as they passed, giving no sign of the pounding in her heart.

Outside, George leaned against the wall, drawing deep breaths until he felt sufficiently in control of himself to make his way to the bar. For an instant, he considered going straight to his room, packing his portmanteau, and walking right out of Verity's life for good. Instead, he ordered a large whisky and sat alone, ignoring the stares of the two old boys on the settle.

What a pair they made, Verity and Mortimer. When he'd first met them, courtesy of Mortimer's employment as a lawyer, Verity was her usual self: opinionated, assertive, manipulative and… utterly charming, when it suited her. Mortimer, her twin, largely went along with her. True, they sparred a little, but Mortimer always lightened their disagreements with humour.

Mortimer's accession to the baronetcy changed him. He developed a harder edge. Stood his ground and, more than that, exerted his will where necessary. For the first time in her life, Verity had to contend with opposition, a will almost as strong as her own.

Caught in the middle, there were times when George increasingly felt as though he was walking on eggshells. It made no sense. They'd braved mortal danger together and depended on each other to come through. And yet… this.

George downed the remains of his whisky. Eyeing the empty glass, he contemplated ordering another. Hang it, why not?

'George. George, over here.' Ambrose stood in the entrance to the passage, beckoning.

Good old Ambrose. George put his glass down and crossed the room.

'How is she?'

'Come and see for yourself.' Ambrose squeezed George's arm encouragingly.

Verity sat in one of a pair of armchairs with her hands clasped in her lap, head bowed. She didn't look up.

Ambrose pointed George to the other chair. 'Don't say a word. Let her speak first,' he murmured.

'George,' Verity spoke in little more than a whisper, her vocal cords thickened by emotion. 'I owe you an apology.' She raised her head, blinking back tears. 'Ambrose has told me what you did, what all of you – Ambrose, Mortimer and you, George – did for Lady Ternan. You acted nobly, as you always have. Then you came here at my request without a thought for yourself, and I treated you appallingly. Can you find it in your heart to forgive my dreadful ingratitude?'

'I'm still here, but you'll never know how close I came to walking out on you for good. Your singlemindedness can be a strength, but there are times when it badly clouds your judgement. Sitting there in the bar, I rehearsed what I'd say to you. How I'd unleash the resentment and hurt I felt. How I'd get my own back. But… as soon as I walked through that door, the feeling vanished.' George smiled. 'Neither of us is suited to emotional scenes. We've both said what we needed to. Now, let's get down to business.

By the way, your taste in dress has taken an interesting turn.'

Verity smiled despite herself, dabbing at her eyes. 'Oh, yes. It's not really me, is it? All on account of playing a part, I'm afraid. The Chase Manor community regards fashion as a distraction. They aim for simplicity in dress, and this, I'm sorry to say, is the result.'

'Oh, but on you it looks becoming,' Ambrose perched himself on the arm of George's chair, striving to keep a straight face.

Verity grinned. 'Thank you, Ambrose, spoken with such sincerity.'

Her voice regained its normal tone. Squaring her shoulders and sitting upright, she addressed herself to the business at hand.

'Have you discovered where Devil's Bridge is, George?'

'Yes. It lies in the hills of mid-Wales. A few miles inland from the coastal town of Aberystwyth. Not a part of the world that I'm familiar with.'

'Nor I. Anyway, let me tell you what I need you and Ambrose to do.'

Chapter 38

'There you are,' Ambrose sat opposite George in the compartment. Dimly visible through the rain-streaked window, a scene of sheep-strewn fields, woodland and occasional farmyards unfolded as their train negotiated the Cambrian Line. 'Rain, rain and more rain. Now you can thank me for purchasing gabardine capes for us before we left London. Judging by the weather since we crossed into Wales, a suit of oilskins might have served better.'

George looked at his wristwatch. 'Another hour to go.' He turned his attention back to the book resting on his knee. 'According to my Bradshaw's Guide, there are several hotels to choose from. Here's one that sounds quite promising. Ah, perhaps not. It's described as a temperance hotel.'

'Perish the thought.' Ambrose shuddered.

'Hmm. What else? Yes, this one sounds more suitable. The Belle Vue Hotel on the seafront. I think it will do.'

***

'We have two of our most well-appointed rooms available on the first floor. Lovely views of the bay when the weather's better. It's a shame you weren't here last week; we had a glorious few days – glorious it was.'

'I'm sure it was,' George replied, anxious to get out of his wet clothes.

'Only the two nights, was it?' the desk clerk produced two room keys.

'Yes, to begin with. It depends.'

'Depends?'

'We have business in the area. Can you tell me how we may get to Devil's Bridge?'

The desk clerk scratched his head. 'Now then. Hopkins the carter goes out that way now and again. He's round in Queen's Road. Or perhaps –'

'We must go there tomorrow morning,' George interrupted.

'Well, you can hire horses if you fancy riding, or, I'll tell you what, how would a pony and trap suit? My cousin Dilwyn rents his out. I can have it waiting in our stables across the road for you tomorrow morning. As a matter of fact, there's talk of building a railway line to Devil's Bridge. It's popular with travellers, you know.'

'The trap will do. Shall we say nine o'clock?'

'Leave it with me, Mr Benson.' The clerk clicked his fingers, summoning a lanky youth in hotel livery. 'Take the gentlemen's suitcases upstairs to rooms eleven and twelve. Here are your keys, Mr Benson and Mr Mallard.'

***

Ambrose nudged George. 'There, by the turnpike. The signpost to Devil's Bridge.'

The sunlight that greeted their departure from the Belle Vue Hotel failed them as they drove through the town. Steely clouds rolled in from the sea. With ten miles to go, the prospect of a soaking was ever present.

Mercifully, only a few spots of rain came their way. They encountered little traffic other than a farm cart or two, and made good time apart from a five-minute hold-up while a shepherd herded his flock across the road and into a nearby field, assisted by two skulking sheepdogs.

High above, a pair of buzzards wheeled lazily. The landscape, which at first appeared softly bucolic, gradually took on a starker edge. To their left the land fell away, revealing a rushing river. On the opposite side of the valley, clumps of woodland sprouted amidst bare heaths and rocky gullies, channelling dashing streams of crystal-clear water.

Out of sight of the valley, the road led them between low hedges and dry-stone walls. A sprinkling of houses suggested they were approaching their destination. Then a timber road sign with the name Devil's Bridge inscribed upon it in white lettering confirmed it.

'More of a hamlet than a village. Do you suppose this is it?' Ambrose asked. 'Just a few houses?'

'At the Belle Vue, they said that there was a hotel,' George responded.

As the trap rounded the next corner, the Hafod Arms Hotel revealed itself. The impressive four-storey building in slate-grey stone dominated its surroundings.

A porter at the door directed them to the stables at the rear. With Nancy, the pony, consigned to the ostler's care, George and Ambrose entered the hotel. A counter bearing the inscription Reception occupied the far wall of the vestibule.

'Gloomy old place,' Ambrose muttered.

George took in his surroundings. Dark oak panelling covered the walls. A mounted stag's head took pride of place on one side of the room, accompanied by the heads of half a dozen snarling foxes and one disgruntled badger. The opposite wall held several landscapes that George assumed to be views of the surrounding area, with dense foliage and waterfalls much in evidence.

Ambrose was peering closely at a gilt frame just inside the front entrance. George looked over his shoulder, finding not a painting but a poem:

To the Torrent at the Devil's Bridge, North Wales, 1824

George read the opening lines.

How art thou named? In search of what strange land
From what huge height, descending? Can such force
Of waters issue from a British source ...

Briskly scanning the remaining lines of verse, his eyes were drawn to the poet's name – William Wordsworth. 'Not one of his that I'm familiar with.'

'Nor I,' Ambrose agreed.

'Can I be of assistance to you, gentlemen?' Emerging from behind the counter, a spare bespectacled figure with thinning grey hair came towards them, leaning heavily on a cane. 'Ah, I see you've discovered the work of one of our most esteemed visitors. Of course, that was well before my time.' The man gave a small chuckle. 'Hywel Morris is my name. Proprietor.'

'Good morning, Mr Morris. I am George Benson, and this is my travelling companion, Mr Ambrose Mallard.'

'Yes, yes, pleased to meet you both.' Morris's head bobbed up and down. 'Is it accommodation you are wanting?'

'We're staying at the Belle Vue in Aberystwyth.'

'Oh, just up for a visit then, are you?'

'That… depends.'

Morris arched his eyebrows. 'Oh, yes?'

'Mr Mallard and I are dedicated birdwatchers. We're travelling through Wales, and we thought we'd undertake a reconnaissance to gauge whether this spot has possibilities.'

'Well, well.' Morris's face brightened. 'You've come to the right place. Oh, yes. Birds galore we have here. People come from all over to watch them. Only last week I had a gentleman all the way from America. Delighted, he was.'

'I see. That seems to bear out what we were told by a bird-watching acquaintance in London. In fact, he remarked that he'd observed several rare species in the vicinity of… what was the name of the place?' George's brow furrowed. 'Dear me, what was it now? Ah yes.' George reached into his waistcoat pocket and produced a slip of paper. 'This is the place.'

Morris squinted at the paper in George's hand. '*Nant-y-Geifr* Farm.'

'Is it far?'

Morris frowned. 'Not far. About a mile.' The frown deepened.

'Is something amiss? You look troubled, Mr Morris.'

'Amiss, you say? Well, I've no reason to doubt what you were told, but I can't imagine that your friend would have been welcome at *Nant-y-Geifr*.'

'Indeed. Is the farmer an unfriendly sort?'

'Ha. It was a farm, but no more. Calls himself Dr Floate, the man who lives there now. He's no farmer, but Twm Cadno runs a few sheep on the property and does odd jobs about the place. Mind you, he's not one you'd want to meet on a dark night. His real name is Twm Hughes, but he's a sly one, so he's called Cadno. That's Welsh for fox. And there's other people coming and going from time to time, outsiders.'

'I can't imagine that a couple of bird-watchers would pose a problem to this Dr Floate. Perhaps we'll take a walk up that way, get the lie of the land. A walk will do us good. Then we could have lunch here.'

'Lunch? Of course you can. If you're set on going up there, go straight up the road and over the bridge, or bridges, I should say. You'll see an iron gate with the name *Nant-y-Geifr* on your left. The house is down a track.'

'Thank you. Mr Morris. Come on then, Ambrose, a brisk walk to summon up an appetite.' George made for the door.

'Just a moment, George. May I ask you another question, Mr Morris?'

'Yes, Mr Mallard. What would you like to know?'

'You said bridges. Is there more than one Devil's Bridge?'

Morris beamed. 'Ah, now, the story goes that many centuries ago, before there was any bridge, an old woman lost her cow. When she went in search of it, she saw it on the far bank of the river but had no way to reach it. Then the Devil came along and offered to build a bridge on condition that he would take the soul of the first living thing to cross it.'

'Quite a dilemma for her.'

'Yes, it was, Mr Mallard, but that old woman was clever. When the bridge was finished, she threw a crust of bread across, and who should run over to get it but her dog. That's what the Devil got – the dog's soul. Anyway, Devil or no Devil, what you will find is two stone bridges, one built right above the other. The lower one is medieval, and the one above which you will walk over, was built in the last century, almost a hundred and fifty years ago.'

'Thank you, Mr Morris, most illuminating. Right then, George, a brisk walk before lunch it is.'

'No sign of old Nick.' Ambrose quipped as he and George crossed the bridge. A fine mist of rain enveloped them, but protected by their gabardine capes, it did little to dampen their resolve. With binoculars in leather cases strung around their necks, they trusted that they'd pass muster as amateur ornithologists.

Other than sheep grazing unconcernedly in the drizzle, there was no sign of life, human or animal. George was content to let Ambrose regale him with tales of his return from India on board the *SS Aeneas*. 'Came through the Suez Canal and spent a few days in Port Said. Teamed up with the First Officer for a run ashore. By George, George, some of the shenanigans people get up to there. Never saw anything like it, not even in the seediest parts of Bombay. Do you know, they even –'

'Tell me later. Ambrose. Look, there's the gate.'

After a quick look up and down the road, George examined the gate, a solid iron-barred affair between squat stone pillars, painted white and bearing a wooden plaque inscribed with the name *Nant-y-Geifr*, just as Mr Morris had said. Beyond it, a pot-holed gravel track ran slightly downhill, hemmed in by rhododendrons and fir trees. The house was out of sight, but a column of grey smoke rising above the trees betrayed its presence nearby.

A metal latch on the right-hand side of the gate held it closed. George tried it. The gate swung open with little effort. Waving Ambrose through, he closed it behind them.

Although the rain had stopped, an intermittent sprinkling of drops fell from the surrounding trees. The track had a mournful air, a gloomy foliage-lined corridor, reminding George of an illustration in a book of fairy tales from his childhood. Hänsel and Gretel on their way to the witch's gingerbread cottage.

Two hundred yards of cautious progress brought them to a bend in the track. George eased forward step by step, with Ambrose at his shoulder. Nothing yet. Five more steps. Another five. George signalled Ambrose to stop. The track continued on a gradual gradient for fifty yards until it reached the farmhouse. Dark and forbidding, as Verity had described it to them at the Wheatsheaf, it stood to the right of the track overlooking a broad craggy valley. George lifted his binoculars.

'Any sign of life?' George shook his head in answer to Ambrose. 'I can't make anything out from here. But if we get any closer, we'll be too exposed.'

'What then? Return to the Hafod Arms? Surely there must be some way of finding out what's going on in there. I have it. Why don't we knock on the door, say we're lost and need directions? Perhaps Dr Floate will ask us in, then I could engage him in conversation while you scout around. You know, ask to visit the lavatory.'

George turned to face Ambrose. Given to flights of fancy, it was often difficult to tell whether he was being serious or flippant. 'You read too many penny dreadfuls Ambrose, we're here to observe, not blunder into the lion's den. When we've established the lie of the land, then we'll come up with a plan of action… Ambrose, are you listening?'

'Certainly, but what about that chap?' Ambrose nodded toward the house.

George swung round. Outside the front door, a man stood smoking a cigarette and gazing down into the valley. Not Dr Floate, unless he dressed like a farm labourer, and a slovenly one at that. George adjusted the focus. Short and wiry, with a grizzled beard, and a black cloth cap pulled well-down on his forehead, the man wore a stained cotton smock, dark trousers and leather gaiters. A double-barrelled shotgun rested in the crook of his arm. Tossing the stub of the cigarette aside, he stepped onto the track.

'Out of sight, quickly,' George hissed, dragging Ambrose back into cover.

'Do you think he saw us?' Ambrose stumbled as George marched him back towards the gate. 'Steady on, old man, I'm not as nimble as I used to be.'

Halfway along the track, George risked a glance behind. So far, so good. Despite Ambrose's protests, they reached the gate unseen, passed through it and out into the road.

'Where the devil are we going now?' Ambrose panted, as George, maintaining a grip on his arm, led him further up the road. 'The hotel's back that way.'

'I'm not wasting this opportunity. Come on, we'll find another way in.'

George found the spot. A fallen branch had dislodged a small section of the dry-stone wall forming the boundary to *Nant-y-Geifr*. Beyond it, dense woodland sloped steeply upward.

Ambrose leaned on the wall. 'Leave me here, George. I'm all in.'

'Out of the question. If that fellow with the shotgun comes along, what are you going to do? Ask him where you can find the nearest willow-warbler? You're hardier than you give yourself credit for, Ambrose. Come along. This way.'

Picking his way through a mass of ferns and briars, George forged a path through the woods, pausing frequently for Ambrose to catch up. Having gained the brow of the rise, they descended at an angle, hoping to glimpse the house through the trees. George nudged Ambrose. 'That way. I see smoke.'

The woods ended abruptly. A slope covered in coarse tussocks of grass, gorse bushes and a few large outcrops of rock ran downhill to a yard at the rear of the house. A stone barn stood along one side at right angles to the farmhouse itself.

George and Ambrose crouched low, edging towards a group of rocks directly overlooking the house. A narrow gap between two of the taller rocks gave George the perfect vantage point. Steadying his binoculars, he observed the house. The four windows on the ground floor yielded little. Two had curtains drawn across them. One, adjacent to the back door, allowed George a grime-blurred impression of a kitchen table and some shelves, while the fourth window was obscured by a potted aspidistra on the windowsill. The windows on the upper floor revealed nothing at all. Dark green wooden shutters covered each one.

George muttered an oath. 'May as well go back to the hotel.'

'Go back? Shame on you, George.' Ambrose grinned. 'Where's the never say die spirit? Perhaps knocking on the door wasn't such a bad idea after all. I –'

'Shush. There's something happening.'

Ambrose scrabbled for his binoculars.

The back door was open. The figure that emerged stood gazing up at the sky, palms held out as though to check for rain. George focussed on his features. A halo of thick black curls receded a little above a broad forehead. Beetling brows, concave-cheeks, a chiselled nose and jutting chin combined to form an arresting countenance. But above all, it was the man's eyes. Even from a distance, their intense dark irises projected a smouldering inner power.

'Dr Floate, I presume,' whispered Ambrose.

Floate moved to the centre of the yard, turned and beckoned. George pointed his binoculars at the doorway, emitting a low whistle as a wicker bath chair emerged, pushed by a tall young man. Its occupant, legs shrouded in a blanket, and face obscured by a broad straw hat, lolloped listlessly as the chair bumped its way over the uneven farmyard.

It came to a halt in front of Floate, and the young man pushing it stepped back to stand a few paces away.

'What on earth is going on, George? Can that poor devil in the chair be Gregory Manning?'

'Just wait and see, Ambrose, and keep your voice down.'

Floate circled the chair in loping strides, stopping every few paces to speak to the chair's occupant. Round and round. Too far away to hear, George imagined a repeated incantation. A ritual? A spell?

The figure in the chair showed no reaction, or so George thought, but, almost imperceptibly, the hands gripping the sides of the chair twitched spasmodically. The movement spread to its legs and torso until the whole body convulsed. The blanket slipped to the floor, and the straw hat tipped onto the man's knees, revealing a pale pink face, eyes obscured by thick spectacles.

'It is Gregory,' George hissed, recalling Verity's description of the young man she and Caroline had befriended. 'And that chap pushing his chair must be Dornford Lamont.'

The convulsions abated. Gregory's body went rigid – head upright, eyes wide open. Floate came closer. Stooping, he positioned himself directly in front of Gregory, their faces a foot apart.

'Now what?' Ambrose watched with rising disgust.

In Float's right hand, a bright silver sphere dangled on a ribbon. He set it in motion, swinging back and forth.

'Mesmerism, Ambrose. Floate is hypnotising him.'

With their view obscured by Floate, neither George nor Ambrose could see Gregory's expression. 'Do you suppose it's working?' Ambrose murmured.

'The poor fellow appeared to be stupefied when they wheeled him out. Drugged, no doubt, to make him all the more susceptible. Hold on – Floate's stepping away. Look, Gregory's speaking.'

'Can't tell what he'd saying. I don't suppose you're a lip reader, George?'

'Now he's stopped. Whatever he said seems to have excited Floate. Look.'

Down in the farmyard, Floate was beside himself. Pacing one way, then another, clapping his hands in delight and emitting a high-pitched laugh, which floated up the slope.

George and Ambrose exchanged bemused looks.

Dornford came striding across to Floate. The two men shook hands vigorously, clapping one another on the back and laughing uproariously. Gregory, immobile in the chair, gazed vacantly ahead, as though unaware of the hubbub, and remained so until Dornford took charge of the bath chair and returned to the house followed by Floate.

Ambrose put his binoculars away. 'Are you thinking what I'm thinking?'

'They think they've persuaded Gregory to sign over his fortune. Just what Verity feared might happen.'

'Then we must act. Go down there now and rescue Gregory. You have your revolver. What are we waiting for?'

'Hold your horses, Ambrose. My revolver is in my suitcase at the Belle Vue. This calls for sober consideration, not a rush of blood to the head.'

'But, George –'

Ambrose stopped in mid-sentence. George's eyes flashed a warning. He held a finger to his lips, urging silence.

Ambrose followed George's gaze. At first, he saw nothing but the surrounding woodland. Then movement. Just twenty yards away through a tangle of shrubs, a figure on higher ground, carrying a shotgun and, thank the good Lord, moving away from them.

'Come on, this way. Quietly,' George whispered.

Ambrose needed no urging.

Safely back on the road, they didn't tarry, but set off at a brisk pace back to the Hafod Arms, neither speaking until they'd passed the entrance to *Nant-y-Geifr*.

'Forget lunch. We're going straight back to Aberystwyth.' George quickened his pace.

'But surely…' Ambrose struggled for breath.

'Hear me out. We'll stay there tonight, then pack our things and return in the morning – with my revolver. I'll inform Mr Morris that we will be checking into the Hafod Arms. We'll get Gregory out of there, Ambrose, one way or another.'

***

Caroline took Verity's arm as they walked from their cottage to the refectory for supper. 'When do you expect to hear from that private investigator and your relative? Ambrose, wasn't it?'

'They only arrived in Aberystwyth yesterday. They planned to visit Devil's Bridge today. Once they've found The Blessed Plot, it's all in George's hands. He'll decide what to do.'

'And if Gregory is being detained there?'

'They must get him away safely.'

'What then?'

'I can't be sure. But those holding him should be brought to justice. That means Dornford and any accomplices. Then, the trail should lead back to this place. Oswald and Ursula. Elspeth too, if she's involved. Whatever happens, we must be prepared. Look, there's Arnold waiting for you, Caroline. Is he still minded to help?'

236

'Of course. If there's trouble from any quarter: Oswald and Ursula, or Aquinas and his henchmen. His fellow craftsmen look up to him. Regard him as their leader. If matters take an ominous turn, we can count on them as well.'

'Will he be walking back with you after supper?'

Caroline smiled. 'Yes, he will.'

'Then we'll talk further. I'll be brief, Caroline, I promise. Far be it from me to intrude on your courting.'

Chapter 39

'Damn this weather,' Ambrose blinked as water dripped off his hat into his eyes. Even swathed in his gabardine cape, the rain, borne on occasional gusts of wind, found its way through.

George grunted in agreement. Nancy trotted on doggedly, head down. 'Only another mile and a half to go, by my reckoning. We should see the outskirts of the town before long.'

Fate, being tempted, intervened.

At first, George put it down to the wet road. Nancy's steady gait became hesitant and awkward. After a few paces, she slowed to a walk.

'Whoa,' George reined her in and jumped down. Nancy stood stoically while he examined her hooves.

'Has she picked up a stone? My pocket knife has a hoof pick.' Ambrose offered.

George shook his head. 'Her right hind leg is lame. Jump down, Ambrose, we'll have to lead her in.'

Ambrose joined George. 'Never mind, old girl, just take your time,' he whispered, patting the mare's neck. 'At least the rain's easing,' he added brightly.

They'd reached the turnpike at the junction of the main road into the town when the sound of a rider coming up behind at a fast trot caught their attention.

Showing no sign of slowing, the rider failed even to acknowledge their presence as he passed, showering them both with water from a muddy puddle in the roadway.

'Ugh!' Ambrose wiped a smear of mud from his cheek. 'Damned ungentlemanly of him. I'd like to give him a piece of my mind.'

'Never mind that. Did you see his face?'

'Eh?'

'It was the man pushing the bath chair back there. That was Dornford.'

'The deuce it was. Do you think he's on his way back to Chase Manor?'

George shrugged. 'He could be heading for the railway station, or perhaps he's some other object in mind.'

***

'Oh dear, gentlemen, the weather has not been kind to you.' The clerk at the reception desk shook his head in sympathy. 'How did you find Devil's Bridge?'

'Interesting. In fact, Mr Mallard and I will be returning there tomorrow. We will be staying at the Hafod Arms Hotel.'

'Oh yes. Please give Mr Morris my regards. My name is Jenkins, Gareth Jenkins. I worked for Mr Morris at one time, up there in Devil's Bridge. Now then, when you get out of those wet clothes, there's a nice fire going in the lounge bar.'

'Good, a seat by the fire with a whisky and soda sounds just the thing. However, we will be requiring transport again. The trap is outside, but I fear the horse has gone lame. We'll need an alternative.'

Jenkins frowned. 'Dear, dear. Dilwyn won't be best pleased. Still, these things happen, don't they? I'll have a word with him. What time are you thinking of departing tomorrow?'

'The earlier, the better. Let's say eight-thirty?'

'Eight thirty. Right you are, Mr Benson.'

***

'I took the liberty of ordering you one,' George nodded at a glass of scotch and soda on the table in front of him.

Ambrose grinned, settling himself into an armchair and gazing appreciatively at the blazing fire nearby. 'Just what the doctor ordered.'

'I've been thinking.' George leaned back, nursing his drink. 'About tomorrow. We can't afford to delay. We must get Gregory away from there tomorrow.'

'My thoughts exactly. Stick your revolver under their noses, George. We'll see what they think of that.'

'I doubt it will be that simple. There's the fellow with the shotgun, for one thing. Mr Morris mentioned a fellow named Twm. I assume it must be him.'

'Hmm, see what you mean. What do you think we should do? If only I had that blowpipe I used at Larkford Grange.'

George smiled. 'I doubt we'll find poison darts hereabouts.'

***

'That one's name is Trojan, the other one is Antoinette.' Jenkins pointed to two horses standing between the shafts of a shabby four-wheeled cart outside the Belle Vue. 'Dilwyn uses it for deliveries. He carried a load of coal the

240

other day, so you might find it a bit dusty. He said he's hosed it down and there's a tarpaulin to wrap your luggage in. Sorry, gentlemen – best I could manage at short notice.'

He might also have mentioned Trojan's unfortunate habit of nipping spitefully at Antoinette from time to time, and his regular bouts of flatulence. Any privations they'd felt in the rain the previous day seemed as nothing as they trundled bumpily along the road. At least the weather held fair, but by the time George and Ambrose drove into Devil's Bridge, their tempers were well and truly frayed.

'Dear Lord, every bone in my body aches.' Ambrose arched his back and swivelled his neck. 'I'll be as stiff as a board tomorrow.'

George grunted wearily, flicking the reins to encourage the horses round the last bend before they reached the Hafod Arms, thinking of what he'd say to Dilwyn if ever their paths crossed.

'Ah, at last.' Ambrose sighed, 'and there's Mr Morris.'

The proprietor stood near the hotel entrance speaking to the driver of a gig standing outside. George drew the cart up behind it.

'Good morning, Mr Benson, I'll be with you in a moment,' Mr Morris called out, then returned his attention to the occupant of the gig. 'Good to see you, Justin. Remember me to your father now, won't you?' He took a step back, waving goodbye as the gig drove off.

'Sorry to keep you, gentlemen. That was Justin Pryce-Thomas. His father and I were in school together. He's followed in his father's footsteps, solicitor down in Aberystwyth. Off to see Dr Floate at *Nant-y-Geifr*, as it happens. I invited him in for a cup of tea, but that fellow with him kicked up a bit of a fuss. Rude, I thought.'

'Good morning, Mr Morris. Did you say he had someone with him? We didn't see anyone?'

'Oh, a young man on horseback. They rode in together. He's staying up at *Nant-y-Geifr*, apparently. Anyway, I don't know why I'm telling you all this. You'll be tired after your journey, particularly in that.' Morris gave the cart a withering look. 'Come on in and I'll show you to your rooms.'

Chapter 40

'Let me look at it again, Caroline. Yes, it's very fine.' In the parlour at Sylvan Cottage, Elspeth inspected Caroline's triptych. 'Exquisite detail; you've captured them perfectly. Now, let me see if I can recall their names. The one on the left with the spindle - that's Clotho. And in the middle we have… Lachesis? Yes. And finally, in every sense, the one with scissors. Hmm, it's on the tip of my tongue.' Elspeth shook her head. 'No, it won't come; you'll have to tell me.'

'The third Fate is Atropos.'

'Ah, of course. Now that it's finished, what next? Will you sell it?'

Caroline pondered. 'Perhaps. But now, Arnold and I are planning to produce a range of furniture with decorative motifs.'

Elspeth arched her eyebrows 'Do I detect that you and Arnold have more in common than artistic collaboration?'

'We have a meeting of minds, one might say.'

'Only minds?' Elspeth smirked, eyeing Caroline's glowing cheeks. 'Forgive me for teasing. I'm really pleased for you both. Now, I must take my leave. I promised to look in at the Manor.'

Caroline stood at the window, smiling to herself as Elspeth skirted the pond and disappeared down the path to Chase Manor. But despite her good humour, unwelcome thoughts wormed their way into her mind. Elspeth, her supporter and mentor, the woman who was unfailingly encouraging to Caroline. Behind the smiles and gentle teasing, that same Elspeth was party to Gregory's abduction. Whatever sinister activities went on at the Blessed Plot, she'd be aware of them. Complicit. Could it be otherwise? Surely not; she was practically a part of Oswald and Ursula's family.

***

Elspeth hung back in the shadows out of sight of the Manor, raising a hand to her mouth to cover a yawn. Her shoulders slumped with the weariness that enveloped her body and clouded her mind. Two sleepless nights had taken their toll. Everything had once seemed so simple. A life dedicated to following her artistic passions. Marriage to Dornford. Nurturing the Chase Manor Community and its ideals. What more could she want?

But she could pretend no longer. The canker beneath the surface. The deception. The lies. A young man abused and cheated. How many others had suffered similar fates? Whisked away to that place. What had become of them? Were they simply cast aside? Consigned to an asylum? Or… worse?

She imagined Oswald and Ursula as two lurking spiders waiting to consume those who became trapped in their web.

And what of Dornford? She'd tolerated his vanity. In her mind, they would have become the inspiration for a new chapter at Chase Manor, their youthful vitality shining forth while Oswald and Ursula faded into the shadows. No longer. Marriage was out of the question. Did she dare to tell them now or wait for Dornford's return? Confront the three of them together.

That would be the end of everything. She groaned inwardly, head bowed.

'Are you quite well?' The words were spoken curtly, without feeling. Elspeth looked up.

'Are you ill? You appear distracted.' Millicent tapped her foot. 'I can't delay. I must tell Oswald and Ursula immediately.'

Elspeth frowned. 'What must you tell them?'

'About the boy, of course. His father came for him.'

'Do you mean Jeremy, Stella's son?'

'For heaven's sake, yes. Not that it's any of your business.' Millicent shook her head in exasperation and turned away, muttering to herself as she hastened toward the Manor.

Elspeth started after her, then checked herself. Her first impulse had been to confront the Lamonts and give Millicent a tongue-lashing. To vent her anger and frustration, whatever the consequences. But was there a better way?

***

'Back so soon?' Caroline poked her head out into the hall. 'Goodness, has something happened? You're trembling.'

'It's Stella. Her son. He has him. Everything is… falling apart.' Elspeth pushed past Caroline and dropped into a chair.

'Do you mean Aquinas has taken Jeremy away from the school?'

Elspeth stiffened. 'What did you say? How on earth do you know about Jeremy?'

'Verity told me. She accompanied Stella to the school. It's appalling, Elspeth. Keeping the boy from his mother is awful enough. And now you say he's in the hands of that brute, Aquinas. How can you associate yourself with such things? You and Dornford – and his parents.'

'But… but I do not.' Elspeth spluttered.

'Nevertheless, you're one of them. Or soon will be,' Caroline retorted.

Elspeth shook her head vigorously. 'No. No, I will not marry Dornford. I've been foolish, I grant you, wilfully foolish perhaps. Unwilling to face the truth. But I will face it. Oswald and Ursula are not the selfless idealists that they purport to be. But I can see that you already know that. And Dornford is following in their footsteps. Chase Manor is a sham, Caroline.'

'So you say. But tell me this: what truly goes on at The Blessed Plot? Don't pretend you have no knowledge of it. Gregory is being held there. Don't bother trying to deny it.'

'I've had my suspicions.' Elspeth willed herself to meet Caroline's gaze. 'And, yes, I'd be a blind fool not to realise that Oswald and Ursula have designs on Gregory's fortune, and the others who have gone there. But I was not a party to their scheming. Neither was Dornford to begin with. It's only now that he's been drawn into it. But…' Elspeth stifled a sob, 'but I'm determined to bring matters to a head, whatever it costs me.'

'How?' Caroline snapped.

Elspeth shuddered. 'All I can think of at this moment is Stella. I dread to think what this will do to her. Jeremy is all she has. He's the reason she hasn't done away with herself. Truly. I would feel the same if Aquinas had done it to me.'

'Done it?'

'Need you ask?'

Caroline sighed and moved to sit beside Elspeth. 'Look at me.'

Elspeth turned her head, blinking away tears.

'Can I trust you?'

'Yes,' Elspeth whispered.

'Then listen to me. Not only do we know that Gregory is being held at The Blessed Plot, we also know where it is.'

'We, being you and Verity?'

'Yes, it's near a place called Devil's Bridge in West Wales.'

'Oh, is it?'

'You mean to say you didn't know?' Caroline scoffed.

'No. Truly. No one told me. Not even Dornford. I always imagined it was in Scotland.'

Caroline hesitated. 'What I'm about to tell you must not go any further. Swear it.'

Elspeth nodded.

'Say it!'

'I swear,' Elspeth whispered, quavering.

'An attempt is underway to rescue Gregory. I won't say more. Oswald and Ursula will be brought down, and this whole charade with them.'

'Dornford too?'

Caroline nodded. 'He must be held responsible for his actions, Elspeth. The blame cannot all be laid at Oswald and Ursula's door. You do see that, don't you?'

'Yes.' Elspeth exhaled deeply. 'I'm done with Dornford.'

'Very well. Now let's return to the matter of Stella's little boy. You say Aquinas took him. When was that?'

It must have been this morning, just before I encountered Millicent, the headmistress. She was on her way to inform Oswald and Ursula.'

'So we must assume that Jeremy is at Myrddin's Keep.'

'Oh no – no, no,' Elspeth gasped. 'Stella will be there working. There'll be the most awful scene, I know there will. Aquinas will taunt her. She'll lose her mind. I dread to think…'

'Verity's there with her. They went off together after breakfast.' Caroline pulled Elspeth to her feet. 'Come on. Outside. Hurry.'

'Where are we going?'

'To see Arnold and then to Myrddin's Keep.

Chapter 41

Verity rubbed her cheek and groaned. A mirror would have shown her the outline of Aquinas's fingers where his gauntleted hand had slapped her. Shocked and dazed, she'd been unable to resist when two of his followers grasped her arms and hurled her through the door of Stella's studio. Dimly aware of Aquinas's command to lock the door behind her and of Stella's screams mingled with the wailing of her son, she lay on the stone floor struggling to regain her senses.

Abruptly, the noises outside ceased.

Earlier that morning, absorbed with thoughts of George and Ambrose and how their quest to rescue Gregory might be playing out, Verity had accompanied Stella in silence along the familiar path across the meadow to Myrddin's Keep. Usually fond of chattering, Stella also seemed preoccupied. Verity had no need to guess the cause. The distressing scene at Jeremy's school was fresh in both their minds.

Entrusted with cutting pieces of glass to form the dragon's scales while Stella busied herself with a section depicting St George's armour, Verity narrowly avoided cutting her fingers when a shrill trumpet blast blared out.

'What on earth?' Stella jumped to her feet. 'What are those fools playing at this time?' she muttered, hurrying to open the door to the courtyard.

Verity followed.

Aquinas's followers were gathered outside. Piers, in his familiar green surcoat, held a long trumpet with a standard displaying the golden dragon hanging beneath it. He put it to his lips and delivered another shattering blast.

Verity turned to face the main gate. There, resplendent in a purple and gold riding cloak, came Aquinas on horseback.

His men set up a ragged cheer as his mount walked into the centre of the courtyard.

Everything about him exuded crude triumphalism, with chin held high and a look of arrogant disdain as his eyes settled on Stella. Applying his heel to the horse's flank, he turned to face her – and opened his cloak, revealing Jeremy's pale, frightened face. Astride the horse's neck, squirming helplessly in his father's grip, he let out a squeak of anguish at the sight of his mother.

Stella's banshee scream drowned out the trumpet blasts. Avoiding Verity's attempt to catch hold of her, she threw herself at Aquinas, scrabbling to reach her son. With one hand holding Jeremy and the reins, Aquinas closed his other fist around Stella's hair, shaking her roughly, then setting his horse in motion, dragging her along the courtyard before flinging her on the ground. Verity's attempt to intervene had earned that swipe across her face.

In the gloom of the studio, Verity took stock of her situation and got to her feet, swaying dizzily for a moment.

More in hope than expectation, she tried the door to the courtyard; to no avail. Finding that the doors connecting

Stella's studio to the adjacent rooms were also locked, Verity sat at Stella's workbench, striving to bring her emotions under control. Pangs of anger, fear and recrimination raced through her mind. Should she have dropped all pretence, cast off her assumed persona, and challenged the Lamonts as soon as she became aware of Gregory's abduction? And why did she not raise merry hell after accompanying Stella to the school?

Gradually, the mental maelstrom subsided. The steely resolve at the core of Verity's character asserted itself. All doubts cast aside, she got to her feet with but one thought in mind.

***

'Arnold! Arnold! Where are you?' Caroline threw open the door to the furniture workshop. 'Oh, there you are.' She hitched up her skirts and ran, heedless of the men she'd interrupted in their work, staring open-mouthed with tools in their hands.

Arnold met her half-way. He listened stony-faced. Caroline sensed his fellow woodworkers gathering around them. No one spoke until she'd finished.

'Brothers, you've all heard Caroline. The rottenness at the heart of this place is laid bare. How often have I said that the Lamonts are only out for themselves? Happy to exploit decent working men and women. Happy to allow Aquinas and his band of privileged louts to ride roughshod over others. To take a young boy from his mother? To treat women as chattels? The age of serfdom is long gone, yet these… vermin, these parasites, for that's what they are, brothers, behave as though it's the Middle Ages. Well, I say, enough. It's time to put an end to their playacting. Jack,

Ted, Davey, I know you are with us. What about it, lads? Who else?'

'Aye, I'm with you, Arnold,' said someone at the back. Then another, and another, until a chorus of voices joined in.

Arnold raised his hands to quell the tumult. 'Alright, thank you, brothers. I can see that there are a few of you shaking your heads and looking doubtful.'

'Come on, lads. Where's your solidarity?' a man standing at Arnold's shoulder called out. 'Happy to be exploited, are you?'

A small group of men muttered in the background, casting dark looks at Arnold and his supporters. 'You're always so fond of making speeches, Arnold,' one of them shouted out. 'You'd put our livelihoods at risk – for what? All on account of some brat we've never seen, and his mother, who's no better than she should be, I'll be bound.'

'No better than she should be!?' Caroline's eyes blazed. 'What sort of man stands back and allows a child to be dragged away, and who are you to cast judgement on a mother desperate to save her son? Why, if I were a man, I'd show you –'

Arnold's restraining hand on her arm allayed Caroline's urge to box the man's ears. 'Every man here is free to follow his own conscience,' he declared. 'I've said my piece. Now let's have a show of hands. Who's with me and Caroline?'

Twelve hands went up with just five dissenters.

'Thank you, comrades. Our first duty is to see to it that the lad is returned to his mother. We're talking about real people here. Jeremy, a boy of only four, and Stella, his mother. Even if you don't know her personally, you all know who I'm talking about. A kind, gentle woman who deserves nothing but our respect. That's enough words. To Myrddin's Keep!'

Elspeth emerged shyly from the doorway.

'Wait, men,' Arnold bellowed. 'What are you doing here? Spying for the Lamonts? Did you hear what I was saying? It's over. For them and for you. We know what your precious Dornford is up to. Have you no shame?'

'She's with me.'

Arnold turned to Caroline. 'What do you mean?'

'Elspeth is here to help us.'

'Is that what she told you?' Arnold scoffed.

Caroline didn't reply. She didn't need to. Her expression spoke for her.

'Ah, forget what I just said.' Arnold adopted a conciliatory tone. 'Elspeth, it's good to have you with us.'

Chapter 42

The ladder-back chair she'd found wasn't tall enough. Verity looked around the studio. She could hardly drag the workbench over to the back wall; it was far too heavy. *That might do,* she thought, eyeing an oak bench in the corner with a panel of stained glass propped on it – one of Stella's earlier works.

Verity placed the panel on the floor. The bench was heavy enough. By the time she'd dragged it into position, her breath was coming in short gasps. She sat on it to recover.

With the chair on top of the bench, she'd be able to reach one of the arched windows on the back wall. That would be the simple part. Not designed to open, the window would only give her a way out if she could remove the glass, and even then it would be a tight squeeze. For a moment she wavered, imagining herself stuck in the aperture. Helpless. '*Nil desperandum,*' she murmured.

The chair teetered as she tried to climb up onto it. Had the bench been wider, she'd have felt more confident, but the width of the chair left a mere inch of leeway. Even a slight movement as she stood atop it could bring her tumbling down. She took a breath and tried again. Planting her left foot first, she paused to steady herself, taking a firm grip of the chair back. On the count of three – one, two, three. Willing herself not to look down, Verity gasped, rigid with fear, both feet on the chair.

Two more deep breaths. Her left hand found the window ledge. She straightened. Good, the ledge was at breast height. Outside, she saw a broad line of trees twenty feet away, while directly below was a meadow of long grass and thistles.

The window was deep enough; its width was the difficulty. Not quite as broad as Verity's shoulders. She'd have to twist sideways as she made her exit, if it ever got to that. She tapped the window, trying to gauge the thickness of the glass. Hard to tell. What would she need to break it? With her mind thus occupied, the precariousness of her situation didn't trouble her. But faced with the prospect of climbing back down to collect some tools, her fears flooded back.

Knees shaking, she held on to the window ledge with one hand while the other groped for the chair. A faint wobble. Verity clenched her teeth. Gripping the back of the chair like a vice, she let go of the window ledge. Now, slowly down with the right foot. How far before she touched the bench …? Ah, there it was. Pause for breath. Almost there. Now the left foot. Such a relief.

Verity stepped off the bench and crossed the floor. The glass cutter? She was proficient in using it at the workbench, but how would she manage perched in mid-air? It would only score the glass. She'd still need Stella's small tack hammer. A proper carpenter's claw-hammer would be much better, but she'd simply have to make do. What else? Pliers.

Stella's capacious velvet shoulder bag was just the thing for carrying them. Emptying Stella's personal bits and pieces on the workbench, Verity replaced them with the tools and hung the bag around her neck. Anything else. Yes, there was Stella's shawl. She'd need that and her own shawl to drape over the windowsill as protection from any fragments of remaining glass.

Was that a noise outside? Verity bit her lip and tiptoed to the door. *Please, God, don't let them unlock the door now.* She held her ear to it. There were no voices, nothing to indicate that Aquinas or any of his henchmen were outside. But what was that?

Low down near the bottom of the door. Snuffling? Scratching? Something was out there. Brans's gruff woof settled the matter.

Verity kept her voice low. 'Bran?'

Silence, then more scratching.

'Shush, Bran. Good dog.'

A whimper.

'Go away. Go, Bran. Shoo.'

Silence. Had he gone? Verity kneeled at the door, straining to hear.

Another whimper. Then a low growl, but further away. She counted to ten. Thank heavens, she mouthed.

Her second ascent was easier. First she tried the glass cutter, scoring intersecting diagonals across the windowpane. Over and over, reluctant to press too hard and risk shifting the chair beneath her. Her shoulder ached with the effort.

Verity put the glass cutter down on the window ledge and fished around in Stella's bag for the hammer. Was it heavy enough? Could she exert enough force to shatter the glass and maintain her balance? Her first effort was so tentative that the hammer-head simply bounced back, almost jumping out of her grasp. Verity firmed her grip. Her second blow carried more conviction, though the glass remained intact.

With her face mere inches away from the window, the danger of flying glass presented another difficulty. Not only would she have to strike out with all her strength while keeping her balance, she'd also have to turn her head away to protect her eyes. Everything depended on maintaining a hold on the ledge with the fingers of her left hand.

Dwelling on her predicament would achieve nothing. Hit out and trust to luck, she concluded. Luck very nearly abandoned her. After two desperate swings, the glass held firm. Doubting that she had the strength for another blow, she swung again, then set the hammer on the ledge while her legs trembled beneath her, resting her forehead on the unresisting glass, eyes shut, panting.

Defeat was all the worse for being unfamiliar. An emotion both alien and deeply humiliating. Verity opened her eyes. So near and yet so distant, the outside world seemed to mock her – were it not for the web of cracks radiating across the glass.

With renewed purpose, she hammered away until all that remained were some jagged edges, which she removed as best she could with Stella's pliers.

Verity put the tools into Stella's bag and lifted it over her head, then let it drop to the floor. She draped Stella's shawl over the windowsill and folded her own on top of it, trusting that the thickness of the two garments would protect her. Any feelings of euphoria she'd felt at removing the glass vanished as she contemplated her next move. Now she must climb further, using the slats of the ladder-back chair, without toppling, all while hoping that the slats would bear her weight.

One step. Verity leaned her head through the window, savouring the breeze on her cheeks. Another step. Now she must twist to allow her shoulders through. Thus contorted, taking the final step was all but impossible. All she could do was kick and heave herself through in one motion, sending the chair clattering to the floor. Gravity did the rest. Had she possessed the dexterity of a cat, she might have landed with more dignity and fewer bruises. As it was, the impact forced the breath out of her, leaving her lying on her back, gazing at the clouds and all too aware of the patch of thistles beneath her.

Chapter 43

At any other time, he'd have found pleasure in his surroundings. Standing near the entrance of the Hafod Arms, a vista of wild natural beauty revealed itself. No wonder Wordsworth had extolled its romantic grandeur.

Would he have been wiser to come alone? Ambrose, despite all his determination and outward stoicism, was struggling with the physical demands of their undertaking. Although he'd not said so, George recognised that his companion would need to rest before setting out for *Nant-y-Geifr*. Not that Mr Morris's offer of lemonade and a plate of sandwiches hadn't been welcome.

George looked at his watch, fretting, anxious to be on the move. One-thirty already. The day half over.

'Sorry, old man,' Ambrose stepped through the hotel door. 'Suffered a bad bout of cramp. Had to lie on the bed for a while. Fighting fit now, though,' he added brightly.

Avoiding the track to the farm, they walked on past the gate and found their alternative point of entry. Within a few minutes, they reached their previous vantage point overlooking the farmyard at the rear of the house.

No signs of life. George focussed his binoculars on the farmhouse, its upstairs windows still shielded by shutters. On the ground floor, there was no movement to be seen through the kitchen window nor behind the aspidistra-shrouded window further along.

However, the yard itself was not empty. Pryce-Thomas's gig was there with the horse standing placidly in the traces, sampling the contents of a nosebag.

'What now, George?' Ambrose asked.

George had been mulling over that very question throughout the journey from Aberystwyth. He had considered Ambrose's suggestion about the two of them turning up at the front door and spinning a tale about being bird watchers. But what then? Might Floate invite them in? Far more likely that he'd send them away with a flea in their ear. Accuse them of being trespassers.

Very well. Forget the bird-watching story. Why not drop any pretence? Demand to see Gregory. Refuse to take no for an answer. Force their way inside at gunpoint, if necessary. A last resort, perhaps. What else?

What if Floate brought Gregory outside again? Might that present an opportunity? George dismissed the notion. Why wait outside, hoping for something that might never happen?

But… George scanned the house and courtyard again. Nothing. No one in sight. He saw it in his mind. A noiseless approach to the back door. Surely it wouldn't be locked. They would look for Gregory first. Then confront Floate and Dornford. Take them unawares with any luck. Brook no opposition and take Gregory away – in his wheelchair if need be.

'I have a plan, Ambrose.' George put his binoculars away. 'Come on.'

'Uh… I think we have a visitor.'

George looked around. Standing a mere three paces away was the man they'd seen the day before. The man with a shotgun. But instead of carrying it in the crook of his arm, his double-barrelled twelve-bore was levelled at George's chest. Twm Cadno, Mr Morris had called him. Sly as a fox. *Stealthy as a fox too*, George thought. And… what else? The eyes - clear, brown, unblinking, with the savage intensity of a predator eyeing its prey.

'Good afternoon, my good man,' Ambrose began, the words dying on his lips when the man turned his shotgun on him and cocked it.

'*Lawr.*' Twm nodded towards the farmhouse. '*Ewch i lawr!*' he commanded, pointing the gun at George and lifting it to his shoulder. With the barrels at eye level, George needed no interpreter. 'He wants us to go down to the house, Ambrose.'

George and Ambrose scrambled down the slope, with Twm close behind. 'Let's hope he doesn't slip,' Ambrose muttered. 'That gun's still cocked.'

Twm marched them across the yard to the back door of the house. With a warning glare at his captives, he lifted the latch.

'Mistar Floate! Mistar Floate!' Twm bellowed through the open door. Ears cocked, he waited for a response, then, satisfied, stepped away, covering George and Ambrose with his gun.

'What is it, Twm? *Beth sy'n bod?*' Floate took in the scene. 'My word, you don't look like poachers. You're not poaching, are you?' he said, turning an amused glance on the captives.

Close to, his features looked all the more striking. George remembered another illustrated book from his childhood in which the villain was a mad professor. Now he came to think of it, Floate was a near match. Then there was his voice – there was something about it. A hint of something continental?

'No, no, forgive me. You are gentlemen, clearly. Ramblers, perhaps?' Floate arched his copious eyebrows theatrically.

George took his cue. 'That's right, Mr?'

'Floate. It's Dr Floate, in fact. I see, you're out to enjoy our marvellous scenery, and who can blame you? However, you've strayed onto my property.' Floate spread his arms. 'No, no, don't apologise,' he continued hurriedly. 'A simple mistake to make. Indeed, I should be apologising to you. Having a shotgun pointed at you, hardly what one would expect on a country ramble.' Floate gestured to Twm to lower the shotgun.

'Allow me to make some recompense. Please come inside and take some refreshment.

Ambrose stood open-mouthed, unable to move, until George nudged him. 'Leave the talking to me,' George whispered as they followed Floate into the house.

A narrow passage ran directly from the rear of the house to the front door. George listened for any sounds as he and Ambrose were led past several closed doors to a sitting room overlooking a narrow patch of lawn, beyond which a wooded valley stretched away in the distance.

'Be seated, gentlemen. Oh dear, how remiss of me. I haven't asked your names.' Floate nodded benignly as George and Ambrose introduced themselves. 'Pleased to make your acquaintance. Now then, let me go and see to that refreshment I promised you; I rather fancy a glass of beer myself, would that be acceptable? Yes? Very well.'

Floate smiled and left the room, closing the door behind him.

Ambrose eyed George warily. 'What do you make of that?' he whispered.

George shrugged.

'Well, we're inside,' Ambrose grinned encouragingly. 'Just say the word. Let's see what Dr Floate has to say with your pistol pointing at his face?'

'Hmm. I thought we might learn something first.'

'What, get the fellow talking, see if he lets something slip?'

'Perhaps. If we set the man at ease. Play along like a couple of artless travellers. Then, it will be easier to surprise him when the time comes. At the moment, he still has every reason to be suspicious. And for all we know, Twm and his shotgun may be waiting in the hall. A glass of beer can't hurt. Just stay alert. If you see me adjust my tie,' George demonstrated the action, 'it means I'm about to draw my pistol. Understood?'

'Absolutely.'

George held a finger to his lips. In silence, they waited for Floate's return.

'Taking his time,' Ambrose hissed several minutes later.

George flashed him a warning look as the door handle turned.

'Forgive the delay, gentlemen,' Floate appeared in the doorway. 'Servants are thin on the ground hereabouts.' He placed a tray on a low table in the middle of the room.

'Allow me,' Floate handed glasses of beer to George and Ambrose. 'I rarely receive visitors, you must tell me all about yourselves.'

***

'You can come in. They're both under.' Floate called out.

Dornford put his head round the door. 'Hmm, what do you make of them?'

Floate considered. 'Are they just ramblers, do you mean? They mentioned birdwatching, although I'm curious as to why one of them had this on his person,' Floate pointed to a British Bulldog pocket revolver lying on the table.

Dornford examined the pistol. 'Not the sort of thing one would expect a rambler to carry. West Wales is hardly the Balkans. I doubt there are many bands of brigands infesting these hills.'

'Not nowadays, certainly,' Floate agreed.

'What do we do with them? Would they be missed if we, you know …?'

Floate shook his head. 'If I had more time, I'd get to the truth, but with things as they are, I think it best we send them on their way.'

'Surely not.' Dornford scowled.

'They're staying at the Hafod Arms. I learnt that from them without the need for hypnosis. If they fail to return, Morris will raise the alarm. The last thing we need is a police search.'

'But the mineshaft. No one would ever know. It's too well hidden. And there are shafts all over this area. If they're never seen again, the authorities will conclude that they've met with an unfortunate accident. Misadventure.'

Floate shook his head. 'No, Dornford. Keep your mind on the task at hand. Gregory's will. The papers are ready. Pryce-Thomas will witness the signature and take care of the rest. As for these two, they'll have no memory of being here. You and I will walk them down to the gate and set them on their way to the Hafod Arms. They will arrive footsore and exhausted, having become lost and wandered around the hills. Tomorrow, they'll return to Aberystwyth. They will have no memory of ever having been here.'

'You're sure?'

Floate laughed. 'My dear Dornford. They are both highly suggestible types. I didn't even use my pendulum. My voice was enough.'

Chapter 44

Nothing seemed amiss. Verity rolled away from the patch of thistles and sat up. Arms and legs in working order, she concluded, flexing each limb. The only casualty of her abrupt descent appeared to be a shoe, lost as she'd exited, and no doubt lying on the studio floor.

Anxious lest she be seen, she removed her other shoe and set off as quickly as her stockinged feet allowed, picking her way through the thistles to the shelter of the nearby wood. Consumed with thoughts of George and Ambrose's quest to rescue Gregory, Verity had given little thought to Oswald and Ursula, and even less to Aquinas. When Gregory was safe, she had a vague notion of confronting them, with Caroline and Arnold's support.

Such calculations were now irrelevant. Aquinas had precipitated a crisis that demanded immediate action. The time for confrontation had come. All that remained was to find Caroline and Arnold.

At the edge of the wood, Verity faced the prospect of crossing open ground to reach the path leading to the settlement. Would anyone be watching at the gate, or up on the battlements? Shielding her eyes from the sun, she squinted back at Myrddin's Keep. Was that a face looking out from the curtain wall? Verity blinked and looked again – it was nothing.

She resisted the urge to keep looking back and struck out across the meadow. Dressed in her hated yellow dress, there'd be no mistaking her. Fifty yards, twenty, ten – she stepped onto the path. Now she must hurry along until a rise in the land would place her out of sight.

When she'd walked this way with shoes on, she'd not noticed the stones embedded in the otherwise smooth clay surface. Now, her stockinged feet made their presence painfully obvious. Torn between the need for haste and preserving her feet, she hobbled the last few paces and sat down heavily, massaging her bruised soles and blinking back tears.

Preoccupied with thoughts of how far she still had to travel, Verity had no warning that anyone was approaching. Getting to her feet, she'd taken only ten paces when they appeared around a bend in the path.

After a moment of dumbfounded silence, Caroline rushed to embrace Verity. 'Thank goodness you're safe. We're here to rescue Jeremy,' she began. 'Arnold, and his comrades, and… Elspeth.'

'Elspeth!' Verity erupted.

'I know. Listen, I beg you. Calm yourself while I explain.' Caroline took a firm hold of Verity's arms. 'It's thanks to her that we learnt that Jeremy was taken.'

'Thanks to her?' Verity's eyes blazed. 'I'll thank her alright. Where is she? I see her, there she is.'

Elspeth cowered behind Arnold.

Caroline struggled to hold Verity back. 'No, you don't understand. She's forsworn them. Forsworn Dornford. Contain yourself. While you're venting your fury, heaven knows what's happening to Jeremy. And Stella. What of her? Is she …?'

'What?'

'For heaven's sake, listen, will you? What has happened to Stella?'

'Oh,' Verity gaped at Caroline. 'He has her. She went for him, but he overpowered her – brutally. They locked me in her studio, but I managed to escape. Thank God you've come.'

Caroline felt Verity's anger subside. She called Arnold to her side. 'It's as we feared. Stella is also captive.'

'Then we must push on,' Arnold eyed Verity warily. 'Do they know you've escaped?'

'No, I don't think so. I climbed out of a window. The main gate is open, and I couldn't see anyone on watch. If we hurry, we can get inside without opposition.'

Arnold looked down at her feet. 'But without shoes, you won't be able to keep up. We'll go on ahead, follow as best you can.'

'No.' Verity shook her head vehemently. 'We go together.'

'Very well,' Arnold got down on his knees.

'What on earth are you doing?'

Arnold ignored her. Grasping the hem of her dress, he began ripping the material apart.

'Arnold, have you taken leave of your senses?' Caroline looked on in disbelief.

'There,' Arnold brandished a handful of strips of yellow cotton. Too dumbfounded to react, Verity raised each foot at Arnold's command, permitting him to bind it firmly with cotton strips.

'Not as good as shoes, but enough to get you to Myrddin's Keep.' Arnold got to his feet and surveyed his handiwork. 'Shall we go?'

***

'Justin. Forgive that untimely interruption. Are all the papers in order?' Floate entered the parlour with Dornford at his side.

'Yes, yes, everything is signed and witnessed. He's been as good as gold.' Justin Pryce-Thomas glanced at Gregory, semi-conscious in his bath-chair. 'But what was that commotion about?'

'Twm found two men up behind the house,' Floate replied. 'English. Not from round here. They say they're ramblers.'

Pryce-Thomas narrowed his eyes. 'Are you sure?'

'I said, get rid of them.' Dornford drawled, leaning an elbow on the parlour mantelpiece. 'Down the mineshaft. Why take the risk?'

'And I've already told you why that's a foolish idea,' Floate snapped.

'Hmm.' Pryce-Thomas shuffled the papers on the table into a neat pile. 'You can't solve everything in that manner, Dornford.' He produced a length of pink ribbon and tied up the bundle. 'I assume you've worked your magic on them, have you, Maynard?'

Floate nodded. 'They'll remember nothing. No need for drastic measures,' he said, casting a disdainful glance at Dornford.

'So, will you be escorting Gregory back to London soon?' Pryce Thomas stood and began to clear away his papers.

'It will take a few days to prepare him to travel. Just enough sedation and hypnotic suggestion to make him compliant without impairing his physical faculties. He'll not need the bath-chair. There's a letter ready to send to his house, informing his housekeeper that he's suffered a sudden breakdown and will be returning, with my assistance, and that he will receive my continuing care at home.'

'Then how long?'

Floate pursed his lips. 'Shall we say, three weeks? The servants will witness their master's gradual decline. And then, phut!' Floate clicked his fingers.

'They will have heard him speak lyrically of his time at Chase Manor and the wonderful woman who gave him such help and encouragement there. A platonic, though deeply emotional, meeting of the minds. When the will names Elspeth as his sole heir, it will not come as a complete surprise.'

'And then Elspeth will become my wife. A most satisfactory outcome all round.' Dornford puffed out his chest and struck a preening attitude. 'Come on then, Maynard, let's set those two ramblers on their way back to Devil's Bridge.'

'Oh, please don't trouble yourselves on our account.'

Floate and Dornford mimicked a couple of scalded cats, while Pryce-Thomas stared slack-jawed at the sight of George and Ambrose in the doorway.

Dornford took one look at the pistol in George's hand and edged nervously away from the mantelpiece.

'You look puzzled, Dr Floate,' Ambrose grinned. 'Had us both in a hypnotic trance, so you thought. And you were half right. George here was indeed under your influence. Took me a few hefty slaps to bring him round. Sorry, George.'

Ambrose warmed to his theme. 'Oh dear, Dr Floate, you seem most discomposed. But you see, I am quite impervious to your powers. I spent many years in India. You remind me of a man I met there. Swami Achyntia, he called himself; played the great Hindu mystic. One of his party tricks was to put his followers in a trance. Oh, I've seen him do it many a time; entire rooms of people, quite out of it, putty in his hands.

'Not boring you, am I, Floate? No, I can see that George's pistol is certainly commanding your attention. Now where was I? Oh yes, got to know the old rogue rather well. Partial to a gin and tonic on the quiet, was the Swami. And I won't mention what he got up to with some of his female acolytes in private. Not the sort of thing he'd want his followers to know. I think that's why he tried it on me – hypnotism – to keep me from letting on that he was not quite the ascetic he professed to be. Not that I had any such intention.

'But he didn't succeed. I remember it quite vividly, a calm, almost disembodied feeling, as though a soft feather bed awaited me, if only I'd slip between the sheets. But I chose not to. And that's how it was earlier on. I simply played along with you.'

Floate stared at George and Ambrose, brows furrowed. Pryce-Thomas, goggle-eyed, clutched his attaché case to his chest, while Dornford fidgeted nervously in the background.

Finally, Floate found his voice. 'Who are you?'

'Sit.'

Floate blinked at George's terse command.

'All three of you – sit. Now!' George barked.

Pryce-Thomas complied instantly, gripping the attaché case more firmly, to keep his hands from trembling.

'You heard me, Floate,' George lifted his pistol, taking aim at Floate's broad forehead. 'Thank you,' he added as Floate lowered himself into a chair.

'Now, you.'

Dornford looked wildly around the room. As George opened his mouth to repeat himself, he made a dash for the door, screaming, 'Twm, Twm, help, murder!'

Ambrose extended a leg.

Dornford's head proved unequal to the ensuing collision with the door frame. Blood streamed from his brow and nose as Ambrose hoisted him by the scruff of the neck and dumped him on a vacant seat.

'That ruffian you call Twm went away down the valley ten minutes ago.' Ambrose handed Dornford a handkerchief. 'I saw him through the window, so he and that shotgun of his are not about to come to your rescue. Now, wipe that blood before it stains your nice clean shirt. Over to you, George.'

George nodded and addressed Floate. 'Who are we? You have our names. Other than that, you need only know that we are here to release Gregory Manning. You may have thought he would not be missed, that no one cared for him. You were wrong, and your villainy will be exposed. I refer not only to the three of you, but those whose bidding you do.'

Floate shot a warning glance at Dornford.

'Ah, now I understand.' Dornford kept Ambrose's handkerchief pressed to his brow. 'I knew there was something about her that didn't seem right. For all that she professed a love of decorative arts and handicrafts, she never struck me as the type to dedicate herself to Chase Manor.'

'That's enough,' Floate hissed.

'Don't presume to command me,' Dornford retorted. 'Verity Mallard, that's who's behind this.'

Chapter 45

Three hundred yards away from Myrddin's Keep, Arnold called a halt.

'I can't see anyone.' Arnold shielded his eyes. 'The gate's still open.'

'It looks quiet enough,' Verity agreed.

'Alright, gather round.' Arnold waited for everyone to form a loose circle around him. 'Aquinas and his band of fools in fancy-dress won't take kindly to us marching into their precious fortress. They may even use weapons. Those swords they use in their ridiculous mock battles aren't toys. And we only have these.' Arnold held his right hand aloft, brandishing a claw hammer. Several of his followers copied his gesture. 'But let's hope we can settle this with no more than our fists if it comes to a fight. Now quickly, with me.'

Arnold and three of his men raced ahead, with the others following. Despite her best efforts, Verity soon fell behind. Cursing, she willed herself forward but could do little more than hobble until an agonizing pain shot through her sole. With a groan, she flopped to the ground, clutching her right foot.

Having covered half the distance to the gate, Arnold had outstripped his three closest companions. They followed twenty paces behind, with the rest of the party, including Caroline, strung out in a line, trying their best to keep up.

Verity watched them helplessly, blinking away tears, clenching her teeth. Her foot pulsed with pain from the thistle spines embedded in her sole. At first, she barely noticed the hands that held her shoulders and the soothing words in her ear. When she recognised Elspeth's face next to hers, she lacked the will to do or say a thing.

A hundred yards to go. The gate remained ajar. Arnold could see into the courtyard now. Empty. Fighting to fill his lungs, he felt his pace slacken. Seventy yards. His breath came in painful gasps. 'Come on,' he grunted. Still no sign of anyone. Fifty yards. He was staggering now, arms outstretched, willing himself through the gate.

With his senses concentrated entirely on the tantalising gap ahead, the trumpet blast sounded unearthly, distant somehow. Then, in what seemed like slow motion, the gates swung shut. With a final desperate lunge, Arnold threw himself forward, crashing into the immovable solidity of the oak timbers and sinking to his knees.

***

'We'll take that.' George nodded at the attaché case in Pryce-Thomas's hands. The solicitor stared, open-mouthed, transfixed by the sight of George's revolver.

'The attaché case – put it on the table.' Spoken with the sharp authority he'd once employed on the parade ground, George's command had the desired effect. With trembling hands, Pryce-Thomas complied, licking his lips nervously.

'Thank you. Now let me tell you all what will happen next. You, Dornford, will lie on the floor.'

'What!' Dornford, one hand still pressing Ambrose's handkerchief to his forehead, attempted to get to his feet.

'No, old chap, he didn't tell you to stand.' Ambrose shoved him back into the seat. 'Now then, these curtain ties we brought from your sitting room will serve to bind your hands and feet.'

'Maynard, for God's sake, do something.' Dornford implored.

'Yes, please, be my guest.' George taunted Floate. 'Oh, don't be concerned about this,' he added, putting his pistol in his pocket. 'Let's test your prowess, man to man. How do you think you would fare?'

Floate's eyes darted around the room.

'Do you think you might make a dash for it, Floate?' George sneered.

'You appear to have the advantage.' Floate shrugged. 'But you seem like practical men. Whomever you represent, consider what you might gain by aiding our little scheme rather than standing in our way. Do you have any idea how much this pathetic individual is worth?' Floate cast a contemptuous glance at Gregory. 'Think, man, a share of the proceeds would far eclipse whatever you're being paid. Two days, that's all we need. You can say that it took you that long to find this place, and that there was no one here when you did discover it. Pryce-Thomas will give you a bank draught here and now. Shall we say… a thousand?' Floate turned to the solicitor. 'You can see to that, can't you, Just –'

George's fist snapped Floate's chin upward, his eyes swivelling in their sockets. He slumped back in his chair without a sound.

George took two thick, braided curtain ties from Ambrose and quickly bound Floate's ankles together, then dragged the semi-conscious doctor out of his seat onto the floor and tied his hands behind his back.

'Now then, Mr Lamont, you were saying?' George moved over to stand in front of Dornford. 'Face down on the floor, if you please.'

Ambrose winked at George as he knelt and trussed Dornford's hands and feet. 'Two down and one to go. Oh, look, I believe our other friend is leaving.'

George turned.

Pryce-Thomas, sidling towards the door, froze.

George shook his head, beckoning with his index finger.

The solicitor gulped and approached hesitantly. 'I won't put up a fight. P… please don't hit me,' he pleaded. 'I'll get down on the floor.'

'No need, Mr Pryce-Thomas. You and your attaché case are coming with us. You won't mind our using your gig, I'm sure. Sit down for a moment. That's it. We won't keep you long. Just sit still and get ready to explain yourself to the police in Aberystwyth.' George viewed the panic in Pryce-Thomas's eyes with satisfaction.

'How are you, my dear chap?' Ambrose leant over Gregory's bath chair. 'I think he hears me, George. There's some sign of recognition in his eyes, I'm sure of it.'

'We're here to help you, Gregory. George and I are going to get you away from here. Do you understand? Can you nod or blink your eyes?' Ambrose waited, staring intently at Gregory's face. 'Do you remember you were at Chase Manor? No?' Ambrose puffed out his cheeks. 'Does the name Verity Mallard mean anything to you?' Ambrose waited in vain for a sign, then shrugged and turned away.

'Poor devil's out of it still, by the looks of it. We'd better get going, George.'

'Look again, Ambrose.'

'Eh? Oh, I'm blessed. He's nodding. And look, his hand is moving. Oh, that's wonderful.' Ambrose grasped the bath chair's handles. Come along, Gregory, we're leaving.'

***

Verity managed a weak smile, then gasped as a wet poultice was pressed to her foot.

'I'm sorry, but it's bound to hurt a little,' Elspeth lifted the poultice. 'Shall I continue?'

'Yes, of course, don't mind me. Please carry on, and thank you, Elspeth, you've been most kind. Especially after I –'

'Shh.' Elspeth bent to her task.

'It's so infuriating,' Verity turned to Caroline and Arnold, sitting glumly side by side in Sylvan Cottage's parlour. Smarting from their ignominious retreat from Myrddin's Keep, they'd said little since their return.

After his failed dash to the gateway, Arnold had picked himself up and walked back to join the others, gathered twenty yards away, gazing impotently at the solid grey expanse of the curtain wall and the gatehouse which loomed in front of them. And there between the crenelations, they saw a row of faces, leering, laughing and shouting, none more raucously than Aquinas, stationed in the centre.

'Well now, if it's not Arnold Wright,' he called out. 'I don't recall issuing an invitation to you and your socialist rabble to call on us. Mighty uncivil of you to come without

278

one, I must say. Would you take kindly to my knights and me barging into your precious workshop?'

'We've come for Stella.' Arnold shouted back. 'And Jeremy.' Caroline added, stepping forward.

'Ah, it's the Lady Caroline. Still associating with your horny-handed socialist, I see. What was that you said?'

'Don't pretend you don't know why we're here. Verity saw it all. You abducted Stella's son, and you brutally assaulted her. But Verity escaped.'

'Did you hear that, men?' Aquinas scoffed. 'I bring *my* son to *my* home and she calls it abduction.' A gale of laughter and crude insults rippled along the battlements. 'Where is Verity the Virtuous, by the way? Ah.' Aquinas shielded his eyes, peering into the middle distance. 'Can that be her?' He pointed to the spot where Verity sat, nursing her foot. 'Who the devil is that with her? It can't be...'

'It's Elspeth,' Caroline exclaimed. 'She's with us.'

'With *you*, is she?' Aquinas smirked. 'Well, well, here's a fine to-do. You'll be telling me that Oswald and Ursula are in your camp next.'

Caroline turned away, shaking her head.

'Where is Stella? We demand to see her.' Arnold advanced to stand directly beneath Aquinas. 'Open the gates so that we can see her.'

Another chorus of laughter rang out.

'Did you hear that?' Aquinas chortled. 'The peasant dares to challenge his lord. What is the world coming to?'

'Enough of your posturing, Aquinas. Let's have this out. Face to face. You and me.'

'Ooh!' A cry of mock alarm went up.

'By all that's holy, I do believe he challenges me to a duel,' Aquinas announced, pulling a face and shaking his hands in simulated terror. 'Oh, dear,' he gasped, dabbing his eyes with his sleeve. 'Tell him, would you, Piers?'

The man standing to Aquinas's right leaned out over the wall. 'The rules of chivalry would never permit a noble knight to sully himself by accepting a challenge from a common churl such as yourself. Now, begone.'

Whether by instinct, intuition or pure good fortune, Arnold's decision to walk away saved him. Seeing the look of horror and revulsion on Caroline's face, he broke into a run, darting a glance back over his shoulder as Piers emptied a chamber pot over the spot where he'd stood.

The bitterness of their ensuing retreat was ameliorated only by the thought of how narrowly they'd avoided even deeper humiliation.

'Infuriating, you say, Verity,' Caroline struggled for words. 'What do we do now? Really, this is… Aagh!' she slammed her fist on the parlour table.

Arnold put his arm around her. 'If we can't do anything, then perhaps…'

'Do you mean the authorities, Arnold? The police?' Verity asked.

'If there's nothing else.' Arnold shrugged.

'Do you think the police would involve themselves in a situation of this nature? Aquinas *is* the boy's father, and I'll wager that they'd have as little sympathy for Stella as for any unmarried woman with a child.'

'But be that as it may.' Caroline recovered her composure. 'A woman is being held against her will – and assaulted.'

'Hmm.' Verity bit her lip. 'Elspeth?'

'Yes.' Elspeth put the poultice aside and sat up.

'You say you've decided not to marry Dornford?'

'That's right, I said so to Caroline this morning. My mind is made up.'

'And what does that mean for your place here at Chase Manor?'

'I imagine that I'll not be welcome.'

Verity nodded. 'No, I dare say Oswald and Ursula will see it as a betrayal. After all, you've been so close. One of the family, in all but name.'

'Oh.' Elspeth met Verity's gaze. 'You needn't beat about the bush. You imply that I am complicit in Gregory's abduction. That I am fully aware of whatever goes on at The Blessed Plot.'

'And are you?'

Elspeth hesitated. 'I'm certainly guilty of blind foolishness, but I swear to you that I am not like them and I'm not party to their... schemes. I don't believe that Dornford was either – until now, that is.'

'Caroline. Do you believe her?'

'I was reluctant to do so at first, but yes, Verity, I do.'

'Then so do I. Elspeth, at this moment two good friends of mine are in Wales. They will find and release Gregory and take him to safety. If Dornford's there... who knows? However, you must realise that Dornford will face justice. When Gregory is free, his abduction and any other wrongdoing associated with Chase Manor will become a matter for the police.'

Elspeth nodded. 'I know,' she whispered. 'Good heaven's what's that?'

The crash of a door slamming echoed through the cottage. Heavy footsteps sounded in the passage. A heartbeat later, the parlour door flew open to reveal the embodiment of a Fury, in the shape of Ursula Lamont.

Chapter 46

'Mr Morris will make sure that the cart gets back to Dilwyn in Aberystwyth.' George climbed up on to the seat of the gig and took up the reins. Designed to carry only two, it made for a tight squeeze, with Pryce-Thomas perched disconsolately at one end of the seat, George at the other, and Gregory in between.

Ambrose stood to one side, mounted on the horse that had carried Dornford to Aberystwyth and back.

'What did he say?'

'Not a great deal. He's quite dumbfounded. Hardly surprising,' George flicked the reins. 'Let's get going.'

With more than its usual load to carry, the horse tossed its head with displeasure but eventually settled into a trot.

As they left the village of Devil's Bridge behind, George felt Gregory stirring next to him. When they'd succeeded in helping him out of the bath chair and onto the gig, he'd shown a small sign of consciousness, muttering what sounded like 'thank you.' Now he made a sudden growling sound deep in his throat. Alarmed, George turned to look at him. The growl subsided. 'Where ...?' George leaned closer, straining to hear. 'Where am I?'

'You're safe,' George gave a smile of reassurance as Gregory turned his head to face him. 'We're taking you to safety. Do you understand?'

The eyes behind the thick spectacle lenses blinked. 'Safe?'

George nodded. 'Ambrose, he's speaking,' he called out.

'Oh, good God, no!' The cry of alarm came not from Ambrose but from Pryce-Thomas, pointing up the road.

Just ten yards away, Twm Cadno levelled his shotgun, a finger curled around both triggers of his twelve-bore.

George pulled back on the reins. 'No!' Pryce-Thomas screamed. 'Twm, *na!*' he repeated in Welsh, waving his arms frantically. '*Peidiwch â saethu.* Don't shoot.'

Twm showed no sign of recognition, eyeing his target along the twin barrels of his gun. The booming discharge echoed across the valley, sending a flock of crows cawing and wheeling overhead.

Convinced that his time had come, George hardly registered the slight movement of the shotgun barrels, an elevation of a few degrees, which nevertheless sent a shower of shot perilously close to the occupants of the gig. The horse flinched and whinnied, straining in the traces as George gripped the reins to hold it back. Not so Ambrose, whose mount hurtled down the road with its rider clinging on for dear life.

Pryce-Thomas had launched himself into the ditch as the shotgun discharged. Thinking at first that he'd been hit, George watched anxiously as the solicitor, on all fours in the mud, groaned, but showed no sign of injury. When he returned his attention to the road, Twm was nowhere to be seen.

***

With an avalanche of invective, Ursula held forth, barely pausing for breath. Verity and Caroline were roundly condemned as ungrateful meddlers who had betrayed the generosity of their hosts. 'To think that Oswald and I welcomed you into our community. How dare you involve yourselves in matters that do not concern you? And you,' she continued, pointing at Verity, 'you, I never trusted. I should have followed my instincts and sent you packing before now.'

Arnold was next. 'You've been nothing but trouble, Arnold Wright. We give you a workshop and everything you need to follow your craft, and what do we get? Nothing but complaints. Oswald is too indulgent. He laughs your insolence off. But you've met your match in me. Take your tools and go, you and your poisonous socialist ideas.'

Finally, her blazing eyes came to rest on Elspeth. 'Vile, treacherous hussy,' she spat.

Elspeth shrank back.

'Oh, you don't fool me. I can see through your devious plan. You think by marrying my son, you'll become the power behind the throne. Foolish girl. You can forget any thought of becoming Dornford's wife. The wedding is off.'

Elspeth gathered her courage. 'Oh, you needn't worry on that account. You can keep your precious son. I would as soon marry a passing tramp.'

Ursula stood smouldering, cheeks purple with rage and eyes radiating hate. 'Filthy bitch!' she screamed, following with a foul-mouthed, barely coherent rant.

'That will do!' Verity stood shielding the cowering Elspeth. 'Enough of your threats. Desist now, or –'

Ursula gave a harsh laugh. 'Or what?'

'Or I'll take you by that greasy plait hanging down your back, march you to the door, and throw you in the pond. Do you doubt me?' She moved closer, locking eyes with

Ursula, seeing surprise give way to defiance, then doubt, followed by a flicker of fear.

'Clear off and get out, all of you.' Ursula's parting shot came in little more than a whisper as she turned on her heel.

Like the calm after a great storm, an unnatural silence pervaded the parlour of Sylvan Cottage. The human whirlwind that was Ursula Lamont had gone, again slamming the front door with shuddering force.

Elspeth buried her face in her hands, sobbing silently.

Arnold cleared his throat and took Caroline's hand. 'Are you alright?'

Caroline nodded. 'What a tirade, and such language! I'm broad-minded, but some of the things she said… What on earth do we do now?'

Arnold shrugged. 'She made it plain. She ordered us to leave.'

'No one is leaving.' All eyes turned to Verity. 'Although they don't realise it, Oswald and Ursula's comeuppance is at hand, Dornford's too. Soon, when I receive the news that Gregory is safe, they will be brought to book for their crimes. If I'm right, they will face charges of abduction and possibly murder.'

'Can you be sure?' Caroline asked.

'Certainly, as far as Gregory's abduction is concerned. So, are we agreed?'

Arnold and Caroline glanced at each other. 'Yes,' they replied.

'And you, Elspeth?'

Verity waited while Elspeth dabbed at her eyes and composed herself. 'Yes,' she nodded. 'But…' Elspeth's eyes filled with tears again. 'But what about Stella and her little boy?'

Chapter 47

'How are you feeling? This will do you good' Ensconced in the comfort of the lounge bar at the Belle View Hotel, George handed Gregory a glass of scotch and soda.

'Uh… thank you.' Gregory eyed the glass suspiciously. 'I don't usually take alcohol. Perhaps this once?' He hesitated, then took the drink from George's hand.

'Forgive me, Gregory, I didn't realise. You needn't if you –'

'No. I don't usually drink, as I said. But then again, these are unusual times.' Tentatively, Gregory raised the glass to his lips. 'Whisky?'

'With a dash of soda.' George recalled his first introduction to whisky. He'd coughed, spluttered, pulled a face, and fought the urge to retch until the spirit reached his stomach and spread its glow.

To his surprise, apart from a widening of the eyes magnified by his thick lenses, Gregory showed little reaction as the liquid passed his throat. After gazing at the glass for a few moments, he took another sip.

'There, just the tonic after all you've been through at that place,' Ambrose patted Gregory's shoulder. 'Not to mention that maniac with the shotgun. How I kept my seat on that horse, I'll never know.'

Gregory smiled. 'I was still only half aware. It just sounded like distant thunder to me.'

'You can put all that behind you now. At least you were sufficiently compos mentis to make a statement at the police station.' George sat back and stretched his legs, allowing a comfortable weariness to replace the tension of the day's events. 'Justin Pryce-Thomas collapsed like a stack of cards. His evidence will cook Floate's goose and Dornford's too, not that it will do him much good. He'll not practise as a solicitor again, and, depending on what the police may find at that farm, the outlook could be grim indeed.'

'My memory of it is quite hazy. Perhaps it's for the best. But tell me again, how did you two come to my rescue? You said that Verity sent you?'

'Yes. You have her to thank. Verity is a force to be reckoned with.' George gave Ambrose a sidelong glance.

'Oh, indeed, an absolute force of nature,' Ambrose concurred.

'Hmm. You know, she didn't strike me as the type.'

'The type who would enter a utopian community?' George offered.

Gregory nodded.

'She's a journalist. Verity entered the community in search of a story, and she's certainly got one.'

'Oh. Do you mean that I will be mentioned in her story? I'm a private person, Mr Benson. The thought of my name appearing in the newspapers…'

'I'm sure that anything Verity writes will be sympathetic and measured, where you're concerned,' George did his best to sound reassuring. 'But, it can't be denied that when this whole business comes to light, and now that the police are involved that's inevitable, it will cause a sensation. At least you can trust Verity to tell the true story without embellishment.'

Gregory's face dropped. George and Ambrose stayed silent, watching his expression as he mulled over what he'd been told. Abruptly, he raised his glass and drained it. '*C'est la vie.* What now, George?'

***

Everyone felt it. The refectory was filled with tension, an oppressive atmosphere like the gathering of a thunderstorm on a hot summer's day. The usual clamour of conversation was muted to a murmur.

All eyes turned on Verity as she entered, arm in arm with Elspeth, Caroline and Arnold following, and made her way to her usual place. At any moment, she expected Ursula to react, to assert herself in front of the community and order the four of them to leave.

Verity risked a glance in her direction. Ursula sat stony-faced at the head of her table, mechanically spooning soup into her mouth. At the head of the next table, Oswald tried to engage those nearest to him in conversation, feigning a bonhomie he clearly didn't feel.

Food was served in the usual way. The serving maids placed meals in front of them, while studiously avoiding eye contact. The four outcasts ate in silence, conscious of being surrounded by eavesdroppers. Soup, cold cuts and salad, platters of fruit. A typical supper.

Then it happened.

Oswald got to his feet. A hush descended on the room. 'Friends,' he began, 'for many years our community has flourished. Co-operation and harmony have been our watchwords, and Ursula and I have derived the greatest pleasure from seeing our venture succeed and for all of you, our dear friends, to find happiness and contentment here at Chase Manor.' Oswald extended his hand to Ursula who rose and joined him.

'But now, we are faced with a matter so grave that it threatens to undermine our very existence. To put all that we have built together in jeopardy. We have in our midst those who wish us harm.' A buzz of indignation greeted Oswald's remarks. 'Yes, my friends, even though we have invited them to share our bounty. Even though we have opened our hearts to them and wished them nothing less than to prosper among us, they, for reasons I cannot fathom, have met our kindness with antagonism.' Oswald paused while another wave of outraged murmuring swept around the refectory.

'I hear you, my friends. Their perfidy is written on their faces. There they are, daring to sit among us.' Oswald raised his arm and pointed. 'Note them well, the vipers in our bosom – Arnold Wright, Verity Mallard, Caroline Hislop and, a person whom Ursula and I loved as a daughter, but who has utterly betrayed us – Elspeth Forsyth. Know them and shun them. Shun them one and all.' Oswald's voice rose to a shrill crescendo.

At some signal, unseen and unheard, everyone around them rose to their feet. Everyone, even Arnold's erstwhile woodworking comrades. Led by Ursula and Oswald, they filed silently out of the refectory.

'They mean to freeze us out,' Elspeth was first to speak. 'Oswald and Ursula have been busy turning everyone against us, it seems.'

'No matter, we have only to wait until my friends have done their work and Gregory is safe.' Verity said. 'Then the game will be over.'

'But we can't simply return to our quarters and carry on as before, can we?' Caroline turned to Arnold.

'I think it best if we stay together. There's a great deal of animosity out there. Someone might take it into their heads to do us harm. I propose that we all stay at the Fairy Cottages. If Elspeth takes what she needs from Sylvan Cottage, she could move in with you and Verity. I'll sleep next door. Let's hope your plan succeeds, Verity, because I doubt we'll be able to hold out for more than a day or two.'

They arrived in the fading dusk.

'Arnold,' Caroline said at the threshold, 'I think it would be safer if you also stayed here with us. I think we can put normal standards of propriety aside in the circumstances. It will mean bedding down as best you can in the parlour.'

'Well, yes, if Verity and Elspeth are agreeable.'

'Perfectly,' Verity concurred. 'I was about to suggest it myself.'

'Oh, yes,' Elspeth nodded enthusiastically, 'let's all stay together.'

'There are scant rations, I'm afraid,' Caroline announced half an hour later as they sat around the parlour table. 'Most of a loaf, some butter, honey, and a jar of blackberry jam. I don't imagine that Tamsin will be calling in the morning to make breakfast, so we'll simply have to make do.'

'I dare say we'll manage,' Verity said briskly. 'I'm more concerned with our safety, to be frank. As things stand, it seems that the entire community is against us, and let's not forget Aquinas and his followers. There may have been a falling out between Oswald and Ursula and the Myrddin's Keep faction, but we are loathed by both sides. For all we know, there may be someone out there now.'

'Oh, surely no one would creep up on us at night,' Elspeth scoffed. 'This is England after all, not some wild, lawless place. And don't try to scare me by staring at the window like that. I'll not fall for –'

'Verity isn't playing games, Elspeth,' Caroline insisted. 'I saw it too. Someone passed the window. There, did you hear that? Someone's at the door.'

Arnold was already on his feet. Holding a finger to his lips, he stepped noiselessly into the hall. The doorknocker rapped twice. Not, Arnold thought, the sound of someone aggressively demanding admission, simply loud enough to gain the attention of those within. He pressed his ear to the door. 'Please open the door. I mean no harm.' A low voice called out. A man's voice. Not one he recognised. Arnold slipped the bolt and lifted the latch.

For an instant, the sight that greeted him confirmed his worst fears. The man wore a dark cloak around his shoulders, underneath which his knightly surcoat was revealed.

'My name is Oliver. Please don't be alarmed. I bring news of Stella and her boy.'

'Who is it, Arnold?' Verity stood at the parlour door. 'Oh, I see. If you've been sent to threaten us, you can think again. Should anything untoward befall Stella and little Jeremy, you will regret it. You, Aquinas, and all your preposterous crew of misfits will answer for it. Do I make myself –'

Arnold interrupted. 'He says he has news of Stella. His name's Oliver.'

'Yes, I'm here because I want to help. Allow me to explain,' Oliver pleaded. 'Aquinas and the others have no idea that I'm here, I swear.'

'Very well. Come through to the parlour.'

'This is Oliver. He says he wants to help,' Verity announced to Elspeth and Caroline, their faces a picture of suspicion and concern.

'Thank you,' Oliver began nervously. 'I realise that you have no reason to trust me. But not everyone at Myrddin's Keep is –'

'A boorish, loud-mouthed oaf?' Elspeth interjected, eyes blazing.

Oliver flinched. 'Aquinas has gone too far. You failed in your attempt to rescue Stella, but there is a way. There's a hidden entrance to Myrddin's Keep – a sally port. In the woods behind the Keep, there's a small stone tower, shaped like a pepper pot. Unless you knew its location, you'd not notice it. It has no windows, only an iron-bound oak door. A tunnel connects it to the Keep. Gain entrance to that sally port, and it will bring you to the heart of Myrddin's Keep.'

Elspeth looked doubtful. 'I've never heard of this sally port.'

'It's well concealed. But I can assure you –'

'So, you have just left Myrddin's Keep through this sally port, have you?' Verity interjected.

'Yes.'

'Then why did you not bring Stella and Jeremy with you? Surely, if you want to help, you would have brought them to us.'

'I would have done so. But Stella is being kept under lock and key, and Aquinas has the boy in his chamber.'

'Is the man mad? We are on the verge of the twentieth century, yet he behaves like a medieval seigneur.'

Oliver shrugged.

'Let's get down to brass tacks.' Arnold stuck his thumbs behind the lapels of his jacket. 'Will you take us to this back door?'

'I must return at once before I'm missed.'

'And we will come with you.'

Oliver shook his head. 'Aquinas has set a guard overnight. One man above the main gate, and another within the great hall in the keep itself. I'm that man, but only for another half hour, until I'm relieved. I must get back at once. Come at dawn. I'll do what I can to clear the way. Take this.' He took out a folded sheet of paper and handed it to Arnold.

Arnold unfolded the paper. 'A map?'

'Use it to find the sally port. I've also drawn a plan of the keep. It shows where Stella is being held, and where Aquinas's chamber is. You had several men with you this afternoon; once inside, they should prove enough to overcome any opposition.'

Arnold gave a hollow laugh. 'My comrades have been turned against me.'

'You mean to say that it will be only the four of you? One man and three –'

'Have a care, Oliver,' Verity snapped. 'Three determined women are not to be dismissed lightly. Now go before you're missed.'

Oliver turned to leave. 'The sally port door will be unlocked. Bring a lantern to light your way through the tunnel.'

Chapter 48

Sergeant Davies was a man of few words. After twenty years on the beat, he'd found it hard to adjust to being out of uniform when he was first assigned to the detective branch, but soon found he'd discovered his vocation.

At first light, he waited with a small portmanteau in hand at the entrance of the Belle Vue for George, Ambrose and Gregory to emerge. When they'd arrived at the police station the previous afternoon with a petrified Pryce-Thomas, and a pale young man in tow, he'd listened patiently to their tale of abduction, hypnotism and conspiracy to commit murder, with a good dose of scepticism. It might have remained that way if Pryce-Thomas had kept his head, but the man panicked, all but admitting the whole thing.

Superintendent Llewelyn shook his head in disbelief at first but soon realised the gravity of the case and took firm charge. 'Davies, you will take these men's statements, then you will accompany them to Hereford on the early train tomorrow morning. I will telegraph the Hereford Police to expect you. In the meantime, Inspector Jenkins and I will pay a visit to *Nant-y-Geifr* farm. We'll see what this Dr Floate has to say for himself. And that other chap, Dornford Lamont, isn't it?'

'Good morning, Sergeant.' George led Ambrose and Gregory down the hotel steps.

'Good morning, gentlemen. It's only a short walk to the railway station. Let's stretch our legs before we sit on that train for the next few hours.'

***

Dornford shivered, turning his collar up against the early morning breeze blowing in from the coast. He moved along the platform seeking shelter in the small waiting room. Ignoring the curious glances of the old couple occupying a wooden bench on one side, he perched uncomfortably on a bench opposite. His pocket watch showed seven more minutes to wait.

Dear God, what a night. He'd always viewed Twm Cadno with a mixture of disdain and wariness. More wild animal than man, he slinked around the farm and surrounding countryside like the fox he was named after. A fox in human form. Smelt like one too. But if it weren't for Twm, what then? He'd not be sitting here waiting for the train to get him far away from Devil's Bridge. Away from that bleak, unforgiving landscape, and away from the grim secret that lay at the bottom of the mine.

He'd been consumed by rage, lying trussed up on the floor at the farmhouse; rage and then fear. Pryce-Thomas was as weak as he was grasping. When those two – that swine Benson and his insufferable companion – arrived at Aberystwyth and presented the spineless solicitor and the contents of his attaché case to the police, the game would be up. Unless? Was there any other way?

Floate's groans interrupted his train of thought.

It took half an hour to free themselves. When Floate had regained his senses, they gradually manoeuvred themselves until, back-to-back, they could untie each other's hands and then remove the bonds from their ankles. Dornford was first to his feet.

Floate remained on the floor, rubbing his ankles and wrists.

'How are you, Maynard? You look deathly pale.'

'Eh? Oh, I… I feel rather strange. Perhaps some air?' Floate shakily attempted to get up.

'Steady now. Let me give you a hand.'

Dornford helped Floate to stand. How curious to witness such a commanding presence, the malevolent intelligence who took such obvious pleasure in wielding power over others, rendered almost helpless – weak as a kitten. This would be easier than he'd thought. As long as he didn't delay.

'There now, Maynard. Some air, you said? Let's get you out in the yard. That's it, take my arm.'

Dornford guided his companion outside.

Floate stood unsteadily outside the back door. 'I'll get you a chair from the kitchen.' Dornford dashed back inside, returning with a chair, and helped Floate to lower himself onto it. 'Deep breaths now, Maynard. Close your eyes and take deep breaths. One… two… three. That's right, keep breathing.' Dornford reached for the shovel propped against the wall, the one Twm used for clearing up the horse manure in the yard.

'Four… five.' The shovel reverberated with the force of the blow. Face down on the cobbles, Floate felt nothing as the shovel came swinging down a second time, and a third.

Dornford stood back and considered his options. The wheelbarrow might do. It wasn't far to the shaft. Or…yes, he noticed the bath chair standing where George and Ambrose had lifted Gregory from it; that might work better.

It took all his strength. He failed twice when the chair rolled away at the critical moment, but with determination and a volley of curses, Dornford finally deposited Floate's body in it. He looked with distaste at his stained hands and the pool of blood on the cobblestones and stepped to the pump over the horse trough to clean himself and draw a bucket of water to sluice down the yard.

Fifty yards – that's all. The distance from the corner of the yard to the copse of stunted trees and gorse bushes concealing the mine shaft. *Hidden in plain sight*, Dornford chuckled to himself as he pushed the bath chair toward it. While it was awkward enough to propel the chair on cobbles, the broken ground beyond almost defeated his efforts. Only by turning and dragging the chair backwards could he make any progress.

Panting and sweating copiously, he finally reached the copse. Now the only way forward lay in tipping Floate out and dragging his body through the dense undergrowth. Sheer desperation drove him on. No one familiar with the effete aesthete he presented as at Chase Manor would credit him with this display of strength and endurance. Dornford's chest heaved as he contemplated the next step. Here at the centre of the copse, the mineshaft remained hidden, covered by a metal grille. A casual observer would have no idea that under two moss-covered boulders lay the entrance to a long-abandoned silver mine. A narrow vertical shaft. Floate had mentioned it took five seconds for a dropped stone to strike water.

Steeling himself for one last effort, Dornford rolled the boulders aside. The grille was harder to shift, but gave way at last. The chasm lay open to receive Floate. He'd not be alone down there. A dull splash confirmed his arrival at the bottom of the shaft. Dornford quickly replaced the grill and rolled the boulders back into position. There – all done. He felt suddenly light-headed. Not faint, but euphoric.

The stench filled his nostrils a mere instant before he heard the man's voice. Low and guttural. 'Mistar Floate?' Twm pointed at the concealed shaft. '*Lawr fyna?* Down there?' His feral eyes displayed no emotion. He turned away. '*Dere*. Come.' Twm gestured toward the farmhouse.

Though reluctant to do so, Twm showed a greater command of English than Dornford expected. The bargain was simple enough. Twm's silence and his help to get Dornford safely away in return for… *Nant-y-Geifr*. 'I will have the farm,' he pronounced with an expression that said, *It's no use to you anymore, is it?*

The discovery that his horse was no longer in the stable threw Dornford into a panic. But the wiry pony that Twm produced proved a better choice of mount for their journey across the wild terrain. By-passing Aberystwyth, he led Dornford overnight to a village by the unlikely name of Bow Street, one stop up the Cambrian Line, Dornford's lifeline out of Wales and back to Chase Manor.

What would he say when they arrived there? The authorities with their accusations. What better than to play the victim? He'd accompanied Gregory to The Blessed Plot in all innocence. *Why the pretence that Gregory was leaving on account of his ailing father?* That's because Gregory was being offered a privilege coveted by all at Chase Manor. The community would be up in arms at the notion that a newcomer was being favoured in such a way. *And why was he being favoured?* Dornford had an answer for that as well. Gregory was a wealthy man. He'd offered a tidy sum to be elevated to The Blessed Plot. A place, as he saw it, to nurture and expand his aesthetic sensibilities. *Nevertheless, you were party to a conspiracy to coerce Mr Manning into signing a fraudulent will and complicit in a plot to murder him.* Oh no, you see, Dr Floate and Pryce-Thomas were the conspirators. I, like poor Gregory Manning, was under Floate's nefarious influence. He'd hypnotised me. I was not responsible for my actions. Thank heavens those two men, Mr Benson and Mr Mallard, stopped him. Not only did they save Gregory, they also saved *my* life. With Dr Floate incapacitated, I regained my senses, and I fled. It was in blind panic. I simply had to get away. *Where is Dr Floate? He was not at the farm.* I have no idea. I pray that you will find him and bring him to justice. That man is a danger to society.

Dornford ran through it all in his head until the sound of the approaching train brought him back to the present. Stepping onto the platform, he hurried to the nearest empty compartment. The guard blew his whistle, and with a slight jolt, the engine took up the strain. Little did he know that in the carriage behind his, George, Ambrose, Gregory, and Sergeant Davies occupied a compartment, equally oblivious to his presence.

Chapter 49

At the first hint of daylight, they neared Myrddin's Keep.

'Let me see Oliver's map again.'

Verity handed the paper to Arnold.

'We need to go further to our right. That way we'll stay out of sight. Another ten minutes and we'll be there.'

It was easy to miss it – and they did.

Only after retracing their steps and peering through the trees did the squat pepper-pot tower reveal itself. Cloaked in ivy, it defied discovery by any casual passer-by.

Had Oliver fulfilled his promise? Arnold pushed. The door creaked open.

Pausing only to light his lantern, he led them in single file along a brick-lined passage. The roof glistened with moisture. After the freshness of the dawn, the air felt dank and oppressive.

Caroline followed closely in Arnold's footsteps. Elspeth, who had confessed to a fear of confined spaces, came next, willing herself forward despite her galloping heartbeat. Verity whispered encouragement to her as she brought up the rear.

Curving to the left, then to the right, the passage wound its way to the Keep. Oliver had not said how long it was. 'Can't be much further,' Arnold mumbled. Another curve to the left, ten more paces, and there it was: a stout wooden door.

What lay on the other side? Oliver's sketch showed the tunnel emerging into the cellar. From there, a spiral stone staircase would give them access to the floors above, winding all the way to the top of the tower.

Arnold gritted his teeth and lifted the iron latch. Softly, he pushed at the door, inching it open, fearful of making a sound. If Oliver had played them false, led them into a trap, this was the moment of truth.

He put his face to the gap, shining the lantern into the cavernous cellar, and illuminating… an empty space.

'What do you see?' Verity hissed.

Arnold opened the door wider. 'See for yourself.'

'Come on then,' Verity urged. 'The steps are over there.'

Arnold stood aside to allow the women through.

'Hurry. Come along. I'll take that, Arnold,' Verity pointed to the lantern. 'Quickly, there's no time to waste. We must find Stella.'

Verity took it from him.

'Wait for us,' Caroline called out, grasping Elspeth's hand and rushing to catch up. Arnold shook his head despairingly, then followed.

Verity did not wait. Reaching the steps, she climbed rapidly, leaving the others to scramble after her. How far? Twenty steps, thirty. The first door leading off the staircase opened into the great hall on the ground floor. According to Oliver, Stella was confined in a room on the third floor – at the top of the tower.

Outside the door to the great hall, Verity halted and turned to the others. 'Door,' she mouthed. Satisfied that they understood her, Verity turned to continue her ascent.

Exposed in the flickering light of the lantern, a dark figure stood in a recess. Cloaked and half in shadow, the silent presence emerged into the light.

'Oliver!'

Placing a finger to his lips, he stepped to Verity's side and pointed upwards.

The next door led to Aquinas's private apartments. Oliver stopped and pressed an ear to it. Hearing no sound, he resumed climbing. The others followed, glancing warily at the door as they passed.

Oliver reached the top of the staircase. 'Stella,' he whispered, pointing to the last door. Lifting the latch, he stepped inside.

After the airless confines of the spiral staircase, the space they entered was light and airy, with a doorway opening onto the battlements encircling the top of the tower. Narrow windows at intervals, admitted the early morning light. Directly opposite, a wall decorated with a mural depicting a hunting scene bisected the tower, beyond which, Verity assumed, must be Stella's chamber.

Oliver gathered them round. 'We must tread warily.' He kept his voice at a whisper. 'The door to the chamber's locked, but the key is over there.' He pointed to a table outside the chamber door. 'We must do our best not to startle her. She must see a friendly face. Yours.' Oliver nodded to Verity.

'Very well.' Verity crossed to the table and took the key. To her relief, it turned smoothly in the lock. Cautiously easing the door ajar, she surveyed the interior. It contained only a table and chair, a washstand, and a bed, on which Stella lay on her back, hands clasped and fully clothed – asleep despite the light intruding from the undraped windows. Verity prepared to tiptoe over and gently wake the sleeper.

Elspeth's gasp behind her was all the warning she had. With a scrabbling of feet and a yelp, Bran burst through the doorway. Heart in mouth, Verity followed, all hope of waking Stella quietly, now dashed. Knowing how she herself would react to being woken rudely by an excitable, slobbering canine, she rushed forward hoping to stifle Stella's inevitable scream.

Far from confirming her fears, the dog sat on its haunches and rested its head on the bed, gazing devotedly at Stella.

'Good dog.' Verity stroked Bran's head.

'Stella,' Verity shook her shoulder. 'Stella.'

A sigh. Stella slept on.

'Stel…'

Her eyelids flickered open.

'Shush. It's Verity.'

'Uh?' Stella frowned.

'It's Verity, Stella.'

'Not you too? Aquinas has –'

'No, no, Stella, I'm not a captive. I'm here to free you. Caroline and Arnold are waiting outside. Elspeth is also with us.'

'Truly?' Stella sat up. 'Oh, and Bran.'

'Yes, Bran has joined us.' Verity laughed. 'Now, let me help you up.'

Verity emerged with Stella on her arm. 'You see, your friends are here.'

Stella's smile froze. Cowering, she pointed at Oliver. 'What is he doing here? Have you betrayed me?' she gasped.

Caroline and Elspeth embraced her. 'No one has betrayed you. Oliver is with us. Without him, we couldn't have found you.'

'It's true,' Elspeth stroked Stella's cheek.

'Is it?' Stella turned to Oliver. 'Do you swear it?'

'I swear it.'

'We can go now.' Verity took Stella's arm.

'Go?' Stella pulled her arm free. 'Not without Jeremy. We must find him.'

'And you need look no further.' Aquinas's voice echoed as he emerged from the stairwell, holding his son by the hand. Too frightened to make a sound, Jeremy quivered at his side. A moment later, Piers followed.

'It seems we have a traitor in the camp,' Aquinas shot Oliver a look laced with scorn. 'Clear out, you turncoat, and count yourself fortunate to escape a thrashing.'

'Save your breath, Aquinas. You're in no fit state to issue threats. Your arm is only good for lifting a cider jug, but if you wish we can have it out now, man to man, down in the bailey.'

Aquinas scoffed, 'I wouldn't sully my hands with you. Piers, you may have the pleasure.'

'What …?'

'A duel, Piers. Trounce the upstart.'

'I hardly think that's necessary, Aquinas.' Piers looked uncertainly at Oliver. 'I mean, he's obviously not one of us anymore. He'll just go. Isn't that right, Oliver?'

'Is it? You make such a show of being Aquinas's champion, or do you lack the stomach for a fight?'

'For heaven's sake, stop this foolishness now,' Verity stepped between them. 'We are not in Camelot. You are all subject to the laws of the land – Queen Victoria's, not King

Arthur's. You've detained Stella against her will, and you'll answer for it. Hand Jeremy over now, Aquinas, or it will be the worse for you. Your fanciful idyll here is at an end.'

'Ha! Go back to London. Chase Manor is no place for you.'

'Chase Manor? You mean Oscar and Ursula's criminal enterprise.' Verity laughed. 'It's over. The Blessed Plot, as they call it. The place near Devil's Bridge in Wales. There, I see it in your face, Aquinas. You know where I'm talking about, and I'll wager you know what goes on there. The police will know too, by now. What do you intend to do when they arrive? Shut the gates? Cower in your ridiculous mock castle?'

Aquinas bolted. Before anyone had time to react, he ducked out onto the battlements, Jeremy held firmly in his arms.

'Jeremy!' Stella wailed.

Arnold was first in pursuit, with Verity close behind. Oliver made to follow. 'No, you stay and see to it that Piers doesn't interfere,' she yelled as she stepped outside.

The battlement jutted out from the tower, encircling it, and having a walkway wide enough for two to pass between the tower wall and a crenelated stone parapet.

Aquinas stood near an embrasure. Lifting Jeremy to sit in it, he roared defiance, holding his son steady with one hand – perched precariously ninety feet above the ground.

'Not a step further.' Aquinas's eyes blazed. 'If you value his life. You – common scum,' he glowered at Arnold. 'And that harridan.' Red-faced and shaking, he pointed at Verity. 'Get back. Leave, or, by heaven, I'll –'

For the second time, Verity heard Bran hurtle past her. Had Aquinas not raised his free arm, the lurcher's jaws would have found his throat. As it was, the force of Bran's impact sent him staggering. With nothing to steady him, the terrified boy teetered. The force of gravity exerted itself. Arnold couldn't say how he did it, but with a desperate lunge, he locked his hand around Jeremy's ankle.

Aquinas backed away, driven no longer by rage, but fear.

Bran advanced, growling deep in his throat, hackles raised.

Verity rushed to help Arnold, gathering the shocked child to her. Ten feet away, Aquinas babbled incoherently, eyes fixed on Bran. His right hand moved to the belt at his waist. Unsheathed, the dagger gleamed wickedly. 'Come, you cur,' he spat.

Bran growled deeper, gathering himself.

'No Bran!' Verity called despairingly. 'No!'

The dagger flashed… as it clattered to the floor. Aquinas clutched his breast, face contorted, turning puce. His strangled cry was cut short as his knees buckled.

Chapter 50

Ambrose snorted, but didn't wake. George shook him again.

'Mmm. Eh?'

'Wake up. We're arriving in Shrewsbury. We have to change trains.'

'Oh, was I asleep long?'

'Dead to the world for the last hour.' George grinned. 'Vivid dream, was it?'

'Dream?'

'You were most animated.'

'In what sense?'

'You kept calling out. Sergeant Jones and Gregory were quite intrigued.'

Ambrose narrowed his eyes. 'What did I say?'

'A name. A woman's name.' George smirked.

'Oh dear, Violet?'

'Correct. My word, you certainly had an eventful life in India, Ambrose.' George winked at Sergeant Jones. 'It's just as well we had the compartment to ourselves.'

The shriek of the engine's whistle drowned out Ambrose's stammered response. Red faced, he stood to lift his portmanteau from the luggage rack.

'All change. All change,' the guard called.

Out on the platform, George consulted the station timetable. 'We have twenty-five minutes to wait for the Hereford train. Can I suggest we attend the buffet?'

'Yes, indeed, I'm quite parched,' Sergeant Jones rubbed his throat.

'Yes.' Gregory concurred.

'What do you say, Ambrose?' George turned around. 'Ambrose? Where the deuce are you?'

'There he is.' Sergeant Jones pointed. 'See, he's waving at us.'

George crossed the platform. 'What is it?'

Ambrose whispered in his ear. 'Over there – don't look yet. On a bench next to an old lady. Just glance out of the corner of your eye. It's him.'

Sergeant Jones joined them.

'Dornford Lamont.' George murmured. 'Over my left shoulder, sitting on the bench. Do you see him?'

'Aye, young chap, no hat. No sign of the other one, Dr Floate, is there?'

George shook his head.

'Must have been on our train. But we didn't see him at the station in Aberystwyth.' Sergeant Jones pondered. 'Unless he went from Devil's Bridge to Bow Street and got on the train there.'

'Let's go and ask him. Are you prepared to make an arrest, Sergeant?'

Jones hesitated. 'Perhaps we should wait and see if Floate is with him? He might have gone to visit the gents.'

Gregory watched them conferring. Consumed by curiosity, he wandered over. A pair of tardy passengers rushed across the platform to catch the Cambrian Line train before it returned to Aberystwyth, one of whom cannoned into Gregory in his haste. Gregory came off second best, sent sprawling onto his hands and knees, scrabbling to find his spectacles.

All eyes were drawn to the commotion, including Dornford's.

'Ambrose, would you go and help Gregory while Sergeant Jones and I apprehend Dornford?' The words were hardly out of George's mouth when the policeman grabbed him by the sleeve. 'He's seen us. Come on.'

No longer on his bench, Dornford strolled along the platform with the collar of his coat pulled up, hoping to exit the station unobserved.

At the sound of Sergeant Jones's boots pounding toward him, he glanced over his shoulder, spun on his heel and broke into a run.

The Aberystwyth train was pulling out. George wondered if Dornford might try to jump aboard.

But Dornford ran on as the carriages glided by until the guard's van at the rear drew level. As he jumped down onto the tracks, intent on crossing to the opposite platform, the train whistle blared – obscuring the sound of the goods train passing on the down-line.

George and Sergeant Jones waited until the last goods-wagon trundled past, revealing Dornford's mangled remains.

Chapter 51

Oliver, Piers and Arnold struggled to carry Aquinas's lifeless body down to the Great Hall. Covered by a sheet, it lay on the table at the centre of the hall, a facsimile of Arthur's fabled Round Table.

His followers gathered. The men gravitated to Piers, talking in an urgent hubbub, all save Oliver who stood apart. Lavinia and the other two women whispered together in a corner.

'Time we left.' Verity announced. 'Stella, are you and Jeremy ready to come with us?'

'Nothing would induce me to spend another minute in this place,' Stella took her son's hand.

'Come then, we'll leave by the front gate.'

They crossed the courtyard. Arnold lifted the bar across the gate and pulled it open. As they passed through, Bran's familiar bark heralded his arrival. 'Mama!' Jeremy yelled. 'Can Bran come?' Both boy and dog looked beseechingly at Stella.

'Of course, come along, Bran.'

Arnold swung Jeremy onto his shoulder, and Bran fell in at his heel. The four women linked arms and followed.

Back at Eileen Cottage, they crowded into the parlour. 'Now we wait,' Verity said, sounding more confident than she felt.

'Until your detective arrives?'

'Yes Elspeth. When he's freed Gregory.'

'Oh, I'm blessed, well I never,' Tamsin's startled face appeared in the doorway. 'I've been clearing out the scullery. They told me, you was gone. I don't understand.'

Elspeth sat up. 'Who told you that, Tamsin?'

'The master and the mistress said so. Told me to come and clean the place and to lock the door after.'

'As you can see, Verity and Caroline have not gone. They will remain for the present.'

'Oh dear, what will I say to them?' Tamsin wrung her hands.

'Just tell them that I instructed you. Don't be fearful. There are changes coming, Tamsin. But you will not suffer, nor will your family. Do you trust me?'

'Suppose I'll have to, miss.'

'Very well. Go now and remember what I just told you.'

Tamsin curtsied and turned on her heel.

'One moment,' Verity called after her. 'Before you go, will you promise me one thing?'

'What, miss?'

'I'm expecting a friend of mine to pay a visit. He may have Mr Gregory with him.'

Tamsin's expression showed her confusion.

'His name is George Benson. He will not know where to find me. When he arrives, you must send him here. Do you understand?'

Flustered beyond measure, Tamsin nodded and turned tail.

'Poor girl,' Elspeth remarked. 'It just shows that this whole situation affects so many people, not only ourselves and the Lamonts.'

'Yes.' Verity agreed 'Let's hope that we can at least honour your promise to Tamsin. I'll do what I can.'

'I wonder what's happening at Myrddin's Keep,' Caroline mused, stroking Bran's head. 'If ever a seizure was timely. It may be considered bad form to speak ill of the dead, but it's almost enough to make one believe in divine intervention.'

'The man's excesses caught up with him,' Arnold said, standing at the parlour window, 'and it looks as though we're about to have company.'

Caroline joined him. 'It's Oliver and those three women. The ones Aquinas referred to as Guineveres.'

With no chairs available, Oliver stood by the mantelpiece while Lavinia and her two companions, whom she introduced as Miranda and Lydia, perched together in a window seat.

'Piers has assumed command at Myrddin's Keep,' Oliver began. 'You should hear them. They talk as though Aquinas were some mystical leader, rather than the drunken sot he really was. They seem to think the whole charade can continue. There was much talk of a grand funeral and then…' A frown crossed his face.

'Then what?' Verity asked.

'Then things took an ominous turn. I was denounced, and Piers vowed revenge.'

'On us?'

Oliver nodded. 'I slipped away and advised the ladies to come with me.'

'We needed no persuasion,' Lavinia remarked dryly.

'Do we really have anything to fear?' Stella hugged Jeremy. 'Surely, they wouldn't harm women or a child.'

'They're in a belligerent mood. Piers stirs them up. Add drink to the equation and matters could boil over.'

'They're drinking?' Verity asked anxiously.

'They've broached a keg of mead.'

'What should we do?' Stella looked at Verity.

'Perhaps this place is too isolated? Although we're not welcome, we might be safer at the heart of the community. Sylvan Cottage, Elspeth?'

Elspeth shrugged. 'We'd be bursting at the seams. Then again, we're almost sitting on top of one another here. But I think you're right, Verity. Piers and his louts would surely not assault us in full view of the community.'

'Are we agreed then?'… 'Very well. Once we're outside, we must stick together and make haste.'

'I think you'll find it's too late.' Lavinia's warning drew all eyes to the window. On the lawn outside, two riders sat looking at the cottage. 'It's Piers, and that's Quentin with him. They're drunk, you can tell.'

Miranda and Lydia moved smartly away from the window seat.

'At least there are only two of them.' Verity joined Lavinia at the window. 'And yes, I see what you mean. They certainly don't look sober.'

Outside, Piers and Quentin shared a joke, staring at the cottage and laughing uproariously, each holding a goblet and gesticulating wildly, to the point that Quentin slid awkwardly out of his saddle, landing on his back on the lawn, where he struggled to get up.

'I doubt they'll cause us much trouble,' Verity declared. 'Come on…' The words died on her lips as the remaining Arthurians trotted into view. The horsemen halted on the lawn, all in high spirits, one balancing a wooden keg on the pommel of his saddle.

In Eileen Cottage, everyone crowded behind the window, except Miranda and Lydia, who clung to each other in a far corner.

The Arthurians dismounted. A conference took place with Piers at the centre of the group, then he approached the cottage.

'Here's trouble,' Arnold muttered.

In his green surcoat, with a sword hanging from his belt, Piers swaggered across the lawn and up to the garden gate, goblet in hand.

'What's he saying?' Caroline strained to hear the muffled voice outside.

'I can't tell,' Verity cupped a hand to her ear. 'Arnold, open the window, would you?'

Arnold eased the window open.

'… is dead because of you.' Piers's harsh tones came through loud and clear. 'There you all are, cowering in your little fairy cottage.' A ragged roar of approval came from his comrades. 'Well may you cower.' Piers raised the goblet to his lips and drank. 'We have come to lay siege.' Another roar. 'Surrender yourselves or we will storm your puny stronghold.' Piers took another drink, swaying slightly, then walked away, to the thunderous acclaim of his henchmen.

Verity turned to Oliver. 'Are we to take him seriously, or was that the drink talking?'

'Piers has a vicious streak. The drink accentuates it, but the man takes delight in violence. Especially to women.' Oliver nodded toward Miranda and Lydia.

'And you? You were one of them. What did you do, Oliver?' Verity snapped.

'I… should have done more to stop…' Oliver hung his head.

'He was the only decent one among them.' Lavinia moved to Oliver's side. 'He has nothing to be ashamed of – save his gullibility – and he's no friend of Piers.'

'No, I believe he isn't.' Verity agreed. 'But the question remains: what will Piers and his gaggle of drunken savages do?'… 'Where are you going?'

Oliver edged past Verity. Moments later, he stood at the open cottage door.

'Enough of your threats, Piers. You avoided my challenge earlier. I renew it. Single combat. When I give you the beating you deserve, you will take these fools and skulk back to Myrddin's Keep.'

Piers turned unsteadily, screwing his eyes to focus on Oliver. Quentin whispered in his ear and beckoned the others to gather round. They all turned to face Oliver and drew their swords.

'Come back in, you damned fool.' Arnold grabbed Oliver's arm and pulled him into the cottage, slamming the door behind them and sliding the bolt into place.

'Shut the window,' he bellowed, dragging Oliver into the parlour. 'I've bolted the door, but I doubt that will stop them. Everyone, get upstairs. Oliver and I will try to keep them out.'

'Don't be absurd. I have no intention of hiding away,' Verity retorted.

'Nor I,' Caroline and Elspeth chimed in.

'When you've finished with the histrionics,' Lavinia said coolly, standing at the window. 'You'll find they've stopped. See, they're huddled together out there.'

Everyone watched as the Arthurians sheathed their swords and ambled back across the lawn. Apart from two of their number, who walked off toward the neighbouring cottage.

'They're going to Elaine, see, they've gone inside,' Elspeth frowned. 'What on earth for?'

Her question was soon answered. They soon emerged, one swinging a metal can.

'Oh Lord,' Elspeth whispered. 'Paraffin. That can contains paraffin for the lamps.'

'What? You can't mean they intend to set fire to the cottage?' Verity asked.

At the mention of fire, Stella, with Jeremy on her lap, broke down in tears, sobbing silently and clutching her son tightly to her. The frightened boy trembled in her arms and began wailing piteously. Cowering in their corner, Miranda and Lydia whimpered.

Lavinia made no move to comfort her two companions, maintaining her post at the window. 'I think they mean to roast us,' she said without emotion. 'You see.'

Piers took the can. Holding it aloft and shaking it, he gave an approving nod to the others and made a great show of unscrewing the cap before turning to face the cottage. Quentin fell in at his side, grinning madly and holding his right hand aloft.

'What's the fool got in his hand?' Arthur muttered. A moment later, it was obvious. 'Matches.'

'Out!' Verity screamed. 'Get out, everyone. Down the passage, to the scullery, and out through the back door. Elspeth, you take Stella and Jeremy. Caroline, show those two the way,' she commanded, pointing at Miranda and Lydia. 'You too, Lavinia.'

Lavinia stood gazing out of the window, deaf to Verity's entreaties.

The odour of paraffin spread through the cottage. 'Come on, Lavinia,' Verity insisted, expecting the flash of ignition at any second.

'We have more visitors,' Lavinia announced.

Verity recognised the carriage. Seth had already jumped down from the box seat. Piers and Quentin turned on him belligerently, shouting insults and threats. Seth hardly broke his stride, shouldering Quentin to one side, wrenching the paraffin can from Piers's grip and hurling it across the lawn.

Verity and Lavinia watched the drama play out. Piers attempted to draw his sword, but before the blade was halfway out of its scabbard, Seth delivered a most unchivalrous headbutt to the bridge of his nose. Dazed and bleeding, Piers staggered blindly, holding his hands to his face until Seth tripped him and put him on his back. Engrossed in the action, Verity hardly noticed the figure who followed at Seth's heels and sent Quentin sprawling with a forceful shove. Only when George had disarmed his victim and held his sword aloft in a mock salute, did recognition dawn.

On the lawn, the remaining Arthurians were being herded by a police sergeant and two constables. Meekly, they threw their swords down before being marched away.

After Piers and Quentin had been pulled to their feet and taken in charge by the police, Verity emerged, wrinkling her nose at the reek of paraffin as she stepped across the threshold.

'Seth, what can I say? It seems that no Knight of the Round Table is a match for Seth Cooper.'

Seth grinned self-consciously. 'Don't know 'bout that, miss. 'Tis all playacting if you ask me. They're daft young gentlemen, that's all.'

'George, you took your time,' Verity remarked mockingly.

'What was that?' George grinned and cupped a hand to his ear. 'Thank you, George, for rescuing Gregory and saving me from a conflagration. Isn't that what you just said, or did I mishear?'

Expecting one of Verity's typically barbed responses, he almost lost his balance as she threw herself into his arms. 'Yes, of course it's what I meant, George, and it's wonderful to see you.' Dazed by such a spontaneous gesture, George returned her embrace somewhat stiffly, cursing his awkwardness.

The moment passed all too quickly. 'Now then, tell me everything.' Verity detached herself and stepped back. 'Where's Gregory? How is he? And Ambrose. What about Dornford? Are Oswald and Ursula under arrest?'

Peppered with questions, George did his best, describing Gregory's plight at *Nant-y-Geifr* and the events leading to his rescue.

'Dear Lord, it sounds like a plot from a gothic novel. A sinister mesmerist, a crooked solicitor, and a wild Welshman. Good old Ambrose, he's always full of surprises. And the police are involved. Does that mean that Dornford is sitting in a police cell in Wales, together with Dr Floate and that Pryce-Thomas fellow?'

George hesitated.

Verity read his expression. 'You're not about to tell me they're still at large, are you, George?'

'Pryce-Thomas is in custody. The police were on their way to the farm when Ambrose and I left Aberystwyth, so Floate may be in their hands.'

'And Dornford?'

George told her.

Verity's face fell. 'Oh, I would not have wished that on him. He was a stupid, vain fool, but Oswald and Ursula are the real culprits in all of this. It is they who must take the blame.'

'That's in the hands of the police now. There are three forces involved: the police in Aberystwyth, of course; the local police from Hereford, and the Shrewsbury force – because of Dornford's death at Shrewsbury station. I saw Oswald and Ursula being taken away. Arrested and informed of their son's death at the same time, imagine that.'

'Like a Shakespearean tragedy, in a way. Oh well, let's speak of brighter things. Where are Gregory and Ambrose?'

'I left them at Chase Manor with Sergeant Jones from Aberystwyth. Come on, Seth can drive us over there.'

'In a moment,' Verity pointed back at Eileen Cottage. Arnold and Caroline stood arm in arm in the doorway, the others crowded behind the parlour window. 'We must tell my companions first. Come on, George, and be sensitive where Dornford is concerned. The woman who was his fiancée is among them.'

Chapter 52

Two months later

'Goodness, hasn't she grown?' Verity whispered, bent over Sylvia's crib. 'Still, you'll be glad to get back to Thorneycroft, I expect. The country is much the better place for a child.'

'We've stayed in London for longer than either of us expected.' Olivia gently tucked the coverlet around the sleeping infant. 'The estate will need a great deal of Mortimer's attention. Now then, we'd better make an appearance downstairs.'

'Does Ambrose have any suspicions?' Verity tiptoed to the nursery door.

'Not an inkling. Mortimer's taken him along to a meeting with our bankers in the city. That will keep him safely out of the way until everyone's arrived. It will be quite an occasion, especially after your recent adventures.'

'No doubt. Ambrose never ceases to amaze me. There he was, careering around the wild Welsh countryside with George; despite his age, he's quite irrepressible. Not that he's ever divulged how old he is.'

'Well, we won't embarrass him. His birthday cake will have only a single candle,' Olivia grinned. 'Ah, could that be our first guest arriving?'

Guests, in fact. Alfie and Dick were first. George appeared five minutes later and, to no one's surprise, Mary arrived last, offering profuse apologies.

Olivia glanced at the drawing-room clock. 'Any minute now,' she announced. 'George, would you do the honours with the champagne?'

George obliged. With glasses charged, they waited.

'Yes, there's their cab,' Olivia turned away from the window.

'He was a dry old devil,' Ambrose's voice floated in from the hall, 'I know bankers aren't considered the most entertaining of fellows, but it was all I could do to keep my eyes open.'

Mortimer chuckled. 'Actually, you didn't. Never mind, you won't be the first to nod off in Barker's presence.'

'Sorry, old chap, perhaps I should take a nap before lunch. I'll just pop upstairs and get my head down.'

'Ah, before you do. There's something I need to show you in the drawing room. Come along.'

'Very well. What is it you want… oh, my word!' Ambrose succumbed to the unfamiliar sensation of being lost for words. With a glass of champagne pressed into his hand, he blinked away a tear and beamed with pleasure to a rousing chorus of 'Happy Birthday'.

'Oh, my dears, my friends, what a wonderful surprise. Could there ever be a better way to mark one's birthday than with the finest people in the land – nay, the whole world.'

Lost for words no longer, Ambrose became as ever, the life and soul of the gathering. Luncheon passed in a tide of chatter and good humour, with much recounting of the events at Chase Manor and Wales.

After Ambrose blew out his candle and the cake was served and eaten, a relative calm descended. He sat back contentedly, ruminating over his glass of port. 'Well, what a time we've had. But never mind all that. What does the future hold? Alfie and Dick, does the pawnbroker's prosper?'

'Can't complain,' Alfie grinned. 'Brings in a decent quid or two. And to be honest, it's all down to Nel. She's a marvel, right enough. With her running the place, it leaves me and Dick to pursue our other business interests, if you get my meaning.' Alfie winked at his brother.

'I think we get your drift, Alfie,' Ambrose nodded.

'And what about you, my dear? Still dazzling the world of the theatre, I'll be bound.' Mary flashed a smile. 'I'm in rehearsals for a new play. By the Bard.'

'Shakespeare!' Ambrose trumpeted. 'I knew it. The finest actress deserves nothing less than the finest playwright.'

'Before you ask, it's as Miranda in *The Tempest*, and there's something else… I'm engaged.' Mary held up her left hand. 'There, you see.'

'Look at your faces,' Verity cast an amused glance around the table. 'You men, sitting there open-mouthed. You might as well be blind. Mary's engagement ring has been staring you in the face all this time. Of course, Olivia and I spotted it the moment she arrived and removed her gloves. Well, come on, Ambrose, aren't you going to congratulate her?'

'Y-yes, of course, heartiest congratulations, my dear. Who is the lucky man, may I ask?'

'His name's Douglas Hartnell.'

'A fellow thespian?'

'No, Douglas is a physician. Oh, please stop staring at me, everyone. It's worse than being on the stage. I promise I'll introduce him to all of you very soon. Now let's hear from someone else. You, Verity.'

'As you are all very well aware, my entire purpose in going to Chase Manor was to write an article about life in a utopian community. And little did I imagine that it would provide such sensational material. However, with court cases pending, I must delay publication for the present. In the meantime, I've been writing another of my pieces on *History's Forgotten Women*. I doubt that any of you have heard of the subject, it's Hildegard von Bingen. There, blank faces all round, I think. I… yes, George?'

'Twelfth century Benedictine Abess, scholar and composer. Do I have the right Hildegard?'

'Bravo, George.' Ambrose chortled. 'That's taken the wind out of Verity's sails.'

'Yes, George, it has.' Verity conceded. 'How on earth…'

'All in the line of business. A client of mine. Professor of Divinity. Something of an authority on dear old Hildegard.'

'Capital, George. Oh dear, you should have seen your face, Verity.'

'No doubt you will take pleasure in reminding me of it, Ambrose. Let's move on and hear what George is up to. Oh, no, wait. One more thing… I'm going to France next week.'

'Jaqueline will be so excited to see you.' Olivia gave Verity a warm smile.

'And I her. You see, I'm bringing her back with me.'

'How wonderful! How long will she be staying?'

'Forever. It's time to drop the pretence. She is my daughter, and I will acknowledge her as such. Yes, I realise that it may come as a shock, but my mind is made up. If anyone has concerns, we can discuss them later.' Verity looked pointedly at Mortimer.

'I would simply…' Mortimer hesitated, unsure how to express himself and wondering whether it should be a sentence best left unfinished.

'Mortimer and I are delighted, my dear.' Olivia came to the rescue. 'You have our unconditional support. That was what you were about to say, wasn't it, Mortie?'

'Of course, my dear.'

Seizing the moment, Ambrose dispelled the tension. 'George, your turn, I think.'

'Thank you, Ambrose. I also have some news.' George produced a letter from his jacket. 'This arrived yesterday. Addressed to both of us, Verity. It's from Gregory Manning.'

'From Gregory. How is he?'

'Very well. He sends his fondest regards to you. And you too, Ambrose. I think you'll both be pleasantly surprised by what he has to say.' George paused, slowly smoothing the letter out on the tablecloth.

'Well? Are you going to tell us?' Verity voiced her impatience.

'I won't read it out. You're all welcome to peruse it afterwards. I'll give you the gist.'

'Which is?' Verity tapped the tablecloth

'Chase Manor has been sold.'

'Sold? The Lamonts have sold it? To whom? What –?'

George put a hand up to forestall Verity's flood of questions. 'The Lamonts were gravely in debt. The place was mortgaged to Stribling's Bank, and they have foreclosed.'

'So, the bank owns Chase Manor?'

'You'll learn what's happened a great deal more quickly if you refrain from asking questions constantly,' George grinned. 'Shall I continue?'

Receiving a curt nod, he went on. 'The bank has sold Chase Manor, lock, stock and barrel, to Gregory Manning Esquire.'

'An unusually quick sale.' Mortimer remarked.

'It seems that the Chairman, Sir Septimus Stribling, was an old friend of Gregory's father.'

'Hmm, rather irregular.' Mortimer muttered. 'Still, if the board was satisfied…'

'We must assume that they were, Mortimer. Now, Verity, I can see you straining at the leash, so I'll try to anticipate your questions. Chase Manor will continue as a community dedicated to the decorative arts. It will operate under the guidance of a board comprising Gregory himself, Arnold Wright and, this may surprise you, Elspeth Forsyth.'

'Actually, I don't find it altogether surprising. Elspeth will be a tremendous asset. Is there more to tell?'

'Yes, happy news. Gregory writes that Caroline Hislop and Arnold are to be married.'

'Ha! I knew it. Marvellous. Does he mention Stella and her little boy?'

'Let me see.' George leafed through the letter. 'Yes. She and Jeremy are well, and it seems she has expanded her stained-glass workshop. Taken on some female apprentices. What else should I mention? Oh yes, Myrddin's Keep. The Arthurians are gone. Gregory says he thought of demolishing it, but he's decided to use it for workshop space. In fact, he's founding a print works. Fine hand-printed books along the lines of William Morris's Kelmscott Press, he says.'

'A case of all's well that ends well,' Ambrose quipped.

'Except for the Lamonts,' Verity said. 'I understand that the police have discovered bodies in a mineshaft, one of whom is Dr Floate.'

***

What a day. Back in her drawing room at Eaton Terrace, Verity kicked off her shoes and stretched out on the sofa. It was so unexpected. She'd thought nothing of it when George invited her and Mary to share a cab. Mary's lodgings were nearest. After they'd waved goodbye to her, Verity was about to ask George another question about Gregory's letter. He forestalled her. 'Verity?'

'Hmm?'

'I have a request.'

'Yes, George? What is it?'

'Uh. It's… um.'

'Heavens. George. What can be so difficult about –'

'Would you please allow me to invite you to have dinner with me?'

Oh, the expression on his face. Verity smiled at the thought. Facing up to the King brothers was as nothing compared with the dread he must have felt at posing such a question.

'George, of course, I'd be delighted.'

The words had come naturally enough. Now she wondered. Was it wise? Verity tried to push the thought aside. She must think of something else.

What was it Mortimer had said on her way out? 'Here's a letter addressed to you. The sender must be unaware of your new address.'

She got up reluctantly to fetch her handbag and retrieve the letter. The envelope had a London postmark. The handwritten address was unfamiliar. Not a woman's hand, she concluded.

Who could it be? None of her acquaintances came to mind, and her close friends had all been told of her new address.

Verity crossed to her desk for her letter opener. *Hmm, now then, let's see who you are. Only a single sheet. No sender's address, how curious.*

Dear Verity,

Do you find that the passage of time serves to soften painful memories? After all, you have your career, the comfort of your genteel existence in Montagu Square. Oh, and those gallant friends of yours.

How vividly I recall that night at Larkford Grange. Every last detail is etched in my memory. Not a day passes without my thinking of the woman who condemned me to the life of a fugitive. Everything I had, everything I was – gone.

Consolations are few. Save for one abiding hope, that your downfall will be even more bitter than mine. It's what I long for, and I will bring it about. Tomorrow? Next month? A

year hence? Who knows? Remember that. As you go about your life, I am out there somewhere with only one object in mind.
Yours vengefully,
Anthony Spencer

Author's Note

Present day visitors to Devil's Bridge will still find the Hafod Arms Hotel (now named The Hafod Hotel) presiding over a landscape of rugged beauty. The waterfalls that inspired Wordsworth still flow beneath the bridges which give the place its name.

Whereas George and Ambrose saw two bridges, one above the other, there is now a third bridge spanning the valley, passing directly above the other two. It was built, in 1901 just a few years after the events described in this book.

Nant-y-Geifr is translated as Goats' Brook.

Acknowledgements

My gratitude goes to my publisher, Ian Hooper, for his unstinting support, shrewd advice and humour throughout the publication process.

A very big thank you also to Jo Smith for her excellent work in editing the manuscript and for her suggestions, which have undoubtedly improved the finished product.

Once again, Brittany Wilson's eye-catching cover design has brilliantly captured the essence of the book.

About The Author

R J Williams was born in Aberystwyth in Wales and now lives in Perth, Western Australia.

After a busy career in information technology and management consulting, in the UK and Australia, retirement has given him the opportunity to indulge his interest in history and pursue his long-held ambition to become an author of historical novels.

He enjoys writing, cycling, travelling, and volunteering with Para Quad industries, who provide employment to people with disabilities.